Mystery at Mistletoe Place

BOOKS BY CLARE CHASE

Tara Thorpe Mystery series

Murder on the Marshes

Death on the River

Death Comes to Call

Murder in the Fens

Eve Mallow Mystery series

Mystery on Hidden Lane

Mystery at Apple Tree Cottage

Mystery at Seagrave Hall

Mystery at the Old Mill

Mystery at the Abbey Hotel

Mystery at the Church

Mystery at Magpie Lodge

Mystery at Lovelace Manor

Mystery at Southwood School

Mystery at Farfield Castle

Mystery at Saltwater Cottages

Mystery on Meadowsweet Grove

Mystery at Lockley Grange

Mystery at Mistletoe Place

CLARE CHASE

bookouture

Published by Bookouture in 2025

An imprint of Storyfire Ltd.
Carmelite House
50 Victoria Embankment
London EC4Y 0DZ

www.bookouture.com

The authorised representative in the EEA is Hachette Ireland
8 Castlecourt Centre
Dublin 15 D15 XTP3
Ireland
(email: info@hbgi.ie)

ISBN: 978-1-80550-000-1
eBook ISBN: 978-1-83618-999-2

For Alison

1

As Eve Mallow approached Arthur's Yard, she was already in a good mood. The weather was unseasonably mild for November, though it was only the first of the month. The air was fresh and the sun bright in the blue sky – the sort of day which made her especially conscious of her own luck. Here she was, within minutes of her home, strolling along a tranquil estuary in one of the most beautiful counties in England.

She was part of a happy group, too. Her best friend Viv was at her side, her hair a rather intense berry-red this season, and just ahead of her walked Viv's eldest son Jonah and his wife, Stevie. They were holding hands and turning to each other at regular intervals to exchange smiles or fond words. The sight was clearly making Viv feel mushy and their joy made Eve sentimental too. At the front of the group was Simon, Viv's brother, who was dashing ahead with the keenness of a schoolboy, despite the fact that he was nearing fifty. Bringing up the rear was Eve's beloved dachshund, Gus, who'd got distracted by a rustle in the reeds that lined the brackish water.

'Simon can't wait to pick up his new toy.' Viv laughed as her brother put on an extra burst of speed.

He was about to take possession of a beautiful sailing boat that had been lovingly restored at the boatyard. He'd been talking about it breathlessly for weeks now, describing every bit of it in such minute detail that even Eve had felt a slight sense of overkill. Not that she'd said anything. Simon's happiness made it worth it.

He knocked on the door of the boatyard and a good-looking dark-haired man with a short beard and a ready smile opened up. Anthony Mottram. Eve knew him casually. He had a dog too, so they'd bumped into each other in the early mornings, on the beach. Gus was paying a lot of attention to the boatyard doorway, almost tripping Simon up. She ushered him out of the way to be met with an indignant look.

'She's all ready for you.' Anthony pointed towards the yard's moorings, beaming.

Eve could see the small crane they'd used to get the boat into the water. Simon's eyes were bright as he stepped towards the craft, its name painted on the hull: *Angel of the Marshes*.

Viv let out a pleased sigh.

'She's a beauty, isn't she?' Anthony said, turning to her. 'Mahogany on oak ribs.'

The boat gleamed in the sun. The topmost part of the hull was painted racing green. The rest had been varnished to let the rich, old wood shine through. Eve had the urge to go over and stroke it; it looked so warm and smooth.

'Ah, and here's Hal,' Anthony said.

His second in command, Hal Osborne, had appeared from round the side of the yard, his eyes scrunched against the sun. He was a lot paler than Anthony, despite plenty of outdoor work, and his eyes were bloodshot. Eve felt a moment of unease. She'd seen him around, but never looking like this before.

Hal didn't acknowledge Anthony but nodded towards Viv's brother.

'Simon.'

It was the tersest of greetings, and before Simon could reply, Hal disappeared into the bowels of the yard and out of sight. As he went, Eve heard him swear under his breath.

Eve took in Anthony's blush. Hal's rudeness was clearly making him squirm.

Poor Simon looked disconcerted too. Eve knew he was friends with both Anthony and his deputy. The snub would have stung. It wouldn't be anything Simon had done – he was far too friendly to offend anyone – so Hal's behaviour was odd. Even if he was out of sorts, you'd think he could override it for a minute, given the occasion.

Anthony shook his head. 'Let's get the paperwork sorted, then you're ready to roll.'

The boatyard's interior captured Eve's attention, making her forget Hal's unfriendliness for a moment. In front of her and to her left were offices and stores, but to her right, the space opened out. A handsome sailing boat, its hull gleaming with varnish, was supported on wooden struts while Anthony's team worked on the finishing touches. The place was a hive of activity, and the smell of paint, varnish, oil and wood filled the air. Arthur's Yard was coming up to its centenary. It was stirring to think of the generations of craftspeople who'd gone before, operating with their hands but also their hearts.

Eve was almost distracted enough not to notice Gus trying to sneak down the stairs towards the main workroom, but not quite. She snatched his leash from her coat pocket and attached it to his collar.

'I know, Gus. I like the smell and the hubbub too, but take it from me, you wouldn't want a varnished nose.'

Anthony laughed and came out from behind the oak desk where he and Simon had been dealing with the admin. 'It's true it's not the best place for dogs. I never dare bring Hamish here – he gets way too excited. But come back any time if you'd like a tour unencumbered.' His eyes shone. Eve could see

how much he adored the place, and how keen he was to show
it off.

He bent to ruffle Gus's fur too, which touched Eve.

At that moment, there was a crash which made her start.
Gus barked. Anthony's sunny look turned to alarm, but instead
of rushing in the direction of the noise, he ushered them
towards the door. Eve wondered if the commotion was anything
to do with Hal. He'd seemed angry. Perhaps he'd thrown something in his frustration.

They were now back outside, approaching the *Angel of the
Marshes*, but the incident had marred the feelings of peace and
happiness Eve had been enjoying. Arthur's Yard was a staple of
Saxford St Peter life. The business had been a byword for quality, reliability and friendly openness ever since Anthony's
ancestor, Arthur Mottram, launched the place.

Its backstory was full of the village lore Eve loved. Arthur
had been given the required land by an Osborne as a thank you,
after he had daringly rescued said Osborne from a sinking boat
on rough seas. The connection between the two families had
deepened when Arthur married a distant cousin of the man
whose life he'd saved. The closeness had persisted down the
years, but now, something seemed to have disturbed the reassuring continuity.

It wasn't Hal Osborne's bad temper that bothered Eve –
though it had made her tense. It was the way Anthony had
reacted to the enormous crash. By rights, he should have rushed
over to see what the matter was, not walked in the opposite
direction. That told her he could guess what had occurred, and
that he was determined it should stay private.

2

Eve looked on as Simon, Jonah and Stevie donned life jackets and boarded the *Angel of the Marshes*.

She and Viv waved them off as Simon used the motor to head towards the sea.

'I'll make him take us next time,' Viv said, as the sound of the engine receded.

Eve turned to her. 'That's all right. With Jonah and Stevie heading home tomorrow, it's only fair to let them go first.'

Viv bit her lip suddenly. 'I feel like I've made them guinea pigs, sending them out on Simon's maiden voyage.'

'They'll be fine. He was a model student on the sailing course and they've got life jackets. Besides, it's a beautiful day for it.'

The plan was for Eve and Viv to follow them along the estuary, then cut through the village to the sea, so they could see the boat on the open water.

Twenty minutes later they were on the shore, walking over the pebble-strewn sand. Gus dashed ahead, ears flipped back, eyes rather wild. The seagull he'd been chasing flapped off with a scornful cry. Poor Gus. Eve didn't want him decimating the local wildlife, but his look of pained astonishment still gave her a pang.

After giving him a consoling pat, she unbuttoned her coat. The brisk walk from the yard had made her warm.

Next to her, Viv's berry-red hair blew wildly in the sea breeze. She had a pair of binoculars trained on Simon's boat a couple of hundred metres away, out on the water. Eve could tell from her white knuckles that she was tense. Tenser than Eve would have expected, in fact.

It might be kind to distract her. 'What did you think of Hal's behaviour back there?'

Viv let the binoculars drop for a second. 'Weird. Simon always says how friendly he is.'

'He and Anthony go way back?'

The binoculars were back in place. 'Oh yes. Hal's mum died when he was young and after a bit his dad decided London was no place to bring up a child and sent him back here to live at his uncle's with a nanny. Even before that, Hal spent a lot of time in Saxford visiting his grandparents.'

'So he and Anthony grew up together?'

'Pretty much. Simon says they had lots of larks. Hal's dad had instructed the nanny to keep Hal on a tight rein, but Anthony helped him slip away. They were allies – like brothers. Anthony led, and Hal followed.'

'I guess it's no wonder they ended up working together.'

Viv nodded, though her eyes were still on the boat and its precious cargo. 'I think the boatyard equalled freedom for Hal. He and Anthony used to hang around there even when they were small. They weren't supposed to, of course. Health and safety and all that. But it was their happy place. Anthony started mucking in for his dad as soon as he was big enough, and Hal would sneak along too, from what Simon says. I—'

She broke off suddenly, instantly putting Eve on high alert.

When she spoke again, her frantic whisper was almost lost on the wind. 'Oh no, oh no, oh no!'

In a flash, Eve's eyes were on the boat, but it was too far out to see what was going on. 'What is it?'

Viv's binoculars were fixed on the craft. 'Something's wrong. Simon was shouting to Jonah and now he's disappeared. Jonah's taken charge and Stevie's scrambled over to Simon. Jonah's panicking. You know how he waves his hands around? He's doing something to the sails, but he's all over the place.'

As the one who'd done the sailing course, surely Simon wouldn't abandon his post to Jonah without good reason. Viv's face had drained of all colour and her anxiety was contagious. 'Maybe something blew overboard, or—'

The boat's main sail flapped wildly.

'Oh, Eve!' Viv grabbed Eve's sleeve with one hand, her other still clutching the binoculars. 'Stevie's bailing water!

'Simon's taking over from Jonah. Thank goodness. He'll know what to do. But he's pointing. Shouting. And Stevie's disappeared. I can't see her. Oh, Stevie!'

Eve had tugged her phone from her pocket. 'I'll call the coastguard.' The life jackets were all very well, but the water would be frigid. The sun was enough to warm Eve's face, but it wouldn't have mellowed the bitter North Sea.

She dialled 999.

'I'd swear the waves are getting bigger.' Viv swallowed. 'Oh, Eve. I can't bear it. Especially if Stevie goes in. I just don't know—'

Eve summed up the situation at speed for the coastguard, listened to the woman on the line, who was trying to be reassuring, then rang off. 'They'll send someone. The operator says they won't be long. What about Stevie?' Eve had seen Jonah's wife get a dunking before, though in warmer weather. She'd been impressively brave and a strong swimmer.

'She— I—' Viv's teeth chattered and she glanced quickly in

Eve's direction. 'I overheard her and Jonah when they arrived. She's pregnant.' Her gaze was back on the boat. 'It's very early days. They haven't told me. But what if she falls in?'

Fear for Stevie flipped in Eve's stomach now.

Viv had waded into the water, as though she could help by being two feet closer, and Eve went in after her, struggling to catch her breath as the intense cold hit her. *Heck.* Viv was right to be worried. She leaned in to give her a hug. 'I'm sure they're a long way off sinking. They'll be rescued before you know it.'

'I knew it was a mistake for them to sail this late in the year.' Viv continued to gaze through her binoculars, then suddenly, the tension went out of her shoulders. 'Wait! I can see Stevie again. She's next to Jonah. Oh my goodness, they're all laughing!'

'Right.' Eve redialled 999. Better cancel. She explained to the operator, then hung up.

Viv was laughing too now, but crying as well. 'Thank goodness! They're bringing the boat around.'

'Shall we get out of the water then?'

'What?' Viv was smiling beatifically, but after a moment she looked down at her wet jeans. 'Oh, yes. Good idea. Blimey, it's freezing!'

That evening, Viv was round at Eve's seventeenth-century house, Elizabeth's Cottage, a mulled cider at her elbow, a bowl of cashews in front of her. Robin, Eve's husband, was out with a friend, so it was just the two of them and Gus, who was stretched out in front of the blazing fire in the inglenook. One very relaxed dog. The logs shifted as wood turned to charcoal, and Eve shuffled nearer the flames. She hadn't felt properly warm since that morning.

'So what did Simon say?'

Viv had announced her intention to 'have it out with him'

the moment he was back on dry land. She sipped her drink, then kept it cupped in her hands for extra warmth. 'He claimed they'd had a wonderful sail, until I told him I'd been watching.'

'What went wrong?'

She put down her cider and took some nuts. 'Something about a cracked ball valve. He mentioned a seacock too. I wasn't sure if he was having me on, but I suppose he knows what he's talking about. Just as well he paid attention during his course; it was his instructor who recommended the putty stuff he used to mend the leak. He fluffed it though; the water only stopped when he shoved his *Sailboat Maintenance Manual* on top of the putty and pressed it down with his foot. Hardly foolproof, but I guess he's made use of the book already – that's what they were all laughing about. But if they hadn't had the book, they might have sunk!' Viv took up her drink again. 'What I want to know is, what is Arthur's Yard playing at? Surely they checked the boat before handing it over?'

Eve put another log on the fire, crouching to stroke Gus's warm fur as she did so. 'Will he talk to them about it?'

Viv nodded. 'But you know Simon. He'll play the whole thing down and be as nice as pie, because he's friendly with Anthony and Hal. He's only agreed to talk to them at all because I said I would if he didn't.'

That explained it. Viv didn't mince her words when she was riled.

She still looked hunched and tense. 'What if Simon hadn't had the putty in his pocket, and they'd been out with a newborn or some other vulnerable passenger? Someone could have drowned.'

Just over a week later, Eve was at Monty's, the teashop Viv owned, working on a batch of sticky ginger loaves. Her part-time job there was a godsend, providing a regular income as

well as good company. Eve was in charge of chaos reduction –
always a challenge when Viv was around, but a satisfying one.
She listened as Viv produced a series of tuts, followed by an irri-
table sigh.

'Are you planning to share your worries, or keep me in
suspense?'

Viv was stirring a batch of plump raisins, candied peel and
angelica into some fruit-cake dough, an activity she normally
described as soothing. 'It's Arthur's Yard.'

Eve thought Viv's concerns on that score had been taken
care of. Simon had spoken to Anthony as promised, and
Anthony suspected one of their casual workers was to blame.
He'd promised to question them, then read the riot act. 'There's
a fresh problem?'

Viv looked over her shoulder at Eve, mid-stir. 'That useless
individual Anthony Mottram hasn't kept his word. I got chatting to one of his casual staff about Simon's leaky boat, and he
didn't know a thing about it. He says he and his workmates are
always gossiping over a pint. He's sure he'd have heard if one of
them had been told off, but there's been no hint of it. No one's
even been questioned, as far as I can see. What's the point of
being the boss if you don't boss people?' She dug her wooden
spoon into her batter savagely, making Eve wince.

If Anthony hadn't bothered to follow up, that really was
bad. The sea was beautiful and awe-inspiring, but dangerous
too.

'I marched straight over to Simon's and told him, of course,'
Viv went on.

'What did he say?'

'He's trying to wriggle out of talking to Anthony again. He
doesn't want to ruin their friendship. He keeps saying what a
nice guy he is, and that he probably "dealt with the issue
privately".' Viv snorted. 'Simon's just being a wimp, and I'll bet
Anthony's the same. He clearly let the issue slide.'

Or perhaps it hadn't been one of the casual workers who'd mucked up, but Anthony or Hal. If one of them was getting lax, it could explain the tensions between them.

Three days later, Viv came rushing into the teashop after a dash to the village store for emergency sugar. (She'd accidentally tipped a ten-kilo pack onto Monty's kitchen floor. Eve had been busy getting it up while she was out. It was still rather crunchy and sticky underfoot.)

'I bumped into Gwen Harris on my way back.' Viv was breathless.

'Bad luck.' Gwen's imagination was as overactive as her tongue. She'd once told the police Eve had been having an affair with a murder victim.

'Her husband's boat is stored at Arthur's Yard and they paid to have it spruced up. He went to check the moment it was finished.'

That was entirely predictable. They were a pair of fusspots. 'And?'

'Mr H found a sandwich wrapper and a half-eaten packet of crisps in one of the lockers, along with an empty vodka bottle.'

Eve paused in her sweeping. Together with the leak, it made the outfit look unprofessional at best.

'The Harrises told Anthony Mottram of course. Around a week ago.'

'I don't imagine they were as nice about it as Simon.'

Viv scoffed. 'No. And guess what? Anthony told them the rubbish must have been left by "one of their casual workers".'

That excuse was starting to wear a bit thin. 'It would have been before you asked one of them about Simon's boat.'

Viv nodded. 'And they said there'd been no trouble. So it looks as though Anthony never tackled them about the leak *or* the empty vodka bottle. I'd like to know what's going on.'

3

―――――

Three weeks later, despite much chivvying from Viv, Simon still hadn't got round to having it out with Anthony. It was on Eve's mind when she rang Robin, who was working down in London for a spell. They'd been married less than a year, but they'd lived together for a while before that, and she missed their usual closeness. It didn't help that the work was for the police and could be dangerous. What's more, it was open-ended. Christmas was fast approaching, and she longed to enjoy the run-up together.

After she'd quizzed him about his day and tried to feel reassured, she filled him in on the situation at Arthur's Yard. They had a useful chat and she went into Monty's the following day with a sense of purpose and armed with a plan.

The teashop was in its full festive regalia, hung with decorative holly, ivy and mistletoe garlands, with red cloths and early flowering Christmas roses on each table. Outside, the village green was home to a large Christmas tree, its twinkling lights cheering up the winter grey. The warmth of Monty's was like an enveloping hug and she was met by the sight of various villagers, snuggled in their woollens, tucking into Viv's exquisite mince pies. The heavenly smell made her hungry. Friends and neighbours smiled as she passed them en route to the kitchen. It had taken a while after her move from London, but the sense of belonging now was precious. It made her awkwardly emotional at times.

Once she and Viv were alone in the teashop's cheerful kitchen, warm from the ovens, surrounded by the smell of cake and spices, they exchanged news.

'Jonah still hasn't told me about the baby,' Viv said dolefully.

'You could always admit you overheard by accident.'

Viv chewed her lip. 'But what if I do, and there's something wrong?'

'How did Jonah sound when you spoke to him last?'

Viv cocked her head. 'Normal.'

'I'm sure it's fine then. I expect they'll tell you very soon.'

Viv groaned in frustration and Eve decided it would be a good moment to change the subject. She explained how she'd spoken to Robin about Simon's leaky boat, the night before.

'I tested a theory on him. Perhaps the mistakes at Arthur's Yard are down to Anthony Mottram or Hal Osborne. It would be huge if it got out that the boss or second in command are at fault, especially with the centenary coming up.' The whole village took pride in the yard's expert workmanship and honesty. If those pillars were knocked away, it would be hard for them to recover.

Viv put some sloe gin spice cakes in to bake then turned to her, her cheeks flushed from the oven's heat. 'I can see it would fit, but I doubt Simon will believe it – he's fond of them both, and everyone's always going on about how reliable they are.'

'I know. We need evidence, and we've got the perfect chance to hunt for it.'

Viv's eyes lit up. 'The centenary party?'

'Exactly.' There was a whole-village celebration the

following night, to be held at Mistletoe Place, the beautiful big manor house belonging to Hal's uncle. It was almost next door to Arthur's Yard, which made it the perfect venue. 'Anthony and Hal will be the stars of the show. It should give us plenty of time to observe them. We can ask the gang to help so we don't miss anything.' 'The gang' was comprised of Eve's neighbours Sylvia and Daphne, as well as Simon.

'What if Anthony and Hal don't give anything away?'

'Let's not leave it to chance.' Eve leaned forward to explain her plan.

Eve found it hard to get to sleep that night. Focusing on the centenary party had helped take her mind off Robin's absence, but thoughts of *that* large gathering had focused her attention on another one. In just over a week's time, Eve was due to host a party too: an open house to celebrate Elizabeth, for whom her cottage was named. Back in the 1700s, she'd hidden a poor servant boy to save him from the gallows, after he'd stolen bread to feed his starving siblings.

The open-house dos were a twice-yearly, long-running tradition to raise money for children's charities. Eve was a hundred per cent committed to the cause, and a relatively old hand at the events now, but she still went into planning over-drive each time. There was a lot of baking involved. Thank goodness Viv was so helpful with the preparations. Eve had already ordered all the ingredients, of course. Weeks ago. And made lists. Lots of them. But it was still hard to stop the jumble of thoughts that assailed her.

At last, she managed to switch off and fall asleep. But in the small hours, she woke suddenly, heart thumping, to the echoes of running feet down in Haunted Lane. Then from somewhere downstairs, Gus whined. Eve got up as she so often had before, and went to peer out of the ancient casement window, shivering in her pyjamas. There was no one there. She listened, but Gus had gone quiet again.

Back in bed, the goosebumps didn't subside. The footfalls belonged to the legend of Elizabeth and the servant boy. They were said to be echoes of the hue and cry sent to hunt him down and were only heard in Elizabeth's Cottage. Viv, whose parents had lived there before Eve, swore they signified danger. Eve still didn't believe in ghosts, officially, but she'd heard the footfalls too often to dismiss them. Violence always followed. Mostly death. And invariably within twenty-four hours.

The following day was a quiet, average Saturday in December. Eve began to put up decorations for the following week, tying holly with red ribbon, perching it above the paintings on her walls. She pinned mistletoe to the beams too and thought of Robin. She longed for him to be back for good.

Nothing unusual happened, but that just left her increasingly anxious as time wore on. She tried to push thoughts of the footfalls away as she approached Mistletoe Place for the party that evening.

Eve had visited before and was fond of the old house. It was a wonderful, rustic home, spreading out to either side of a central entrance hall. Its large, well-proportioned rooms were painted in heritage colours. Everything was tidy and attractive, yet lived in, from the big comfy sofas to the warm rugs covering the oak floorboards. It must have been a great place for hide-and-seek for Hal as a child. It would have kept his nanny on her toes. A few years back, his dad and stepmother had moved in too. Eve guessed it was company for Hal's uncle, a widower whose daughter had left home, and the place was certainly large enough.

Tonight, the large party room to the left of the front hall had been transformed. It was festooned with greenery, and each wall light was hung with vintage Christmas decorations: tiny glass baubles and faux leaves that sparkled as though touched with frost. Eve revelled in the prettiness of it. The cosiness was accentuated by the view from the windows, which faced the dark river path and the inky water beyond.

Her previous visit to Mistletoe Place had been thanks to her journalism, which was her true profession. She'd written a profile of Tabitha Osborne's interiors' business – Hal Osborne's stepmum. Mostly, Eve stuck to her speciality, obituary writing, but she was a personal fan of Tabitha's wares, so she'd been keen to do the article. Tabitha had shown her the design room at Mistletoe Place, where she worked up her prototypes. It was part of her business suite, towards the back, left-hand side of the house, also facing the river.

It had been easy to warm to Tabitha. She'd seemed surprised and delighted by the extent of Eve's enthusiasm and it turned out they shared a lot of the same tastes, from perfume to interior décor. Most of the furniture and lights Tabitha favoured would be way out of Eve's price range, though.

Eve's tour had included a second, larger workroom full of sewing machines and desks where the final products were packed, ready for shipping. Eve had recognised the classy ivory notepaper sent out with each item, with what looked like a 'personal' note from Tabitha. She must have a team, copying identical messages to clients in her handwriting. Eve had tried not to feel stupid for believing her note had been written by Tabitha personally. It was just business.

As well as the design and work rooms, there was a storeroom and a kitchenette, which Tabitha kept well stocked with tea, coffee and treats for the staff. The kitchenette opened off the party room. Eve could see its door from where she stood.

People were filing into the party in greater numbers now, women's earrings sparkling in the light, polished shoes gleaming, the smell of expensive scent. Greetings, laughter and kisses on both cheeks.

Eve was happy to see Tabitha crossing the room towards her. She looked sophisticated in a simple black dress, her dark hair swept into a French pleat, a burnt-orange scarf around her neck. Seeing her always made Eve want to revamp her wardrobe. She was clearly onboard with the party, rushing round with drinks and nibbles, beaming at the guests and thanking Eve for the umpteenth time for her lovely write-up.

Eve beamed back and hoped they could gather evidence that evening without offending anyone. 'This is wonderful, Tabitha. Everything looks so lovely! You've done Hal and Anthony proud.'

'I'm so pleased for them.' Tabitha smiled, but looking at her more closely, Eve saw there was something tight about her mouth.

She wasn't the sort to get anxious about organising a party. This must be something else, and Eve's mind lit on the tensions between Hal and Anthony. 'Are you all right?'

Tabitha's smile broadened, but her shoulders were still rigid. 'Of course. Just hoping everything will go well tonight. You know how it is. Excuse me, I must check that the servers are managing all right in the kitchen.'

Her exit was a lot more polished than Hal's at Arthur's Yard, but every bit as hasty.

Eve turned away and found she was standing next to a young, blonde woman with an informal updo. She pivoted to face Eve.

'What a wonderful celebration, isn't it?'

Eve agreed.

'Don't they look pleased with themselves?' The woman nodded at Anthony and Hal. 'But Tabitha's nervous, isn't she? You spotted it. And I'm with her. I'd say the golden boys are riding for a fall.'

Her unexpected nastiness was enough to give Eve a quick, sharp shock, and the woman's tone made her skin crawl. A sort of eager, yet slightly detached, anticipation – as though she was watching a film and waiting for a juicy catastrophe to spice things up.

'I'm sorry,' Eve said, 'I don't think we've met. I'm Eve. Eve Mallow.'

'Ada,' the blonde woman replied. 'Ada Mottram. Anthony's sister.'

Knowing the relationship intensified Eve's unease. A sister wishing her brother ill wasn't pretty.

Ada headed off to talk to another group, and Eve lost track of her amongst the crowds. It was very busy now, and hot, the chatter in the room rising and falling.

It was impossible not to wonder about Anthony and Ada's relationship. Eve needed to concentrate on her plan for the evening, but it might all be related, if Ada's words had been triggered by the situation at the boatyard.

She reviewed their approach. Simon was primed to bring up the issue of the leaky boat with Anthony casually, then politely push for an update. Eve had spent some time warming him up to the idea, suggesting just how to tackle it. Anthony would probably fob him off, but she and Viv would monitor him as soon as the conversation was over. If Simon made him anxious, Eve hoped he'd confide in someone he trusted immediately. It was human nature to share the burden. If she and Viv listened in, they might get the truth.

But Simon was still worried about causing a row.

Half an hour after he'd arrived, Viv had already given him two encouraging shoves in Anthony's direction. The second had been so energetic, he'd slopped his drink. The room was full to the gunnels with guests, all clutching delicately balanced plates of canapés and champagne flutes. They'd probably go down like dominoes if Viv got any more forceful.

'You're going to blow our cover if you carry on like that,' Eve murmured.

'We need him to get on with it!' Viv said, at high volume, through gritted teeth. 'Talk about lily-livered.'

'There's no rush, so long as he tells us once it's done, so we can see what happens.' Eve trusted him to follow through; he'd promised. 'And if you only focus on nagging Simon, you might miss something else.'

Eve nodded subtly to the far end of the room. There was something odd going on with Anthony Mottram right now. His cheeks were flushed and his eyes twinkling as the umpteenth person clapped him on the back, but his expression changed when a powerfully built older man, swarthy with a five o'clock shadow, appeared in a doorway to the right. Eve watched as Anthony tensed and the older guy beckoned, a look of steel in his eye.

Viv took a deep breath. 'You win, Ms Smartypants. I see what you mean.'

Anthony followed the older guy through the door and Eve thought of his sister's words. Were he and Hal really riding for a fall, and if so, why?

Eve raised an eyebrow at Viv. 'Let's follow them. If Anthony or Hal are responsible for the leak and the vodka bottle, then it's out of character. It looks like something's gone wrong and it's affecting their behaviour. Anything out of the ordinary might tell us more.'

Viv nodded, following Eve across the room. 'It definitely looks like there's something brewing between Anthony and the musclebound guy.'

The doorway through which Anthony had disappeared led to a pair of corridors. One ran widthways through the right-hand side of the house, the other went towards the back door. There wasn't any cover. If they followed, they could easily be caught, but if they held back they'd never find out more.

Eve listened until voices told her which direction to go. She trod carefully across the stone floor, thankful she'd worn low slingbacks, not clacky high heels.

In an instant, there was a massive crash, followed by a man's voice.

'I know you're at the root of all this. You're behind her disappearance!'

Eve peered through a knothole in the wooden door as Viv tried to push her out of the way. In the end, she gave up her position and used a slim crack as her viewpoint instead. She held her breath and prayed for Viv to keep deadly quiet.

Heck. The older, thickset man had Anthony by his collar, rammed up against a ceiling-height cupboard in what looked like a dining room. 'I want answers. I want to hear you say it – exactly what you did!'

Anthony was taller than the other man, but wiry. The older man's bulk and his rage filled Eve with anxiety.

'I've told you before, Theo, there's nothing to tell.' Anthony's voice shook. 'Her disappearance has got nothing to do with me.'

Theo? Eve knew who the man was now – Hal's uncle and the owner of Mistletoe Place. She'd heard his name, though they'd never met.

Theo's fist was bunched as he held Anthony tight with his other hand, pinning him in place, pressing on his neck.

'Wrong answer! I know this is all your fault and now you're being a coward!'

Theo drew his arm back, ready to hit out.

4

Eve couldn't watch Anthony and Theo any longer. She'd find out more about the missing woman later. For now, she needed to break up the fight. Theo would surely come to his senses if he knew he had company.

She darted back down the hall before calling out, 'I'm sure the loos were off this corridor! Let's try the doors.'

Viv leaped away too. 'Good idea.'

They'd only opened one – pulling it closed again noisily – when Anthony emerged. He was white and shaking, but Eve pretended not to notice. Instead, she apologised and asked for directions to the toilet. She waited for Anthony to join the throng again before they left.

'What was that all about?' Viv said, when they went to the cloakroom for real.

'I don't know, but it sounded serious. A missing woman? You'd think it would be all over Saxford if someone's really disappeared.' Anthony and Theo must each have reasons for keeping it quiet, which was odd in itself. Eve would have to do some digging. 'Either way, that sort of argument's enough to make Anthony lose concentration at work.'

'And escape his worries in a bottle.'

Eve nodded.

It was five minutes later, when Eve and Viv were back at the party, surrounded by chat and laughter, that Simon came and found them. 'I've done it. Pushed and probed and all that. Anthony said he had a quiet word with one of the casual workers and they were very contrite. He decided to give them another chance, as it's a first offence. I mentioned the Harrises' empty vodka bottle too.' Simon was blushing scarlet. 'Anthony took a moment to reply, but he said it was part of the same lapse. The worker went on a bender, apparently, and mucked up my boat and the Harrises' at the same time. So, there you are.' He grabbed an extra-full champagne flute from a passing server and downed it with indecent haste. 'Please don't ask me to do that again.'

'We won't.' Eve scanned the room for Anthony as she spoke. There he was, and he was making a beeline for Hal. It looked as though he was about to share, just as she'd hoped.

The pair disappeared through the door that led to the corridors. Eve followed cautiously, with Viv on her heels. She was just in time to see them disappear into Tabitha's workroom. Viv's shoulders sagged as Anthony closed the door, but Eve's previous visit played to her advantage.

'Don't worry. There are two ways to listen in. We could nip back and sneak into the kitchenette, but the storage room just here might be a better bet. It's got a connecting door, and there'll be more room.' She approached the first door off the back corridor.

The storage room looked ghostly in the semi-darkness, stuffed with boxes of fabric and cushion pads, but a chink of light came under the door from the workroom beyond. Eve put an ear to the gap between the door and the frame, thanking her lucky stars that Mistletoe Place was ancient, with plenty of ill-fitting woodwork. She picked up the pair's conversation mid-sentence.

'... so that's what I told Simon!' Anthony sounded stressed and angry. 'It's essential we get our stories straight. We should have spoken about it earlier. I might have known he'd ask for an update.'

'For Pete's sake, Anthony, neither of the empty bottles were mine! How many more times?'

'And I have to believe you, don't I?' The anger was still there, loud and clear. 'We've been friends for so many years; I'm hoping that's not all based on a lie.'

'I can't believe you'd even think it! Don't you understand? My career – my whole future – is in your hands. I'd never get work at another yard if you sacked me. No one would trust me with anything. And the job's my passport to freedom!'

What did Hal mean by that?

There was a long silence.

'But you hid that second bottle.' Anthony's voice was tense. 'What the hell did you expect me to think?'

Hal let out a deep, frustrated sigh. 'I knew you'd assume it was mine if you saw it, so I tucked it behind my toolbox. One of the lads must have left it behind; I was going to get rid of it later.' There was another long pause. Eve guessed Hal was getting control of his temper. 'Look, you saw me drunk at work. I was at my very worst, and I'm sorry. But it was a one-off, and you know why. I'd never done it before, and I've been stone-cold sober at the yard since. Neither of the vodka bottles were mine, and I didn't muck up Simon's boat!'

'But you promised you'd get one of the lads to do a final check of it, and you didn't!'

'I knew I didn't need to. I'd done the work myself.'

'You ignored my instructions because you were insulted! And then the boat leaked! So clearly you messed up. You must have finished the ball valve when you were wasted. Can you even remember doing it?' Anthony's tone veered from anxious, to furious.

'A job like that's second nature. I'd never get it wrong.' But that didn't answer Anthony's question. Hal's voice shook but it sounded like fear now, rather than anger. He couldn't be sure, Eve guessed. 'I honestly don't know why it failed.'

There was another long pause. 'All right,' Anthony said at last. 'I'm not firing you. Not now.' Eve could tell he was reaching the end of his tether. 'But no more secrets. No hiding bottles. No arguments. Because if it's not you, it's one of the others and I can't afford for this to go wrong. We've a hundred years of history to uphold.'

'As if I didn't know that!' Hal couldn't keep the bitterness from his voice. 'All I've ever wanted was to work at the yard.' After a long moment, he added: 'What happened out there? You were already shaken up before Simon spoke to you.'

'Just Theo, having a go again.' Anthony's voice had turned quiet.

'You haven't changed your mind? About telling him the truth, I mean?'

Eve could hear Anthony's huff through the door. 'No. And I won't either.'

The whole situation sounded precarious. Anthony was covering for Hal and Eve could see why. The yard's reputation would rock on its foundations if his lapse came out, and they *were* old friends. But Eve sensed Anthony was on the brink of throwing Hal to the wolves. Yet he was in trouble too. Theo had accused him of being mixed up in a woman's disappearance. He was battling problems on multiple fronts.

Back in the party room, Eve watched Hal and Anthony cross the floor towards some journalists from the local paper. Tabitha's eyes were on them; she looked as tense as before. Eve's preoccupation with the scene meant she only caught movement at the back of the room through her peripheral vision. As she turned, she saw the door to the kitchenette close. The figure who'd exited was already hidden behind the chattering crowds but Eve was sure of one thing. She and Viv hadn't been the only eavesdroppers, and Hal's lapse was no longer private.

5

———

Eve updated the gang's WhatsApp group with what she and Viv had witnessed. It had taken them a step forward. Now they needed to decide what to do next.

Simon was upset at the thought of Anthony and Hal's friendship breaking down. 'They've been close for as long as I can remember. And I've always trusted them both.' He looked as though he'd just discovered Father Christmas wasn't real.

Viv declared that was sentimental nonsense ('They risked my family's safety, for heaven's sake!') and was all for having it out with Anthony and Hal immediately. She was muttering 'twerps', 'idiots', 'nincompoops', and a selection of other insults under her breath.

Eve put a hand on her arm. 'I understand. Truly. I want to protect other people from shoddy workmanship too. But we need to know more first. We can't be sure Hal was responsible for the leak or the vodka bottles.'

'It would be a coincidence if there are two secret drinkers at the yard,' Viv said darkly.

'True, but it's not impossible. And if we sound off here, Hal's career will be over.' She glanced at the reporters.

Simon (predictably) thought they should trust Anthony and Hal to sort it out between them.

'Whatever happens, I don't think it'll be that simple.' Eve sighed. 'Someone else listened to their conversation. The news could get out, however hard Anthony tries to keep it quiet. I think we should tell him about the extra eavesdropper. It might shock him into dealing with the situation properly.'

But at that moment Tabitha appeared, and they had to postpone any action they might take.

'All well?' Eve said.

She still looked strained, but produced a bright smile. 'Yes, I think so.'

Eve sought for something to say. 'Didn't I hear you're planning a new line? I think someone mentioned it in the village store.' Get Tabitha onto her interiors business and she tended to relax.

For a moment, she still looked distracted, but then she rolled her eyes. 'Honestly. That must have come from one of my staff. They're not meant to say anything yet! But I've been meaning to talk to you about it. *Suffolk Monthly* say they'll take an advertorial and I'd love you to write the copy.'

Eve wouldn't do it for anyone else, but in Tabitha's case she was happy to accept. She had time to chat about it too, now she'd gleaned what she could about the troubles at the boatyard. She exchanged a glance with Viv all the same, and received a small nod in response. If anything interesting happened while Eve was busy, Viv would be onto it. How she went about it was another matter...

Eve tried not to stress as she and Tabitha chatted about how the article might work.

After they'd swapped ideas, Eve was passed straight onto someone who was hoping she might write about his restaurant in Blyworth. As he started his pitch, she glimpsed Anthony over her shoulder, his mobile to his ear. A second later, he rang off and let himself out of a side door. She saw him pass a window. He was heading up the estuary path, towards the boatyard. Perhaps he'd had enough. None of the gang followed him. She guessed they were focused on Hal. Eve might have gone herself if she hadn't been occupied.

The restaurateur was incredibly pushy, oily in fact, just like his hair, and Eve recognised the name of his eatery. Moira, the storekeeper, had mentioned having 'a funny tummy' after dining there. The entire village had heard the story, with a lot of unpleasant detail thrown in.

Eve fought to extricate herself without causing offence, but it took ages. She'd just managed to get rid of him when she bumped into Tabitha again. The strained look was back.

'Have you seen Anthony? Some of the guests are leaving and they wanted to say goodbye. I've tried his mobile but no joy.' She closed her eyes for a moment. 'In this din, he'd never hear it anyway.'

Eve said she'd seen him walk up the river towards the yard. 'It was a while back. I don't suppose he's still there, but I can check.'

Tabitha looked relieved. 'Oh, would you? That's kind. I'll keep scouring the house.'

Eve nodded and smiled. Mistletoe Place had a lot of secluded corners. Exploring it to find a missing Anthony could take some time...

Viv had appeared at Eve's elbow. 'If Anthony's hiding at the yard in the middle of his own party, it makes you wonder. I'll come with you.'

'We could tell him about the person who earwigged on his and Hal's conversation,' Eve said, as they let themselves out of a side door. 'Perhaps they've already approached him, and that's why he's gone off to hide.' It was bliss to leave the noise and chatter behind as they strode off into the night. Eve didn't want any more men like the restaurateur on her back.

They walked along the River Sax in the moonlight, the water inky black. It was dry and bitterly cold, the reeds touched with frost. The contrast with the heat inside the house was stark and Eve wished she'd grabbed her coat.

But it was only a short distance to Arthur's Yard. Eve could already see a faint glow of light through one of the windows. It looked as though Anthony *was* still there. Why hadn't he picked up when Tabitha called? He must know he'd be needed.

Eve explained about the pushy restaurant owner. 'Did you see anything while I was marooned?'

'Hal went to talk to Theo, but I couldn't hear what they said. Theo hardly spoke anyway, and nothing happened.'

Eve was quite sure there was more to tell. There'd be body language, expressions, pauses. But it might not be relevant and as they neared the yard she was distracted.

Close to, the stark light through the window made the interior feel eerie, unwelcoming, despite the tinsel Christmas tree standing on one of the storage cupboards. The place looked so still in the evening darkness, and the estuary and marshland accentuated its loneliness. Eve clutched her arms around her against the cold. Instinct should have sent her running for the boatyard and shelter, but the lack of any visible presence held her back. Her anxiety was building.

Viv nodded at the window. 'I doubt he's there. The place looks empty. He probably left the light on by accident. My three did it all the time.' Viv often spoke of her desperate attempts to house-train her boys.

But Anthony hadn't struck Eve as careless. Eve approached the side door. It was unlocked and she knocked as she pushed it open. 'Anthony?'

There was no reply, and for a moment she convinced herself that the place really was empty. But even if Anthony hadn't turned the light off, she was certain he'd never have left the place unsecured. Her heartbeat quickened as she walked further into the cavernous building.

It was then that she saw the legs, sticking out beyond a bit of stud wall. The ends of the coffee-coloured chinos. The shoes. So smartly buffed, brown and shiny. She almost tripped over them and the shock made her stomach lurch. She turned to gape at Viv and in an instant felt her friend's hand on her arm. Her eyes were wide.

It probably took half a second for Eve to snap out of her trance, but it felt like longer. As though she'd delayed inexcusably.

She dashed around the wall, beyond the shoes, the legs. To rush to Anthony's side and attempt first aid. If only she could remember what was required in her panic. She had an app on her phone, she could check for symptoms—

But the moment she'd darted into the area – a store, its walls lined with racks full of technical kit – she realised her app would do no good. Anthony was beyond saving, his head battered. Attacked from the front, by the look of it. He'd fallen on his back. A bloody pipe wrench lay next to his body on the cold, hard floor.

6

———

Viv was bent double. For a moment, Eve thought she'd fall. She put a hand out, so that they were supporting each other, then rang the police. After that, she rang Tabitha to break the news, and Viv called Simon.

'Poor, poor Anthony,' Viv said as they finished their calls. 'I was so angry when I realised he'd been protecting Hal. But what if he finally decided to act and Hal killed him over it?'

For once, she was whispering, but her words were still clear in the quiet of the building. For all they knew, the killer was in there with them. Eve glanced around the room, then backed towards the door. 'Let's go outside. We can tell the police everything when they arrive. And Viv?'

Viv blinked at her.

'We need to know every detail of what happened here tonight, whether it seems important or not.' She lowered her voice to a murmur, though they were out on the river path now. 'When you tell the police about the conversation between Hal and Theo, for instance, don't just say nothing happened. Try and remember exactly how they behaved, what you could see of their expressions, that sort of thing. It might not be relevant, but

Theo looked ready to harm Anthony earlier, and Hal clearly knows why. Perhaps they were discussing that. Would you write it all down, when you get home, so you can tell me tomorrow too?'

Viv nodded slowly. 'All right, if you think it's important.'

'It could be. Hal's one suspect and Theo's another. We need to find out if Anthony changed his mind about keeping Hal on, and who this missing woman is.'

It was a long night. Some uniformed officers were first on the scene and after Eve had filled them in, she warned them about Hamish. Poor animal. Someone would need to take care of him. Simon arrived too, with Eve and Viv's coats. His face was immobile with shock as he handed them over, his eyes glistening. 'Poor Anthony,' he said. 'I can't believe I was hassling him about my boat. To have that as our last conversation...'

One of the officers turned, a sharp look in his eye.

'Can I have your name, sir? We'll need to ask you about that.'

'I hope Palmer doesn't decide Simon's a suspect,' Viv whispered, as she and Eve made their way back towards the house. 'We both know he's a lousy detective.'

Viv was right. DI Palmer was closed-minded and keen on easy solutions. Eve had dealt with him before, when she'd written the obituaries of murder victims. Several times, she'd passed on crucial information to the police and Palmer seemed to hate her for it.

As for Simon, Hal would quickly leapfrog him when it came to motive. They'd have to tell the police everything, of course. Eve regretted it. She wished she could understand more first. Know whether she was dropping an innocent man in it.

When they reached Mistletoe Place, Palmer was there already, talking to Theo.

'Perhaps the police have heard about his and Anthony's argument,' Eve said, under her breath. Though they might have picked Theo first because he owned Mistletoe Place.

Eve bumped into Tabitha, who was wide-eyed with shock. 'Poor, poor Anthony. I've told the police we can take Hamish. Ada didn't seem interested.'

Seconds later, DI Palmer spotted Eve. He looked as though he'd got a bit of sick caught in the back of his throat, and Eve felt as though she'd got some in hers too.

Thankfully, he directed the infinitely preferable DC Olivia Dawkins to take her statement. Eve sat down to tell her everything, wondering whether Anthony had changed his mind and threatened to sack Hal after all. Someone had listened to their conversation. They could have sworn to speak out if Anthony didn't act.

Eve was very late to bed that night and she missed Robin's comforting presence more than ever. She didn't text to let him know what had happened. He'd be trying to sleep too; it could wait until morning. She imagined him at the B&B where he was staying, his mind full of the case he was working. It echoed one he'd dealt with long ago, before reporting corrupt colleagues had forced his move to Suffolk under a new name. Now, the network of dodgy cops and crime bosses were behind bars and he was free to be open about his past. It allowed him to combine freelance work for his old force with his other job as a gardener. Eve was happy he was back in his element, but the danger involved tied her stomach in knots. And now there was danger in Saxford, too.

Eve kept thinking of the awful restaurateur who'd trapped her as she'd watched Anthony head up the estuary path. She might have followed him if she hadn't been mid-conversation. She should have listened to her instincts, made an excuse and gone. Regret flooded through her. She might have prevented the murder.

The next day, Eve felt just as sad but clearer sighted. She needed to find out who'd killed Anthony. It was hopelessly inadequate, but the only thing she could do to help now. She messaged her contact at *Suffolk Monthly* to pitch his obituary. Having a legitimate reason to question a victim's contacts was always invaluable.

Thoughts of the tensions the night before filled her head. Had Tabitha sensed something was terribly wrong? Was that why she'd looked so anxious?

And then there was Ada, Anthony's sister, who'd seemed to be anticipating something catastrophic. In her case, she'd seemed eager to watch it play out. Eve shivered, despite the large radiator in her cottage's dining room.

She got up, gave Gus a pat, then donned her coat and went to the village store for milk and news. The place was looking festive, with fairy lights around the window. Moira had sprayed some fake snow in the corners of the glass, too. Eve pushed the door open and the store's bell jangled.

'Ah, Eve dear.' Moira loomed at her over the counter. She was wearing reindeer deely boppers, and had been for the last week. Eve found them terribly distracting. 'What awful news about poor dear Anthony Mottram! We'd left the party before it happened, but a little bird tells me it was you and Viv who found his body!'

Eve could see the excited anticipation in Moira's eyes. The storekeeper viewed first-hand gossip as a robin might view a juicy worm. It would make her the centre of attention for at least twenty-four hours if she could get Eve's full account.

But, as ever, Eve was determined to glean information, not give it up. 'I'm afraid it's true.'

Moira tutted with reasonably well-acted sympathy. 'Terrible. Terrible.' Her boppers bobbed. 'I hear someone hit him over the head?'

'You know, it was such a shock, I can't really remember anything in detail.' Eve met Moira's gaze head-on and tried to look convincing.

The storekeeper sighed. 'That's a shame. For the police, I mean. They must want your account.'

'I told them everything I could. But what about you, Moira? People must have been in here, sharing their worries. I know it's you they turn to in times of trouble.'

Moira simpered. 'Well, I suppose that's true. And yes, I've had lots of people in already. It's only right that I should tell you what they said, if you're looking into this business. You'll write poor Anthony's obituary?'

Eve nodded. 'I hope to.'

Moira leaned forward on the counter and frowned. 'Let's see then.' She proceeded to tell Eve all kinds of irrelevant details, to the extent that Eve had all but switched off by the time something useful came. '... and that's when Deidre Lennox overheard Hal's dad, positively begging Anthony not to tell Hal.'

Eve snapped to attention. 'Hal's dad?'

Moira beamed, clearly delighted by Eve's sudden interest. 'Giles Osborne. He, his wife Tabitha and Hal all live with Giles's brother Theo at Mistletoe Place, you know?'

Eve nodded.

'Of course, Theo had his wife and daughter there in the past, as well as young Hal and his nanny for a time. But then Theo's wife died and his daughter went off to study, so it was him and Hal, rattling around. So, when Giles had that little hiccup and money was tight, Theo invited him and Tabitha to move in. It made so much sense, I thought. Why waste all that space when Giles was in need? Of course, Giles had been in and out before that. He came every weekend to visit Hal, and for holidays and so on. A very attentive father.'

Eve wanted the background. 'What made Giles send Hal to Suffolk in the first place? Viv said his first wife died very young.' It was tragic that both brothers had lost their spouses. 'Did he have trouble coping?'

Moira gave a satisfied smile, so she must know the answer. Eve waited for the goods to drop.

'He'd hired the nanny so he could manage, but then one day, she was mugged in the street, and in front of Hal too! Really quite traumatic. It made Giles very anxious and he decided they'd be safer here, naturally.'

Eve didn't bother pointing out there'd just been a murder in Saxford, and it wasn't the first. 'It must have been hard for Hal, to lose his mum, and then be separated from his dad.'

Moira gave a heavy sigh. 'Apparently he was so young, he hardly remembered his mother.' She lowered her voice. 'I can't imagine what it was like for Hal living with Theo, though. He's such a bear of a man.'

'But he must be generous too – with his home and his time, I mean. He was happy to share Mistletoe Place with Hal and his nanny, I guess?' His character fascinated Eve.

Moira nodded. 'Oh yes. It's not everyone who would change their routine like that. And he never charged Giles rent or housekeeping for either of them from what I hear.' She looked quite perplexed. 'Of course, he was fiercely protective of Giles and that extended to Hal. But fierce is the word! He roared at me once because I'd forgotten to order his favourite preserve. Though he apologised later and bought me a lavish bouquet of flowers.' She coloured slightly. 'His bark's worse than his bite.'

Eve thought of his clenched fist the day before and wasn't sure. 'And you said Giles had a "hiccup". Why did he need Theo to take him in?'

Moira leaned her head in further, though they were alone. 'Well, they say Giles had some kind of breakdown and left his job in London due to the pressure, about ten years ago now. It must have been soon after Hal went full-time at Arthur's Yard. In those days, old Peter Mottram was still in charge.'

Anthony and Hal's lives really had been entangled for a long time. 'What did Giles do, before he got ill?'

'He managed an upmarket crafts gallery down in London,' Moira replied. 'Tabitha was one of the artists he promoted. Theo's daughter was studying interior design back then, and she introduced them. Then romance blossomed.' Moira clutched her hands together and looked a little dewy-eyed. 'Giles is a market gardener now, of course.'

That much Eve knew. She'd bought vegetables at his outfit, though she'd only dealt with his staff.

'It's a family tradition,' Moira went on. 'Theo retired and Giles took over. His team works Theo's land.'

'And Giles is happier?'

Moira put her head on one side. 'I hear he still has problems, but I'm not quite sure of the details.' The regret was there in her eyes.

'And what did Giles say to Anthony last night? And when?'

Moira's expression cleared again. 'According to Deidre, it was as the evening wore on. Around nine maybe? Or ten?'

People would have had a few drinks by then, and got tired. They'd have been less controlled.

'Anthony said something like: "It's just not right. You have to stop it. Please, Giles. If you don't, I'll be forced to tell Hal." And then Giles said: "I will. I promise you I will." So then Anthony said: "You said that before. Do it now! Send a text. I need to see you've done it." Deidre says Giles looked like a rabbit in headlights. He seemed absolutely lost for words. And then he told Anthony he couldn't do it in the middle of the party, but he'd do it as soon as everyone went.'

Eve imagined that had played poorly.

'Anthony clearly didn't believe him,' Moira went on, proving her right. 'Deidre says he put his face very close to Giles's and said: "I don't trust you! You can't expect me to carry on lying to Hal. He's my best friend!"'

Their connection was still strong, clearly, despite the problems at the yard. No wonder he'd been so angry and tense. When it came to the leak and the vodka bottles, his head had been pulling him in one direction, his heart in another.

Eve thanked Moira and walked out of the store in a daze. A short time after threatening to tell Hal Giles's secret, Anthony was killed.

7

Back at home, Eve sat at the dining room table, her laptop open, fire blazing and Gus warming her feet. A moment later, she had a photograph of Giles up on her screen. He was featured in a recent article about the Osborne market garden business in *Suffolk Monthly*. He looked significantly older than Tabitha – maybe sixty to her forty-five – and less conventional, with his wine-coloured scarf, jacket and open-necked grandad shirt. His smile was attractive – in fact he was attractive full stop, just like Tabitha – but there was something anxious about his brown eyes. The article was aspirational: all about the draw of working in nature and his idyllic career change at the relatively advanced age of fifty. There was precious little detail about his previous work at the gallery or why he'd left, though he looked fragile and his London job must have involved endless schmoozing, long hours and complicated, costly logistics, all on a very public stage. Eve guessed market gardening must also be pressured, but not in the same way, and he'd been brought up on it. It had been his parents' and brother's business before it was his.

It might not be relevant, but Eve made a note to find out more. The key thing was that he had a potential motive to kill

Anthony, just like his son Hal and his brother Theo. Even in the photo, there was fear in his eyes. If he'd panicked, he could have lashed out. Eve needed to uncover the secret – see if it was worth killing over. Anthony had clearly felt it was a betrayal of Hal. What the heck was it that could be addressed by sending a text?

She'd just moved on to googling Theo when there was a firm knock on the door of Elizabeth's Cottage. Gus barked like a dog ten times his size and Eve dashed through to the living room to answer.

Eve recognised the woman on the doorstep instantly. It was Ada, Anthony's sister. Eve swallowed. She was joint-top of Eve's list of people to interview, yet she wasn't looking forward to it. The way she'd spoken about her brother and Hal at the party had felt deeply unhealthy.

Even Gus looked a little uncertain, though Ada bent to fuss him.

It gave Eve more time to consider her. Her updo looked just as artfully arranged as it had the night before, with tendrils hanging down here and there. If she was mourning, it hadn't been enough to affect her routine. She stood up straight again, and Eve guessed she was around thirty, with a heart-shaped face and large eyes.

'I'm sorry to bother you,' she said. 'We met yesterday. Anthony was my brother.'

Eve snapped out of it. She was second-guessing the woman's feelings, based on one very brief conversation. That wasn't on. She put a hand on the woman's arm. 'I'm so sorry for your loss. Would you like to come in?' She ushered Gus out of the way. 'How can I help?'

Ada crossed the threshold and Eve shut out the frigid air behind her. It always amazed her how quickly the cold reached into the house. The perils of having no hallway.

'I was talking to Moira in the village store,' Ada said. 'She mentioned you'd be writing Anthony's obituary.' She shrugged. 'I guessed you'd ask to interview me. And I'd love to talk to someone about what's happened. It's all right for the Osbornes.' For a second her tone turned bitter. 'They've got each other. I expect Hal's devastated, but he can offload on his dad and step-mum, and his uncle too. But I'm alone now. My parents are both dead and I've no other siblings.'

'I'm so sorry. Of course, if you feel like talking, you're welcome to talk to me.' But there was something hollow in Ada's tone, as though she'd planned a script and was repeating it back. And it was rare for Eve to get a pre-emptive visit like this. She usually had to request interviews. *Suffolk Monthly* hadn't even confirmed the commission yet. She couldn't help feeling Ada had an agenda. 'Please, take a seat. Can I get you a drink?'

Ada asked for a coffee, and Eve made herself one too, fetching some spiced shortbreads to go on the side. It was her standard practice to provide food. Bereaved people were often too tired or distracted to remember to eat. But something told her Ada had probably breakfasted as usual. She seemed composed.

She sat forward on the couch. 'I hear you help the police with their enquiries sometimes.'

Eve imagined she had Moira to thank for passing that on. She met Ada's gaze, which was disconcertingly intense. 'That always gets exaggerated. I've written the obituaries of murder victims before. I tend to interview the exact same people as the authorities, and if I stumble across something significant, I pass it on.' If she downplayed her involvement, she hoped Ada would relax.

Ada nodded. 'You will tell me, won't you, if you get any hint of who killed my brother?'

'It's not normally that straightforward, I'm afraid.' Promising would make her very uneasy.

'Then just let me know your thoughts, as things progress. Please. I *was* his sister. I need to know.'

'I'll do my best.' Even that was more than she'd wanted to offer. There was something about Ada that put her on edge, and if she was the killer, then of course she'd want to know Eve's thinking. It would keep her one step ahead. 'You were very close?'

'Of course. We were alone in the world, and he was my brother.'

That didn't mean anything in Eve's experience. 'You said last night that you thought Anthony and Hal were riding for a fall.'

Ada laughed. A jarring sound. 'We had our spats. All siblings do. You have to admit, he and Hal looked insufferably smug last night. But we were the three musketeers, growing up. Mine and Anthony's parents lived close to Mistletoe Place, and Hal was around all the time, visiting his grandparents, then living with Theo. We'd grub about together, mudlarking, and sailing too. Hal's nanny was meant to stop Hal coming with us, but Anthony could see how trapped he felt. He was a past master at helping Hal slip away. Anthony and I were like that.' She placed her middle finger over her index one, still looking at Eve unflinchingly. 'I'll take over from him at Arthur's Yard now.'

Eve was curious about that. 'It's in your blood too, I guess.' She wondered if she had the same level of skill as Anthony, but asking would sound rude. She'd find other ways to investigate.

Ada nodded. 'And it's a hundred-year-old family business, of course. Running the yard's not how I thought I'd spend my life, but I don't have a choice now.'

Eve had come across similar situations before, where beneficiaries felt obliged to take over the reins of a family business. 'What had you hoped to do?'

'I've been working for Tabitha.' Ada's smile didn't reach her eyes. 'You know Tabitha, of course. Didn't you write a feature about her? She's such a love, isn't she? It's first-class training, working for someone like her.'

Eve imagined Ada as one of Tabitha's minions, finishing the products on one of the sewing machines, packing orders, writing, 'Hope you adore your new cushion' in Tabitha's handwriting. If she didn't truly like Tabitha, that could wear thin, and her fond words had sounded fake – the tone gushing and over the top.

'I was planning to stay another year or two, then start my own collection,' Ada said. 'But I'll have to step into Anthony's shoes now. It's so unexpected.' At last, she blinked. 'You don't imagine your brother will die at thirty-two.'

'You certainly don't.' Eve said how sorry she was again. 'And Anthony was clearly so well liked. It's hard to imagine who could possibly have wanted him dead.' Eve hoped she might goad her into showing her true colours, but Ada just looked at her placidly.

'I know.' She nodded, a tendril of blonde hair escaping her updo. 'He was almost too good to be true. I *adored* him.' Her tone was saccharine, and Eve was convinced she was lying through her teeth. 'I can only think it was a yob, passing up the estuary. They could have popped into the yard to steal something and found Anthony there. You hear about people lashing out in a panic, don't you?'

Eve nodded slowly. But the light had been on at Arthur's Yard. An opportunistic thief would have guessed there was someone on site. If they'd risked sneaking in, they'd have been prepared, not panicky. Eve didn't believe Ada really thought it was likely either. For the first time during their conversation, she'd stopped meeting Eve's eyes.

8

Once Ada left, Eve found it hard not to shudder as she noted down what she'd said. She'd been deeply hostile towards her brother, and even if she didn't want to work in the boat repair business, she'd just inherited a valuable company. The way she'd appeared on Eve's doorstep was suspicious too. She could easily be the killer, looking for information, not comfort.

Eve was feeling exposed and uneasy as she went back to researching Theo Osborne.

She knew Theo had inherited Mistletoe Place from his and Giles's parents, but not much beyond that. When she put his name into Google, his thickset form appeared, with his grizzled hair, dark eyes and strong eyebrows. Eve found an article dating back nine years in the *Blyworth Advertiser*, marking his retirement from the family business. He must have stuck around to do a handover with Giles, then pulled back. Eve found the announcement of Theo's wife's death too, twelve years earlier, and a mention of Theo's daughter Dora in another article. She'd studied interior design, Eve remembered, and had introduced Tabitha to Giles down in London. Perhaps Dora was the missing woman at the root of Theo and Anthony's fight. It had to be someone Theo really minded about, and a daughter would fit.

But if it *was* Theo's daughter, why wasn't the news all over Saxford, with the police putting out appeals? Eve guessed Theo hadn't told them, but why the secrecy?

She'd just opened an email from *Suffolk Monthly*, accepting her pitch to write Anthony's obituary, when a knock on the door set Gus barking.

He was beside himself with joy when Eve opened up to find Sylvia and Daphne on the doorstep.

Sylvia was looking over Eve's shoulder, her bright, keen eyes surveying her sitting room. 'She's gone?' The wind was getting up and it almost took her words away.

'Excuse me?'

'Ada.'

'Ah. Yes, she went twenty minutes back. Come in out of the cold!' Eve ushered Gus out of the way and her neighbours stepped inside.

As Eve closed the door behind them, Sylvia glanced at Daphne. 'She must have walked towards the estuary path. That'll be why we missed her.'

'You were waiting for her to leave?'

Sylvia nodded. 'We were going to come and see you this morning anyway. We wanted to speak to you last night, only pea-brained Palmer made it impossible.'

'Come and sit by the fire.'

They hadn't put on coats – they were only just up the lane – but the cold was enough to chill you to the bone in minutes.

Eve got them all tea and sourdough toast, spread thickly with butter and gooseberry jam. 'I was planning to knock on your door too, and Viv's and Simon's. I'm trying to amass as much information as I can. You saw something useful last night?'

Once again, Sylvia's eyes met Daphne's as she took up her tea, cradling it in her hands. Daphne nodded.

'We'd slipped out of Mistletoe Place. I'm afraid we weren't enjoying the party that much.'

Sylvia scoffed. 'Who would? Too hot, too much noise, too many people. So once we knew it was Hal who Anthony was protecting, we decided we could sneak off without harming your investigation.'

Eve nodded. It was fair enough. She was the one who'd actually watched Anthony dash up the river and not followed.

'We walked away from Saxford along the estuary, towards the house Anthony rents,' Sylvia said. 'Willow Cottage. You know it?'

Eve did. It was in the opposite direction to the yard. She'd been past it often.

'We were busy dissecting the party guests as we walked—'

'*You* were,' Daphne said, mildly.

'All right, I was. But you laughed several times, Daphne, so you're complicit. Anyway, we were so engrossed we got a little way beyond the cottage. Just as we were about to turn back, there was a loud bang and a labrador shot past us. I could see the whites of the poor animal's eyes. It was absolutely terrified. I'd seen Anthony with the dog on the beach, so I knew it was his.'

'He's called Hamish.'

'Ah. I called after him and ran too,' Sylvia went on. 'It was you that paused, wasn't it, Daphne?'

Sylvia's partner nodded. 'I wondered what had caused the noise and made the poor dog bolt. Then I saw Ada, striding away from Willow Cottage, and as she went, she threw something into the reeds. She was glancing over her shoulder, as though she was checking for onlookers, though I don't think she spotted me.'

'But you saw her face, didn't you?' Sylvia said.

Daphne shivered. 'Yes, in the moonlight. She was smiling.'

'Meanwhile, I was still running hell for leather, after the poor pooch,' Sylvia said. 'In the end it was a pedestrian who caught him, up by the main road. He assumed he was mine and held on to him for me. If he hadn't been so quick, Hamish would have been in amongst the traffic on the A12. I wouldn't have fancied his chances.'

Daphne shook her head, her kind eyes sad, and swallowed a mouthful of toast. 'We assumed he'd escaped from the garden. Though it would be cruel to shut a dog out in such cold weather.'

'Could you see how he'd got out when you got back to Anthony's cottage?' Eve asked.

Sylvia nodded. 'The gate was ajar and odder still, the front door was open. I got the wind up then. Thought Anthony might have had burglars.'

'I said we should call the police,' Daphne said.

'I know. I wish we had now. But at the time, it seemed more sensible to take a look inside. There were two of us, after all.'

Eve had every faith in Sylvia's indomitable spirit, but she was with Daphne on that one. If you could floor a burglar with a look, Sylvia would win hands down, but in a fist fight things might not be so simple.

'There was no one there, anyway,' Sylvia went on. 'And no sign of any disturbance. But Hamish didn't want to go back inside. The bang had clearly spooked him, good and proper. We got him settled in the end though, then closed the door to keep him safe and started back towards Mistletoe Place to tell Anthony what had happened. But then Daphne remembered the thing Ada had chucked into the reeds.'

Eve raised an eyebrow and Daphne shuddered.

'I had a look and found a champagne bottle, minus its cork. It was still two-thirds full.'

Eve understood now. 'You think she let Hamish out, then

popped it to terrify him deliberately?' It was an appalling thought. Eve imagined her making the bang just behind the poor dog's head for maximum effect. There'd been plenty of champagne bottles knocking around at the party. And perhaps Ada had keys to Willow Cottage.

Sylvia met Eve's eye. 'Would it fit with your impression of her?'

Eve's policy was not to pass judgement until she had plenty of evidence, but her gut reaction to Ada had been strong. It had felt essential to invite her in, but after five minutes she'd wished she hadn't. It was as though simply allowing Ada to cross her threshold had made Eve vulnerable.

'Your tactful silence speaks volumes,' Sylvia said. 'For my own part, I believe she set out to send poor old Hamish onto the A12, quite possibly to his death. Hardly the act of a loving sister.' She drained her tea. 'We wanted to tell Anthony about it, of course, the minute we got back to the party.'

Daphne sighed. 'In the end, we never got the chance.'

'No.' Sylvia shook her head. 'We hovered nearby but he was knee-deep in journalists, then on the phone. When I looked up again, he'd disappeared. We had a scout round but there was no sign of him.'

'That's probably when he went off to the boatyard,' Eve replied. The timing would fit.

'There's one other thing you should know too,' Sylvia added, 'though it doesn't relate to Ada.' She looked at Daphne, but it took a moment for her partner to speak.

'Just after we'd got back from our walk, so a little after twenty past nine, I think, I saw Hal staggering.' Her eyes were sad. 'He had to clutch a side table to steady himself. I didn't see him again until the police arrived.'

Daphne went on to point out that most people had been a bit squiffy by that stage, but Hal had apparently been staggering-drunk, and that was different. Eve could barely imagine how angry Anthony would have been if he'd seen him like that, especially after their earlier conversation. It was an important occasion, with the press there. He could easily have decided to sack Hal after all, under the circumstances. And Hal could have lashed out to stop Anthony ruining his reputation.

9

─────────

By the time Sylvia and Daphne got up to leave, it had started to sleet. Eve walked back up Haunted Lane with them, muffled against the cold and sheltering them with a golf umbrella. They let themselves back into Hope Cottage, its door adorned with a wreath made of ivy strung through with tiny glass baubles, glistening in the icy wet. Eve had bought a willow base to make one for her and Robin this year too, having got wreath envy last Christmas. She'd have to get it done before the open house. The decorations and seasonal cheer jarred with Anthony's death but people would want something uplifting.

As Eve walked on towards Monty's, she saw a police car weave its way round the village green. They must be on their way to Mistletoe Place or the boatyard. Eve wondered how the Osbornes were coping. She couldn't get the tensions of the night before out of her head. Viv would have a view on it. She'd already texted Eve three times during Sylvia and Daphne's visit, demanding to share updates, and now was the time. The teashop didn't open until after lunch on Sundays so they could talk while they baked, without any distractions.

Eve had left Gus in the warm, but she'd take him to Simon's

later if the sleet slackened off. She needed Simon's inside knowledge of Anthony and Hal. He might even know something about Theo's daughter – she was Hal's first cousin after all.

Viv was waiting by Monty's door as Eve approached, arms folded, fingers tapping. Despite her obvious impatience, Eve was momentarily distracted. Viv looked different somehow. Eve almost wondered if she was ill. 'Are you okay?'

Viv stepped back, peering at Eve. 'Of course I'm okay. I mean apart from what happened last night. Why are you looking at me like that?' Her frown deepened. 'Ugh. Don't tell me. You think my face looks weird.'

'Well, it's not—'

'No.' Viv held up a hand. 'Don't try and humour me. I can see it in your eyes. It's this wretched new foundation. It promised it was ideal for the more mature woman and would give my complexion a "dewy freshness". But it just makes me look sweaty, doesn't it?' She glistened at Eve rather fiercely.

'All right. Yes, it does. You normally look wonderful, so it's the make-up, not you.'

Viv groaned. 'I kept getting Facebook ads for it. They made it sound like some sort of miracle.'

Eve guessed she must have been googling for ideas. 'You wanted to give yourself a makeover? You don't need to. Truly.'

Viv sighed. 'Thank you, Eve, but you're biased. Forget it, anyway. We need to talk about last night. I can't believe you spoke to Sylvia and Daphne before me!'

Eve had felt forced to explain the delay when Viv texted her the third time.

'They came round to my place after they saw Ada visit.' Eve told her what Ada had said, then passed on Sylvia and Daphne's news.

'Wow. Ada sounds like an A1 cow.'

'I couldn't have put it better myself.' Eve filled Viv in on what Moira had said about Giles's secret, and how Anthony had threatened to tell Hal.

Viv blinked. 'So Ada hated her brother enough to endanger his dog, and Giles, Hal and Theo all have possible motives too.'

'I'm afraid so. I want to visit Simon next, to get his take on the Mottrams and the Osbornes. And I've texted Robin to let him know what's going on. He's promised to get some information from Greg.' Greg Boles was DI Palmer's second in command, and found the inspector almost as vexing as Eve did. He also happened to be married to Robin's cousin. He and Robin secretly chewed over cases, as Palmer was hopeless as a sounding board. 'But in the meantime, let's get on with the baking and you can tell me all about this scene you witnessed between Hal and Theo Osborne.'

Viv opened her mouth to start the story, but Eve pointed to the kitchen. 'The bakes?'

Viv huffed but complied. Eve followed her through, grabbing a bit of paperchain that had come down from the kitchen ceiling and climbing on a chair to press it back into place. Eve liked the fact that Viv had made the kitchen as festive as the tearoom, but the Blu Tack she'd used was wholly inadequate. The paperchain had dropped into her cake batter the week before.

She went on to dump her coat and umbrella in the office and donned an apron and hairnet.

Five minutes later, Viv was zesting in preparation for rich chocolate orange cakes and Eve was embarking on some festive flapjacks with candied peel.

'I wrote it all down like you said.' Viv nodded towards her bag. Inside, Eve could just see an exercise book, its pages still wobbly from when Viv had dropped it in the bath a couple of weeks back.

Eve had the urge to photograph the notes, just in case, but

she resisted. She'd make her own record of their conversation later.

'I thought about what you said, about body language and all the rest of it.' Viv was sifting some dry ingredients now, coating nearby objects lightly in flour. 'It was Hal who wanted to talk. Theo was trying to fob him off. Half turning his back, but Hal wouldn't give up.'

'That's useful.'

'They went into a room to the left-hand side of the back corridor. I think it was the one you told me about, where Tabitha comes up with all her designs, because there was a desk with drawings and scraps of fabric on it.'

'And a standard lamp with an ochre shade in one corner?'

Viv nodded. 'That's the one.' She reached for the cocoa without looking. 'Anyway, they left the door ajar, so I peered in, but they spoke quietly. I was alone in the corridor, but there was so much din from the partygoers that I still couldn't hear.'

'Did anything strike you at all?' Eve spooned golden syrup into a pan.

'Theo kept near the door, as though he'd like to sneak away, but I could see his face reflected in the mirror over the fireplace.'

'Most excellent Watsoning,' Eve said, twizzling two spoons to catch the final drips of syrup.

Viv cocked her head. 'I was hoping for Holmesing. Anyway, he looked angry at first. Like he was really having to hold his feelings in.'

'Like he was with Anthony? As though he wanted to punch Hal?' Eve weighed out some butter.

But Viv shook her head. 'No. It was more controlled than that. But here's the interesting bit. After Hal had been talking for a couple of minutes, Theo's expression changed completely. He suddenly looked desperately sad.'

Eve visualised the scene. 'This really is useful. And what was Hal doing?'

'Wandering around the room. He wasn't looking at Theo, which was odd.'

'Perhaps he didn't want him to feel scrutinised.' Eve popped the butter into the pan with the syrup, and wondered when Viv would remember she was meant to be preparing chocolate orange cakes. 'Or maybe he feared his reaction.'

'I wondered about that.' Viv nodded. 'When I thought back like you said, I remembered that Hal's shoulders were hunched. Almost cowering, like an animal that's been mistreated. He just went around the room, not meeting Theo's eyes, touching some of the objects on the bookcases and shelves. As though he was thinking about them and not Theo at all.'

So Hal had been scared. He'd taken a risk, but he'd managed to change Theo's mind about something. Theo had gone from being angry to sad. 'And you've no idea what they were talking about?'

Viv pulled a face. 'None whatsoever. Unless it was Theo who overheard Hal and Anthony talk about Hal's problems at work. Theo could have faced Anthony with it and got him to promise to sack Hal. In which case, I could see Hal trying to talk Theo round. How's that for a theory?' She glanced at Eve and groaned. 'What? What's wrong with it?'

'I suppose Theo might be tough enough to take a stand against his own nephew.' Eve remembered the hulking man. He certainly looked tough physically. 'But would he talk about the failings of a family member with Anthony, whom he clearly hated?'

Viv deflated. 'Now you mention it, it doesn't sound likely. Perhaps someone else overheard and made Anthony promise to sack Hal. Hal could have lashed out if Anthony dismissed him last night. I'd say he's the sort.'

Eve had a sneaking suspicion Viv would like Hal to be guilty, because of the way he'd messed up Simon's boat repair.

'But they were very old friends,' she said in response,

'Anthony was losing patience last night, but on reflection, I think if he'd fired Hal under those circumstances, he'd have explained that someone was forcing his hand. In which case, Hal would know his secret wouldn't die with Anthony.'

'Bother.' Viv turned back to her ingredients at last. 'You're right.'

'But if Anthony and Hal didn't realise they were overheard, that changes everything. Anthony could certainly have decided to sack him, and Hal could have killed him to try to keep his secret.' Eve told Viv what Daphne had said about Hal being staggering drunk.

'Blimey. Anthony would have been livid. What on earth was Hal thinking?'

'I'll want to talk to him as soon as I can. He's a natural interviewee for the obituary. I also need to discover Giles's secret and dig into the mystery of the missing woman. I'll speak to Simon first, like I said.'

Suddenly, Viv applied herself to her cakes. 'I'll come with you.'

'But there isn't time.'

Viv looked at her watch. 'Of course there is. You really need to learn to relax, Eve.'

10

As soon as her flapjacks were in the oven, Eve messaged the gang's WhatsApp group to ask for the timings of every event they could remember from the night before. She wanted to create a timeline of the evening and work out who was where, when. When the flapjacks were well on their way, she went to fetch Gus while Viv stood by, ready to remove them and the cakes from the oven. The sleet had stopped but the sky was still full of cloud. It was threatening something. Eve got her beloved dachshund into his tartan coat, and headed out again.

Viv dashed onto the village green to meet her, scarf flying. They walked down Dark Lane, twinkling Christmas trees in cottage windows providing beacons of light in the gloom, then branched off south towards Simon's house. He lived next to the riding stables he owned, not so far from the boatyard. Eve had texted him in advance, and he welcomed them into his kitchen, warm from the Aga, mistletoe hanging over the table. A moment later he was dishing up vegetable soup in some beautiful sea-green bowls. The crusty bread on matching plates looked sumptuous too.

'I wasn't expecting lunch!' Viv said.

'Eve told me you'd never have time to eat before opening the teashop otherwise.'

Viv rolled her eyes. 'You two are always organising my life.'

'Someone has to.' Eve and Simon had spoken at once.

'It's nice to cling on to something normal like cooking, anyway,' Simon said. 'Each time I looked out of the window this morning it felt like there was a police car passing. A constable came to talk to me earlier too, to ask about the business with the boat.' He closed his eyes for a moment.

'That's not going to make you a suspect,' Eve said. She felt guilty for pushing Simon into confronting Anthony now. It meant they knew more than they had, but it was possible they'd set the murder in motion as a result.

'Come and sit down, anyway.' Simon gestured towards the scrubbed oak table, which Eve secretly coveted, though it would never fit in Elizabeth's Cottage.

Eve sat and turned to him. 'I'm so sorry about what's happened. I hardly got the chance to say yesterday, but you'd known Anthony for years, hadn't you?'

Simon sat too. 'Yes.' He sighed. 'But you know what it's like. We'd have a beer together if we bumped into each other. Chew the cud. I didn't know him well. You'll try to work out who killed him while you're interviewing for his obituary?'

'That's right, and I was hoping to pick your brains.' Eve spread the holly-and-ivy napkin Simon had provided over her lap. 'You're friendly with Hal, as well?'

Simon nodded. 'He comes to ride at the stables sometimes.' He was frowning. 'He asked me not to tell his dad.'

'Why on earth would he do that?' Viv beat her to it.

'I don't know,' Simon said. 'Odd, isn't it?'

Viv and Eve's eyes met.

'What?' Simon already sounded defensive.

'If one of us ran the stables, we'd have found out years ago,' Viv said.

Simon looked mystified.

'Bless.' Viv shook her head.

Eve added the oddity to her notebook, then brought Simon up to speed on her visit from Ada that morning. 'She talked about her, Anthony and Hal sailing, and how Hal wasn't meant to. Perhaps Giles is the protective sort.' But Hal hiding his habits now didn't sound healthy. He was a grown man after all – thirty or so, at a guess.

'What else do you know about Hal? Is there anything that would tell us more about his relationship with Anthony, or the trouble he seemed to be in at work?'

Simon put his hands over his face.

Viv grabbed them and pulled them away. 'What is it?'

He was wincing. 'I did once have to stop him from riding because he was drunk.'

'What?' Viv looked scandalised. 'Why didn't you say so earlier?'

'It was years ago. After a break-up with another girlfriend. I'd forgotten all about it. Well, pretty much.'

Eve could see Viv took a dim view of Simon's loyalty towards a man who'd put her unborn grandchild at risk. 'Another?'

'He broke up with his latest, Gabby, recently.'

Viv huffed. 'So he can't hold down a relationship and it's not the first time he's tried to do something safety-critical while sloshed.'

'He seems to be unlucky in love,' Simon said. 'I overheard him talking about it to Anthony, saying it was happening "all over again". And he said it always would, as though he was giving up. But he loved Gabby, and I'd swear he treated her with respect. He's a nice bloke. Truly he is.'

'Do you know him well,' Viv demanded, 'or is it another one of those sharing-a-pint-without-any-intimacy situations?'

Simon looked defensive again. 'More the latter. I don't tell my drinking buddies my life story and I wouldn't expect them to tell me theirs either.'

'Very unhelpful,' Viv muttered.

'Did Hal normally have too much to drink when you were together?' Eve asked.

Simon shook his head. 'No, not as a rule.'

'But you always stick up for people, Simon.' Viv tore off a piece of bread, scattering crumbs across the table.

Eve cut in to ask Simon for Hal's email address and phone number before sibling warfare broke out, then switched focus. 'I wanted to ask you about the missing woman Theo and Anthony argued over, too. Theo sounded so impassioned I figured it must be someone very close to him. He has a daughter called Dora – Hal's first cousin. Has Hal ever talked about her? Could it be her, do you think?'

Simon frowned. 'She was in a relationship with Anthony Mottram. They broke up recently. But you'd imagine we'd have heard if she'd disappeared.'

'If they were seeing each other then of course it must be her, you dodo,' Viv said.

Eve thought it was likely too, though the dodo insult was unfair.

Simon looked stung. 'But if Theo thought Anthony had hurt her – physically, I mean – he'd have reported it to the police.'

'You'd certainly think so.' And that was two recent break-ups, Anthony and Dora, and Hal and the ex-girlfriend Simon had mentioned. Was that just a coincidence? 'Do you know why they split up?'

Simon looked helpless and waited for the Viv onslaught.

'It's all right,' Eve said, heading it off. 'It's a sensitive topic. I wouldn't have asked either. The take-home point is that Theo could have gone to the yard to finish the row they'd started at

Mistletoe Place. Maybe they fought again, and Anthony wound up dead.'

'Maybe,' Simon said unhappily. 'There's one other thing. Everyone's unpicking Anthony's relationships and a couple of the stable hands say Ada was undercutting Arthur's Yard.'

'What?'

Simon nodded. 'If she heard someone needed a repair that she could manage in situ, she'd step in and promise better value for money. She's got no premises. People think she was undermining Anthony because she wanted the yard.'

If that was right, Ada had lied to her point-blank – not just about loving her brother, but about not wanting to work at the yard too. Ada was starting to solidify as the top suspect. Several others had motives, but she had lots to gain, and her seemingly visceral hatred for Anthony counted for a lot. The way she'd let Hamish out was horrific.

Viv gave Simon a hug before they left. 'You know I love you really, don't you? And the soup was delicious.'

They walked back through the village, crows cawing in the stark, bare trees.

Eve had a mounting to-do list. She had it all down mentally and would make more notes the minute she was back home.

'You will let me help, won't you?' Viv said, as though reading her mind. 'I still want to know if it was really Hal who almost drowned Simon, Jonah and Stevie.'

'Any news from Jonah about the baby?'

Viv shook her head. 'I'm going to give him what for when he finally comes clean! Keeping it secret's ridiculous.'

But Stevie was a much more self-contained person than Viv. She might not welcome her enthusiasm just yet. 'I understand. I'm sure Jonah's itching to tell you.'

Viv nodded. 'Maybe. Anyway, enough of that. You haven't promised yet.'

'What?'

'To keep me involved in the investigation. Ada could be planning to continue Hal's contract. The danger's not over. And if he killed Anthony, it would be too awful if he got away with it.'

'I'll let you know everything. We'll tackle it together. But there are plenty of other contenders for killer.' Her mind skipped to Ada and the note of eager anticipation as she'd predicted her brother was riding for a fall. 'Robin will be back later.' Eve couldn't wait to see him, though it would only be a flying visit. 'He's got some news from Greg. I'll pass it all on.'

'You're a brick.'

After Viv left to open Monty's, Eve went back to Elizabeth's Cottage so she and Gus could warm up. The large old-fashioned radiators were kicking out heat, but Eve pulled on an extra jumper too, thick and soft with a roll neck, then settled down on a couch in the sitting room to create a timeline of the evening before. She combined the responses to her WhatsApp message with what Moira had told her until she'd got the evening mapped out. Some of the details might be irrelevant, but she'd rather include them than not.

<u>*Saturday 6 December – Arthur's Yard Centenary Party timeline*</u>

7.30 p.m. – Eve, Viv, Simon, Daphne and Sylvia arrive at Mistletoe Place.

7.35 p.m. – Eve talks to Tabitha who seems tense and distracted.

7.40 p.m. – Ada says she thinks Anthony and Hal are riding for a fall. Appears pleased about it.

7.45 p.m. – Eve and Viv overhear Theo accusing Anthony of being implicated in the disappearance of an unknown woman. Theo's daughter Dora??

8.10 p.m. – Eve and Viv eavesdrop on Hal and Anthony who argue about Hal drinking at work. Hal pleads his innocence. Anthony agrees not to tell (reluctantly).

8.25 p.m. – Daphne hears Anthony ask Hal to fetch some paper-

work from Willow Cottage to show to a journalist. Hal leaves the house.

8.30 p.m. – Eve talks to Tabitha Osborne about a new article for Suffolk Monthly.

8.37 p.m. – Daphne and Sylvia decide they need a break and head up the estuary inland.

8.50 p.m. – Viv sees Hal talk to Theo about something. Theo looks angry but then sad. Hal tats with ornaments in the room and doesn't look at Theo.

8.50 p.m. (maybe?) – Sylvia and Daphne hear a loud bang on the estuary path and see Anthony's dog shoot past them.

8.51 p.m. – Daphne sees Ada chuck something into the reeds by the river

9 to 10 p.m. approx – Deidre Lennox hears Anthony tell Giles he must stop doing something or he'll be forced to tell Hal. He insists Giles should take action immediately (via text) and loses patience when Giles won't comply. The text means someone else has to be involved. N.B. Anthony is still fighting Hal's corner at this stage, but see 9.20 p.m. entry below.

9.10 p.m. approx. – Sylvia and Daphne return Hamish to Anthony's house after being helped by a passer-by on the main road. They find Anthony's gate and front door open, but no one inside.

9.15 p.m. approx. – Daphne finds the almost-full champagne bottle in the reeds where Ada threw it.

9.20 p.m. approx. – Back at Mistletoe Place, Daphne sees Hal stagger, having overdone the drink again. Did Anthony see him and decide to sack him after all?

9.40 p.m. – Eve ensnared by horrible restaurateur.

9.50 p.m. – Eve sees Anthony speaking on the phone, then heading up the estuary towards Arthur's Yard.

10.15 p.m. – Tabitha Osborne asks for help to find Anthony as some of the guests want to say goodbye.

10.25 p.m. approx. – Eve and Viv find Anthony's body at Arthur's Yard.

Looking at it written down was helpful. Hal and Ada had both gone to Willow Cottage, it seemed. Ada had been lucky Hal hadn't caught her. Eve thought of her intensity that morning. She'd tried to convince Eve that she and Anthony were close, despite her toxic words the night before, and she'd pushed for updates too. It would make total sense if she was the killer. Eve shivered. Perhaps Ada had taken her loathing out on Hamish the labrador first, then gone to the boatyard, realising that sending Anthony's dog to its death wasn't enough. And it wasn't just emotional satisfaction she'd gain, it was the prize of Arthur's Yard.

At that moment, her mobile rang. Robin. She went to pick up, but the ringing stopped, and when she called back, he didn't answer. What was wrong? She tried to be logical. A colleague had probably walked into the room. Or maybe an urgent call had come through.

But fifteen minutes later, when he still hadn't rung back, she gave in to temptation and tried again. This time he answered.

'*I'm sorry, Eve. I was hoping for a chat but things kicked off again. I wanted to—*' He stopped. '*No. Look, it doesn't matter. It's best if I explain when I get home.*'

All Eve's alarm bells started ringing. What did he want to say? Why was it better to talk face to face? That implied something serious. Something that was going to upset her. 'Okay. Of course.' She wanted to know now, but at the same time she didn't. His voice sounded odd. Not as clear as usual. Was that emotion?

She couldn't imagine what was up, but she knew she'd be thinking about it until he arrived home that evening. Her stomach was in knots.

11

Eve badly needed distractions to pass the time before Robin came home. It was hard to push the memory of his voice from her mind. She turned to Gus.

'I need to be sensible. It's probably fine, and I've got a to-do list as long as my arm. I mustn't lose focus.'

Her dachshund put his head on one side, and stood poised as though he was ready to support her, whatever she decided.

Eve bent to give him a cuddle and tried to shelve her worries as she marshalled her thoughts. She used the email she'd got from Simon to send Hal a message, expressing her condolences and asking if she could talk to him and his family for the obituary. Hal, Giles and Theo would be crucial, but she'd want to quiz Tabitha, too. She was the type to pay attention, and she knew everyone involved.

It was no use bothering them today, though. Mistletoe Place would be crawling with police and Palmer would run her off the grounds if she showed her face. But it wouldn't hold her up. There were other jobs to do.

Following up on Hal's cousin, Dora Osborne, was a priority. As Anthony's ex, she was automatically of interest. If their break-up had been acrimonious, she might even be a suspect. Or her fate might be at the heart of Theo's motive, if she was missing.

Eve googled her and found she had an interior design practice in Blyworth, the nearest market town. Of course, Moira had mentioned she'd studied the subject in London and she had been the one to introduce Tabitha to Giles. Eve scanned her website to understand her background. She and Tabitha must have stayed friends, because, just like Ada, Dora had worked for Tabitha when she was starting out. She'd gone on to source pieces for show homes in new developments. Now she offered an entire service, advising on colour schemes, layout, furniture and accessories. Eve tried to imagine having the money to hire someone like that. It would be fun to see what they suggested, but she'd rather keep control.

She dialled the mobile number on Dora's website, but had to leave a message. After expressing her sympathy, and asking if they could talk as soon as possible, she rang off. The lack of reply didn't mean anything. But Eve had wanted reassurance, and she hadn't got it.

She walked Gus round the village green, her mind flitting between Robin and Dora. 'You're behind her disappearance!' Theo had said, but had he been talking about her, or someone else? Either way, it sounded ominous.

Back at Elizabeth's Cottage, Eve tried to concentrate on her research into Arthur's Yard. It got stellar reviews in general, Simon's boat troubles notwithstanding, but it had had its ups and downs – in particular a serious fire, years back. It sounded dramatic, but it really didn't tell Eve anything. An hour later, she grabbed her mobile and called Dora again, but once more, it went to voicemail. She couldn't shake her feeling of unease.

'C'mon, Gus.' Eve got him into his smart tartan coat and ushered him out to the car. She needed to go to Blyworth anyway, to pick Robin up from the station, and she couldn't concentrate on desk work. Instead, she could head into town early and visit Dora's business address. It wasn't a working day of course, but 14 James Street was on the outskirts of town in a residential area. It might be Dora's home, as well as her office. Perhaps she was busy with something, her phone on silent.

Eve drove past wide, flat fields, bleak in the winter gloom. It was heartening to see lights glowing from half-timbered houses, once she reached Blyworth.

Not far now. Here it was. 'Let's go and knock, Gus.' If Dora was there, a very appealing dachshund could only help. He was the most excellent icebreaker.

But as Eve approached the door, her anxiety built. There was a leaflet sticking halfway out of the letter box. Dora hadn't collected it. And glancing down through a glass panel, Eve saw a pile of more leaflets and junk mail. A flyer for a local gym and an envelope with a tree-shaped logo printed on it in sunshiny colours. It didn't look as though anyone had picked up the mail for days.

She tried to tell herself it didn't mean anything, but her mouth went dry. Once again, she called Dora's number, and once again, there was no reply.

In her gut, Eve was sure it was Dora who was missing. But Theo couldn't have suspected anything criminal, surely, or he'd have told the police.

She was distracted by a text alert. Robin.

On the usual train, but don't worry about meeting me. I can make my own way home.

Was he trying to put off what he had to say? Eve bent to give Gus a stroke for comfort.

She texted Robin back to say she was already in town, then went to sit in the dog-friendly café near the station. Outside, a Salvation Army band was playing 'In the Bleak Midwinter', which wasn't really helping. She nursed a hot chocolate as she stared unseeingly out of the misted windows. What was Robin going to tell her? And where was Dora Osborne?

When the time came, she went into the draughty station foyer, with its vast Christmas tree. Over to one side, a man stood selling roast chestnuts. Eve normally adored the smell, but at the moment, she felt queasy. She huddled with Gus near the ticket barrier.

The train was showing as delayed, but at long last, the display board said it had come in.

And there was Robin, emerging from the shadows, a scarf swathed around his face.

Eve felt awkward. Normally she'd rush up to him, the minute he was through the barrier. But she felt uncertain. Gus, of course, had no such qualms and dashed ahead. Robin bent to fuss him, just as usual, and as he did so, the scarf fell away.

And at that point, Eve did dash forward. 'Oh my goodness, Robin!' She felt breathless, then tearful. 'What happened?'

12

Robin tried his best to smile, though it probably hurt. He had a split lip and bruising to his cheek and a black eye, too. His jaw was swollen.

He laughed, though it sounded off. 'You should see the other guy.'

Eve clung to him, but then pulled away slightly. 'You're wincing. Am I hurting you? Where else are you bruised?'

'It's all right. I've been longing to hug you. It's worth the pain.'

A woman who'd just entered the station stared at Robin disapprovingly. Eve gave her a hard stare back.

'Don't worry,' Robin said. 'I've been getting looks like that all the way home.'

'But you're the injured party.'

'I did get a couple of blows in too, thank you very much. But you're right, the other guy struck first.'

Once again, Eve felt tearful and huddled close. Gus seemed similarly affected. He was walking so near Robin's feet, he was in danger of tripping him up.

'Watch out, little mate,' Robin said. 'I'm bruised enough already.'

They reached Eve's car and she got Gus into his harness, working with muscle memory, her eyes on Robin. 'I'm so glad you're all right. I mean, not hurt worse. What happened? Have you had your injuries looked at?'

He nodded. 'Spent a long time in A&E. I'd been digging and digging for information to support the case we're working on. It felt like I was getting nowhere, but I must have trodden on someone's toes. On the upside, I got a good look at the guy. It might be the breakthrough we need.' He put a hand on Eve's arm. 'Want me to drive?'

She shook her head. 'You're in no fit state.'

'Well, don't set off yet. Take a deep breath. I bought you this.' He pulled a foil-wrapped chocolate Santa from his pocket. 'Eat it before you drive. It might help sort you out.'

Eve, who'd been trying to hold back tears for the last minute, snorted with laughter at the sight of Father Christmas, coming to her rescue. Then the floodgates opened and she was sobbing. It must be the shock. A second later, anger joined the mix.

'How could they put you in harm's way?'

'It was on me. I chanced my arm to try to get things shifting. I'm sorry. I shouldn't have risked it. I wanted to say something on the phone earlier, to prepare you. But I knew how much you'd worry. At least now you can see I'm okay with your own eyes.'

'I was worried anyway.' Eve suspected she might sound a bit grumpy, but she was horrified. 'Your voice sounded odd.'

Robin sighed. 'That'd be the split lip. Let me make it up to you? I can tell you what Greg's told me about Anthony Mottram's death and cook supper.'

Eve turned to him, then leaned in and held him tight. 'Supper's all sorted and you need to rest.'

. . .

But Robin didn't have an uninterrupted evening. Viv must have seen Eve's car draw up, and of course, Eve had told her Robin would have updates. She appeared just after they'd got their coats off, which also happened to be Eve's standard G&T time, and gasped when she saw Robin's injuries.

'I'll go. You don't need me here.'

It was the first time Viv had volunteered to leave when there was an update to be had. She must be as shocked as Eve.

'No, you're all right,' Robin said, standing back, with the grin-wince Eve was getting used to.

Eve went through to the kitchen. 'I'll get us some drinks and nuts.' Though the salt would make Robin's lip sting.

By the time she returned, Viv was sitting on one of their couches, still goggling at Robin's injuries, which were even more heart-wrenching to Eve in the familiar cosy surroundings of their sitting room.

'Blimey, Robin,' Viv said at last. 'You need to be more careful.'

Robin groaned as Eve handed him a G&T. 'Tell me something I don't know.'

'I hope that's a double,' Viv said, nodding at his drink. 'Will they give you some leave?'

It had been Eve's immediate thought too, but she hadn't dared ask, because she could guess the answer.

'I'm afraid not.' Robin's words sent Eve's insides sinking. 'I've helped the team create an e-fit of the guy who attacked me, and leads are coming in thick and fast.' He took Eve's hand and gave it a squeeze. 'I really want him put away.'

She squeezed back. 'Yes, I'd rather like that too. I was just hoping you could hand over to someone else.'

'Sorry.'

Eve found it hard to speak. She was still feeling teary. But Robin glanced at her through his puffy eye. 'Ready for Greg's update?'

'If you're up to giving it.'

'I feel a lot better than I look.'

'Low bar,' Viv said.

'So.' Robin let go of Eve's hand and pulled out his phone. 'Headline facts. Greg says Anthony died between 9.55 and 10.25 p.m., but you'll have guessed that already. You saw him at 9.50, Eve, walking up the river, and the two of you found him dead at the end of the window.' He glanced at Eve. 'Are you okay?'

She hadn't been taking any of it in. She needed to snap out of it. Put her feelings on hold for now.

'Sorry. Yes, I'm okay.'

Robin nodded. 'He was found with a fragment of paper in his hand. No writing on it, but Greg figures there could have been an argument over a document. Perhaps the killer attacked him for it. It might have implicated someone.'

Eve thought of the secret Giles had been keeping from Hal. Anthony could have had written proof.

'He was bludgeoned to death with a pipe wrench,' Robin went on. 'Wiped clean of prints.'

Viv was scrawling stuff on a sheet of paper she'd pulled from her pocket, and raised her eyebrows rather disapprovingly when Eve reached for a pristine notepad to do the same.

'Sorry,' Eve said. 'I can't focus unless I take notes as well.'

Viv's look softened and she reached to pat Eve's arm. 'You go ahead then.'

Eve recorded what Robin had said. 'So the killing looks impromptu? The murderer used a weapon that was lying around, and they didn't wear gloves?'

'Looks that way.' Robin nodded. 'Though one bit of

evidence contradicts that. Several witnesses including you saw Anthony head to the boatyard after taking a call, and that call was from his sister, Ada Mottram.'

Suddenly, Eve felt focused again. She told Robin what she knew of Ada, from her disturbing comment at the party, to that morning's visit and her releasing Anthony's dog. 'She clearly hated her brother,' she finished.

'She might have,' Robin agreed, 'but she didn't kill him.'

'What?' Eve sat forward. 'Are you sure?'

'She left the party early. By the time Anthony died, she was sitting in the Cross Keys, surrounded by clientele. Cast-iron alibi.'

Viv let out a long breath. 'I hadn't expected that.' Her eyes were wide.

Eve was reluctant to accept it. Already she was wondering how carefully people had watched her at the pub. She would check with the Falconers, who ran the place. 'I presume the police asked Ada why she rang Anthony?' She was thinking hard.

Robin nodded. 'She claims she didn't get to say goodbye before she left, so she called to apologise for being rude.'

Eve shook her head. 'Calling as a social nicety? I don't believe that for an instant. It seems far more likely she rang to get Anthony to the yard, in which case it looks as though she's got an accomplice.'

'She might have,' Robin said. 'It would have been risky to plan a murder with so many people about, but on the other hand, it muddies the waters. The partygoers are all potential suspects. And if the killer knows the yard well, they'd be confident of finding a weapon on site. But if it was planned, why wouldn't they wear gloves, rather than just wiping the handle?'

'It's a paradox, but I'm convinced Ada lied about why she called, and why would she do that, unless she's involved? I could certainly see her conspiring to murder her brother.'

'But if she knew he was about to die, why let his dog out?' Robin asked. 'Even if it was killed, he'd probably be dead before he found out.'

But Eve could see it. 'Don't think I'm being dramatic, Robin, but I could imagine her doing it for emotional satisfaction, because she wouldn't be present at Anthony's death. She might have felt she was missing out.'

Robin gave a low whistle. 'Right. Well, you've met her, and I trust your judgement.'

'From what Simon says, she'll be delighted to inherit his business too,' Eve added. 'Though not his house. That's rented, I gather.'

Robin nodded. 'Greg says Anthony and Ada's parents fell on hard times after a fire at the yard a while back. They downsized around then. Bought a tiny cottage which went to Ada, and resurrected the business, which went to Anthony.'

Eve took stock. 'So now Ada's got both. I'm surprised Anthony left her the yard. He must have known how she feels about him. She might lie, but she's not convincing.'

'Greg's chat with the family solicitor explains that. Mr Mottram wanted Anthony to run the place; he thought Ada would be unsuitable. But she was still better than an outsider. He made Anthony promise to keep Arthur's Yard in the family.'

'How did Ada explain the champagne bottle Daphne found in the reeds?'

'Says she went out for some air and discovered it on the river path. She chucked it to one side to "get it out of the way", so no one tripped over it.'

Viv gave a disgusted tut, which echoed Eve's feelings. It was unforgivable to leave litter lying around like that and it was clearly baloney anyway. 'What a load of—'

'I know,' Robin went on. 'Oh, and she denies entering Anthony's cottage.'

'Our timeline shows Anthony asking Hal to pick up some

papers around that time too.' Eve showed Robin. 'I presume he didn't mention seeing Ada?'

Robin peered at the printout. 'I'm afraid not. He says the house was locked up when he arrived and he secured it again on his way out. There was nothing untoward.'

'He probably got there ahead of her, then.' Looking back at her timeline, that made sense.

'So if you're right, and Ada collaborated with someone, who's on the list?' Robin asked.

Eve hadn't noticed any of the key players in a huddle with her at the party, but anyone with a motive had to be a candidate. Eve updated Robin on Hal, Hal's gallery owner-turned-market-gardener dad Giles, and Hal's burly uncle Theo, father of Dora and owner of Mistletoe Place.

Robin frowned. 'Interestingly, Hal should have been at the boatyard when Anthony was killed. There's some kind of process being done to one of the boats that needs checking regularly. But he claims he never went, which is out of character, according to his stepmum.'

'Not from what we've seen,' Viv put in. 'Hal is a drunken mislayer of girlfriends and botcher of jobs.'

Robin shook his head. 'Just the same, Tabitha said it was unheard of for him to miss one of the checks.'

The two versions of his character jarred. Then again, people were complicated. 'What's Hal's excuse for not going?' Eve asked.

'He says he was with his dad, who wasn't feeling well. And his dad,' he checked his notes, 'Giles, backs him up. They alibi each other.'

'We won't have any suspects left at this rate,' Viv grumbled.

'Does Greg think Hal and Giles are telling the truth?' Eve asked.

Robin winced again. 'He said their stories sounded rehearsed.'

Hmm. 'Well, they both have potential motives, and I guess they might cover for each other.' Eve had already decided Giles was protective. He might lie, or even kill, for his son. She'd need to get to know him.

'What did Hal say when the police asked him about his chat with Anthony?' Eve had told DC Dawkins all about it.

'That he'd mucked up recently at work, but that it was a one-off, and Anthony wasn't taking it further.'

Which fitted with what they'd heard, though it glossed over how angry Anthony had been. 'I wonder if Greg knows Hal got drunk later in the evening. It could have made Anthony change his mind. If Hal was already planning the murder with Ada, that might have spurred him on.'

'We should let Greg know.'

'And what about the other person I saw eavesdropping?' Eve asked, taking a handful of nuts. 'Have they come forward?'

Robin shook his head.

'Perhaps they hope to blackmail Hal instead. The police know he messed up, but it's not them he'll be worried about, it'll be potential clients and future employers.'

Robin nodded. 'It'd be worth seeing if anyone seems to be squeezing Hal.'

'So, next we're on to Theo Osborne,' Viv said. 'I wouldn't like to meet him on a dark night. He's all beetle-browed and brooding. He must have had a hard time explaining his and Anthony's argument.'

Eve leaned forward. 'Did the police get to the bottom of this missing woman?'

'Theo claims he was talking about a boat, not a person.'

Eve opened her mouth and Robin held up a hand. 'I know. It sounds far-fetched, but when they checked, they found he had a boat go missing just over a week ago. The *Lady Mary.* Used to be his mother's, apparently. He says it's got sentimental value, and he was convinced Anthony had taken it to sell. Or that's his story. When Greg asked why he'd do that, Theo mumbled something about Anthony being short of money. It sounded as though he was thinking on his feet, but the missing boat's for real. He stormed around Mistletoe Place, bemoaning the fact, apparently. The family back him up.'

'But he didn't go to the police? You'd think he'd report it for the insurance, if nothing else.'

'He says he slept on it, then decided it was a lost cause and the insurance wasn't worth the bother, what with the excess on the policy.'

'It all sounds like rubbish,' Viv said.

Eve agreed. 'I'm still worried he was talking about his daughter.' She relayed what she'd seen that afternoon. 'I'll feel a lot better if Dora calls me back.'

Robin's eyes were serious. 'If you're right, there has to be a reason why Theo didn't report her missing. It could be that he knows she's unharmed. But alternatively, he might be hiding something serious, or be culpable in some way.' He sighed. 'The police will try to trace her now, of course, as Anthony's ex.'

Eve nodded. 'Because another option is that she's the killer.' She could be Ada's collaborator. They must know each other. Ada had talked about larking around with Hal, and he and Dora had been brought up in the same house.

'That's right,' Robin agreed. 'What's more, the first responders last night smelled perfume when they got near Anthony's body.'

'I hadn't picked up on that.' Eve's mind went to Ada rather than Dora before she could stop herself. It was so easy to imagine her standing over her brother, pipe wrench in her hand. Had she really been at the pub?

As for the perfume, it was another oddity to keep track of. They circled in Eve's head. As well as the issue of the scent, who had eavesdropped on Hal and Anthony's conversation?

And if Ada had lured Anthony to his death and it was all planned, why hadn't the killer worn gloves? And finally, why had Theo not reported his daughter missing, if Eve was right and she'd disappeared?

13

———

After Viv had left, Eve let her thoughts settle. As far as she was concerned, Hal and Giles alibiing each other meant nothing and either of them could have planned the murder in collaboration with Ada. Hal's beef with Anthony predated the party, and that was true for Giles, too. Anthony had clearly pressed him to stop whatever he was doing before. There'd been time for them to plot the killing in the preceding days, or hastily with Ada on the night itself. The same was true for Theo.

Dora was the unknown quantity, of course. Victim or killer?

Eve and Robin sent the updates they had to Greg, then Eve reheated the supper she'd prepared: chicken with cream cheese and pesto, buttered green beans and parmentier potatoes. As they sat down to eat, Eve couldn't stop looking at Robin's bruises. Every time she glanced at his face, she felt like rushing round the table to hug him. To make sure he'd really come through it okay. And what about tomorrow, when he went back? What if his attacker had another go?

She took a deep breath and made herself pull back. 'You know I'm proud of you, don't you? I hate that you got injured, but I love how hard you work to protect people. Just don't get killed, okay?' Her voice had gone wobbly, which wasn't in the plan at all.

He gave her hand a squeeze, then grinned as he cut up some chicken. 'I'll try not to, and I'd be obliged if you followed the same rule. Keep calling me with updates, won't you?'

Eve nodded.

'As for my case, at least I'll recognise my enemy now.'

'Always a plus.'

He took a swig of his drink. 'I'm looking forward to their arrest, and then Christmas afterwards. I brought some candy canes home. I thought we could use them as decorations for the open house. The young ones might want them.'

It was strangely reassuring that he'd had time to focus on something so charming yet ordinary, but looking ahead still made her anxious. As though she was tempting fate.

Robin shook his head. 'You're so transparent. Try to stop worrying and enjoy the food. It's delicious.' He raised his glass of Sauvignon Blanc to her. 'Tell me what you're going to do here, instead.'

Eve pulled herself together. 'I'm off to Mistletoe Place to talk to Hal and hopefully his family too.' He'd emailed to confirm he and Tabitha would be around, but said nothing about his dad and uncle. 'For Hal, I want to test the water. Find out how he really felt about Anthony, and if there's any chance he and Ada were in cahoots. I want to track down Dora Osborne's friends, too. I need to know when they last saw her, and what they know about her and Anthony's relationship. Though the police might get there ahead of me. I assume she'll come forward now the news of Anthony's murder's out.'

'Unless she's the killer. Or she's been killed.'

Eve nodded. Both thoughts had been running through her head.

.　.　.

Yet again, Eve found it hard to sleep that night. She was terrified of drifting off and hearing the ghostly footfalls in Haunted Lane. What if they foretold Robin's death?

She woke after way too little sleep feeling ridiculous about her night fears. All the same, she insisted on driving Robin to the station. A tiny voice was saying, *What if it's the last time you see him?* but she pushed it away. She trusted him. He was good at his job. That was what she needed to hang on to. Neither of them would be able to operate if they let anxiety take over.

She waved him off, then secretly carried on peering after him until he boarded the train. It started to snow, tiny white flakes drifting down. Eve drove home, gritting her teeth, and forced herself to focus on Christmas without feeling she was counting her chickens. It would be lovely to celebrate together.

She'd just parked by the village green, which was gradually turning white, when Viv arrived, intensely red hair flying, and gave her a hug.

'I saw you set off. He'll be all right. I mean, how careful would you be, if someone had already beaten you black and blue?'

Eve took a deep breath as the image of Robin's face filled her head. 'Very.'

'Exactly. And he loves you. He'll be back again, all present and correct, before you know it.'

Eve nodded, though somehow, Viv was making her feel slightly worse. 'I know. Thank you.'

Viv clapped her on the back. 'Good. That means you can focus on your Holmesing this morning, and come for your shift bearing news this afternoon. I'll need it as a distraction. Gwen Harris has booked a table with her cronies. One of her is quite enough – the idea of a gang of them is too dispiriting.'

'Shhh!' Eve was too late. If the dog walker who'd just passed was a pal of Gwen's, she'd find out exactly what Viv thought of her.

'I've been doing some sleuthing myself,' Viv carried on at the same volume, snow landing and melting on her hair. 'Moira says the boatyard had a health and safety spot check a few weeks ago! Of course, everyone in Saxford's been discussing the murder, so all the gossip's coming to the surface. Perhaps Simon and the Harrises aren't the only clients who've had trouble, and someone reported them. Ugh. Just got snow down my neck.' She turned to dash back to Monty's. 'Happy sleuthing!'

Eve's first port of call was the Cross Keys pub. It wasn't open yet, but she tried the bell to Toby Falconer's flat overhead and got a reply. She'd opted for him first, rather than his brother or sister-in-law. He was the noticing sort.

He invited her in and she explained what she wanted to know, and why.

Toby nodded. 'Ada was definitely here all evening, from the time the police said until closing. She's kind of hard to ignore, and she was sitting at a table right by the bar.'

'Sorry, Toby, but you're absolutely sure she didn't leave?'

'I think she went to the ladies' once, and into the foyer to make a quick call, but other than that, no.'

So she'd have to have got someone else to do the dirty work, if she was involved. 'How did she look after she got off the phone?'

Toby's brow furrowed. 'Happy. Like the cat who'd got the cream.'

That would fit, if she'd just sent Anthony to his death. Eve shuddered. 'And how did she seem overall?'

Toby cocked his head. 'Loud. As though she was overexcited about something.'

Anger welled inside Eve. She was sure Ada was up to her neck in this.

. . .

Eve went to fetch Gus and headed to Mistletoe Place next. It looked beautiful in the snow, the topiary in the garden iced white, the roof of the house and the orangery next to it covered. As Eve arrived on foot, she saw one of the doctors from the local practice alight from his ancient Morris Minor. He noticed her too, raised a hand and walked over.

Eve explained about the obituary and how she was there to interview Hal and Tabitha.

The doctor shook his head, his black beard collecting snowflakes. 'Terrible business. It's why I'm here. Been such a shock all round, of course.'

They reached the door together and it was Tabitha who answered. Hamish was close by her side and looked nervous. Poor thing – he probably had no idea what was going on, but he was bound to be missing his master.

Tabitha stood back. 'Ah, Eve, and Dr Wincup. Come on in. Giles is in his room, Doctor.' She pointed to the steep wooden stairs. 'Tea? Coffee?'

The doctor thanked her but declined, while Eve digested the situation. She understood the murder must be a dreadful shock to all of them. The Osbornes and the Mottrams were old family friends. But Giles being hit so hard that he'd called the doctor felt odd. Unless he and Anthony had been especially close – which seemed unlikely, given their tense interaction at the party – his extreme upset looked suspicious. It would certainly fit if he was guilty of murder. Eve thought again of the photo she'd seen of him. His attractive face with its sensitive features and haunted eyes. And then she thought of the secret he was keeping from Hal, and how Anthony had been determined to make him stop whatever he'd been doing. Giles and Ada could certainly have had a shared interest in killing him. Eve needed to find out if they'd been hobnobbing.

'What about you, Eve?' Tabitha was saying. 'Can I get you something to drink?'

'I'm fine, thanks.' Eve slipped off her and Gus's coats and hung them on a hook by the door. 'You must have got enough to cope with. I suppose the police were crawling all over the place yesterday?'

She nodded. 'In and out of here, as well as the boatyard of course, and Willow Cottage. And then there were the reporters...' She shook her head. 'I still can't believe it, honestly. It's surreal. And terribly sad, of course. Let's find Hal, and then you're down to see me after that, isn't that right?'

Eve nodded. 'I'd love to talk to Giles and Theo too, though I don't imagine Giles is up to it, with Dr Wincup visiting.'

Tabitha shook her head. 'I'm afraid not. And Theo's a law unto himself, though I'll see what I can do.'

They unearthed Hal in a small sitting room to the right of the entrance hall. It was cosy, with red walls, a generous log fire blazing in the grate and an appealing pair of antique Staffordshire King Charles spaniels on the mantelpiece.

Hal stood up to greet Eve and her heart sank. She could smell the alcohol on his breath and his hand trembled slightly as he reached to shake hers.

Tabitha was clearly aware of it too. Her look was a mixture of sympathy and embarrassment. 'I'll leave you to it.' She withdrew, closing the panelled door behind her.

'I'm so very sorry for your loss,' Eve said. 'I know you and Anthony went back a long way.'

Hal sank down onto a deep-blue twill sofa and motioned Eve to a comfortable-looking armchair – also blue, though not matching. 'That's right. To the very beginning. He was a year older than me and we grew up together. When I was tiny, I came to Mistletoe Place to visit my grandparents, and his mum and dad had a house just up the river. Then a little while later my mother died, and soon afterwards I moved here permanently. Dora, my cousin, was here too. She joined in mine and Anthony's games sometimes.' He sighed.

'You went to school locally?'

Hal nodded. 'Mostly. Dad sent me to boarding school when I was twelve. He was worried we ran a bit wild here. Thought I'd be safer. But then there was a news report about drugs in public schools and he pulled me out again.'

Hal mustn't have known whether he was coming or going. As for Giles, his reactions sounded panicked and uncontrolled. 'You were pleased to come back?' She could see it in his face.

'Very. I missed Anthony. We were as thick as thieves. And I missed the sea and the yard too. We used to grub about there and later, when I was older, I worked for Mr Mottram part-time. I went full-time when I left school. It wasn't long after that Dad and Tabitha moved in.' He paused, his eyes glistening. 'Anthony was already managing the yard when his dad died. He took me on as his second in command then.'

They'd been in each other's pockets, living within yards of each other and working side by side. Perfect if they'd remained close, but a strain, as tensions developed.

Eve resolved to begin with questions about the early days. She needed Hal to relax before she got onto more contentious subjects.

'So what was Anthony like as you grew up?'

Hal pushed his fair hair out of his eyes and his sad, pale face lightened suddenly. 'Like the best big brother.' He was smiling. 'I used to get lonely sometimes with no siblings, and after my mum died, I was Dad's sole focus. It was intense, even after I came to Mistletoe Place. He visited often – always watching out for me. Anthony helped me escape. Running wild with him gave me a taste of freedom. You know how it is when you're a kid.'

Eve was an only child too, though her parents had always been calmly affectionate, not constantly anxious. All the same, she nodded. She could empathise.

'We used to spend hours down by the water, mudlarking,'

he went on. 'It's funny to think of those days when everything was an adventure and nothing mattered.'

She could see the emotion in his eyes. 'Things changed?'

He bit his lip. 'We all grow up.'

Eve needed to be patient. 'I'm so sorry that you lost your mum. Was Anthony a support when it happened?'

Hal nodded. 'I guess, but not in a formal way. He helped take my mind off it. I was very young, and I remember missing her like mad at first. It was devastating. But I adapted. I suppose kids do.' He flushed. 'I've only got the vaguest memories of her now, and that makes me feel guilty.' His fists were clenched. 'Poor Dad. It was terrible for him, of course. He couldn't be expected to move on in the same way. I was very glad when he met Tabitha.'

'I can imagine. It sounds really tough. Ada mentioned you, she and Anthony used to go sailing, but only when your father's back was turned.' She could understand Giles being protective, especially after losing his wife.

'That's right. I'm afraid I was rebellious about it. Took no notice of Dad's warnings and sneaked off whenever I could. He found me out more than once and it led to some terrible rows. But I saw sense when I grew a bit older and understood.'

'You stopped going?'

Hal raised his head, and once again there was a look of guilt in his eye. 'No. I was just more honest about it. Paved the way, explained how careful we were being. That was Anthony's idea. He probably felt responsible. He was always more mature than me.' He gave a hollow laugh.

'And did being more upfront smooth things over?'

He shrugged. 'For a bit. But Dad's fears built again.'

'What did Ada think?' Eve was desperate to get a better handle on Anthony's sister.

'About my trouble with my dad?' Hal shook his head, as though he'd lost the will with Ada a long time ago. 'She didn't care, one way or the other. I still remember the day Anthony talked me into levelling with Dad. Ada broke in to say she was bored, and who cared about his feelings?'

So Ada Mottram had always been a piece of work, and Hal appeared to know it. 'I suppose she might be your boss soon, if she keeps you on.'

Hal shivered. 'I suppose so. She's asked to see me this afternoon.'

He looked deeply uneasy; it was hard to imagine him being Ada's accomplice. 'What about your cousin Dora? Did she and Ada get on?'

Hal put his head on one side. 'They saw each other less often, and they're different types.'

'Do they socialise these days?'

Hal looked muddled. It might be dawning on him that her last few questions had nothing to do with Anthony. She'd only got away with it so far because he was hungover and sleep deprived, Eve guessed. But after a moment, he shook his head. 'Not so far as I know.'

But he wasn't sure. Ada and Dora could be collaborators.

'I must talk to Dora of course, given how close she was to Anthony. She wasn't down to attend the party?'

Hal shook his head.

So, she and Anthony had probably been avoiding one another, which could suggest their break-up had been acrimonious. That might equal a motive; Dora could have sneaked to the yard to kill him.

Eve focused on Hal. 'And what about you and Anthony more recently? Were you as close as ever?'

Hal flinched but then looked Eve in the eye. 'Absolutely. It's like I said, I loved Anthony like a brother.'

It was natural to gloss over their falling-out. Whether he'd killed his friend or not it could make him look guilty.

Eve hesitated, but she couldn't leave without asking about

Simon's boat. It might bring out something important. 'I'm sorry, Hal – this has got nothing to do with the obituary and it's a bit delicate, but I wondered, was it you who worked on the valve that failed in Simon's boat?'

He shrank in on himself again, but looked at his hands this time. 'What makes you think that?'

'Only that Anthony told Simon it was one of the casual workers. He promised to check, but I've heard on the grapevine that he never asked them. It made me wonder if he already knew who was responsible.'

Hal's shoulders sagged. 'You promise you won't write about this?'

'You have my word. It's just that Simon's one of my best friends and we've been worried about it.'

He nodded at last. 'I did work on the boat, and on that valve. Or at least, I know I must have.'

This wasn't good. Sad and worrying in equal measure. 'You can't remember?'

Hal's head was in his hands. 'No.'

His voice was so quiet she could hardly hear him, but then he looked up. 'But you don't lose all sense of yourself when you're drunk. And skills you learned in your teens don't leave you. It was an easy job which I could do like clockwork. It was unforgivable of me to turn up at work like that, but I swear to you, that's the only time I ever have. I was having some devastating personal issues. They put me at the end of my tether.'

Eve guessed he was talking about his break-up with Gabby, but being 'at the end of his tether' felt like an odd way to talk about it. It seemed to give frustration as much weight as his misery. Then again, Simon had said he was unlucky in love and had talked about history repeating itself. Perhaps he felt things would never come right.

'It was awful,' Hal went on, 'because a couple of empty vodka bottles were found at the yard too, but they weren't mine.

Truly. The lads – the casuals – they're a great bunch, but they party hard. And of course they wouldn't admit it if they'd had a swig at work. Who would?'

'But since Anthony had seen you drunk once, he found it hard to believe the empties weren't yours?'

Hal nodded at last. 'He *said* he believed me, but we'd been friends for years. What else was he going to do? I could see he had doubts. He had no intention of giving me away, though.' The last words came out hastily, and there was a flicker of fear in his eyes. 'He backed me to the hilt, same as always. But it made me sad.'

He was putting a positive spin on the situation. Eve was convinced Anthony had been weighing up his approach when she'd listened to them argue, and that he was close to changing his mind. Meanwhile, the smell of Hal's most recent excesses still hung in the air. She wrinkled her nose before she could stop herself.

'My best friend's just died.' Hal must have seen. 'I couldn't sleep last night. I admit I hit the bottle but I'm not a big drinker as a rule.'

He sounded honest, and Simon had said he wasn't, of course. But would Simon really know? Their friendship sounded warm, but not deep.

'I was just so horrified,' Hal went on. 'Bereft. And scared for the future too.'

Eve could see that. Scared of losing his job, quite possibly. Or of getting caught if he was guilty.

'Hal, I'm sorry to mention this, but on Saturday night, I noticed you go off to have a private word with Anthony.'

He frowned.

'Viv and I were close enough to hear what you said.'

His eyes met hers. 'You told the police.'

'I didn't want to. I knew we hadn't got the full story, but I felt obliged. But the point is, it wasn't just us who heard. I spotted someone leave the kitchenette after the pair of you emerged from Tabitha's workroom.' Eve watched his eyes. Surprise and fear.

It was news to him, clearly. The additional eavesdropper hadn't faced him with what they'd heard or tried to blackmail him. But that might yet be their plan.

'You don't know who it was?' he said at last.

Eve shook her head. 'I couldn't see, from where I was standing.'

Hal bit his lip, and was silent for several moments. At last, he began again. 'It might fit. I think I'm being followed. I've never clapped eyes on anyone, but there's this constant sense I'm being watched. Shadows moving, but when I look, there's no one there.'

Eve wasn't sure if it was paranoia, but of course, someone *had* listened in. Heck, if someone really was tailing him, they might know if he was guilty. On the whole, he seemed like an unlikely collaborator for Ada, but she couldn't be sure.

He sighed. 'That day I was drunk at work...' His sentence trailed off.

'I heard you'd broken up with your girlfriend.'

Hal heaved another great sigh. 'Yes, I had. I found myself alone, all over again.'

Eve waited. She wanted to know why his relationships never worked out. She hoped he'd say more, but he sat back against the sofa cushions and closed his eyes.

'Thank you for talking to me.' Eve got up. She wasn't sure he'd heard her. Perhaps he'd get some sleep at last.

But maybe the peace he craved would be hard to find, and not just because of any stains on his conscience. Things were clearly tense in the Osborne household. Through the panelled oak door, Eve could hear angry voices.

14

———————

Eve tiptoed into the hallway, closing the door to the small sitting room behind her.

'You're seriously going to carry on as though nothing's happened?' A man's voice, low and gravelly. 'Offering drinks to the guests, pottering around the kitchen?'

Eve edged closer to where the argument was taking place, until she could see Tabitha and Theo through the kitchen doorway. They were standing on either side of an oak refectory table, the sash window beyond giving a view of the snowy garden, filling the kitchen with a pure, bright light.

Tabitha's hands were on her hips. 'What on earth's got into you? I can't put a foot right! What do you expect me to do? I'm as shocked and horrified as everyone else, but my way of dealing with it is to hang on to normality!'

Theo was looming over her. 'When Anthony's head was bashed in? When he's gone forever and he's not coming back?' It was as though he was rubbing it in. 'Someone took his life, and he was only thirty-two. Doesn't that make you feel like breaking down?'

Tabitha looked utterly astonished. 'Theo, I saw the way you

looked at Anthony at the party. You'd had a falling-out – it was clear as day. I wouldn't have been surprised if you'd wished him dead. Not that I think you did it,' she added hastily. 'But now you're telling *me* off for not being more emotional?' She threw the tea towel she'd been holding onto the table.

Eve went and knocked on the open kitchen door, before one of them could burst out and catch her listening in.

Tabitha looked tired when she came to join her. She emerged into the hallway, leaving Theo leaning against the kitchen table.

'Eve. Sorry. Come on through. Are you sure you wouldn't like that drink?'

But Eve didn't want to force her back into the kitchen. 'I'm fine, thanks.'

They went to Tabitha's design room, where she came up with her ideas and prototypes, and where Viv had seen Hal and Theo talk. Eve loved it in there. It smelled of fabric and ink and was as cosy as the sitting room where she'd left Hal.

Hamish had been lying under Tabitha's table. He got up to investigate Gus, but he still looked doleful and settled down again quickly.

'Please, have a seat.' Tabitha motioned Eve to a button-backed chair close to a window. The room's green velvet curtains glowed in the chilly light from outdoors. 'My apologies for Theo, if you heard him.'

'I'm afraid I did. I happened to finish with Hal at that point. I think he fell asleep.'

Worry lines creased Tabitha's brow. 'Poor Hal. He doesn't have it easy.'

Eve shot her a sympathetic look. 'In what way?'

But Tabitha just sighed. 'Oh, this and that.' She leaned forward. 'But you're here to talk about Anthony. Whatever Theo thinks, I'm horrified that he's dead. But in truth, I feel quite numb – shock, I suppose. I'm sure I'll cry at some point –

for what Hal's lost, and for the sheer horror of it, if nothing else. And I liked Anthony, though I didn't really know him well.' She provided Eve with a couple of anecdotes, which made him sound thoughtful and informal. 'He always seemed like a thoroughly decent man. I don't know why Theo is being so odd about it.' She paused as though still searching for an answer, then shook her head. 'The fact is, he's never quite taken to me. Between ourselves, I think me being younger than Giles has always worried him. He watches me like a hawk whenever we have male visitors – as though I'm going to run off with someone my own age and leave Giles in the lurch.' She smiled. 'As if I would. I adore Giles. Though he has his problems, just like Hal.'

'I gather he lost his first wife very young.'

Tabitha nodded. 'Utterly tragic. And his and Theo's parents died relatively young too, in a boating accident. It's left him looking over his shoulder.'

No wonder he hadn't liked Hal sailing.

'He can't shake that side of his character.' Tabitha's eyes were far away for a moment, her gaze on an apple tree outside, its bare branches laden with snow. 'It wasn't so obvious when we first met. He was down in London running the gallery, life was busy. I was charmed. Without wanting to blow my own trumpet, I think I made him forget his worries for a while. We had a whirlwind romance, and I was hooked, well before I understood his demons.' She sighed. 'But I still love him very deeply. Coming here helped a bit. Or at least, it did at first.'

'The effect wore off?'

Tabitha nodded slowly, then waved at the air in front of her face, as though warding off emotion. 'Sorry. Take no notice.'

'No, I'm sorry. It sounds hard.' Eve hadn't meant to upset her. 'And after what you said, living under Theo's nose sounds tricky too.'

Tabitha took a deep breath, but then smiled. 'I sometimes

wonder if I'd have refused, if I'd known what it would be like, but it saved our bacon, to be honest. Giles's gallery had started to lose money. And I wasn't making a decent living. Theo gave us the space to follow our dreams. And we're not on top of each other – it's a large house. So I can certainly put up with the downsides. Theo and I rub along all right. I'm hurt that he doubts me, but he isn't normally as scratchy as he was just now. We're all on edge.'

'It's understandable.'

Tabitha nodded. 'I asked if Theo would talk to you – we were discussing that before he got so combative in the kitchen, but he was leaving immediately to see his daughter.'

Eve's ears pricked up. The daughter who was mysteriously away from home, the mail piling up on her mat? If she was back in circulation, the police would catch up with her too.

'I suggested tomorrow instead,' Tabitha went on, 'but he brushed me off. Here.' She wrote a mobile number on the back of one of her business cards. 'Perhaps you can call him to sort something out.'

'Thanks.'

'His daughter will feel it of course, as Anthony's ex.' Tabitha shook her head. 'Even after a break-up, it'll hurt. They were together a couple of years.'

'Do you see much of her?'

Tabitha frowned. 'I haven't recently. I imagine she's been keeping her distance to avoid Anthony. We're so close to Arthur's Yard and Willow Cottage. But before that she'd come here every so often. Probably to see me as much as her dad, if I'm honest. Dora used to work for me, as well as being my stepniece. We get on well.'

Eve remembered reading about the time Dora had spent working for Tabitha's Interiors. 'I'd love to speak to Dora for the obituary, when she's up to it.'

Tabitha nodded. 'I'll get Theo to pass the message on.'

At that moment, there was a knock at the door and Dr Wincup appeared. 'I'm just off now, but Giles asked me to check on you and Hal too.'

Tabitha took a deep breath, as though she might be counting to ten. 'I'm fine, Doctor. Thank you.'

Still the doctor hovered. 'You might like to pop up and see him soon. He was asking for you.' Then he nodded and moved towards the door. 'I'll see myself out.'

'Do please go up to Giles if you'd like to,' Eve said, when he'd gone.

But Tabitha shook her head. 'He'll be all right.' She sighed. 'It's best not to leap to it every time he feels anxious, I suspect. A psychoanalyst friend of mine says it's unresolved trauma.'

Eve wanted to ask for more details, but it would be a step too far.

'We're nearly finished anyway, aren't we?' Tabitha said. 'Let's just sort out a time to discuss the advertorial for the new range.'

They pencilled in a slot on Thursday for Eve to come back.

Tabitha sighed. 'I expect Theo would say I shouldn't be carrying on with work given what's happened, but the business is still building. If I take my foot off the accelerator it could all come crashing down. And there's nothing like having a focus to get through difficult times.'

Eve could imagine trying to work her way through it too. 'Don't worry. I understand.' It wasn't as though Tabitha had known Anthony well, unlike Hal. Eve wouldn't expect her to be knocked flat the way he was. It was her husband's reaction that seemed more unexpected. He must have known Anthony as a small boy, of course, and it was harrowing that he'd died so young and in such a horrific way, but to need medical attention? That still rang alarm bells. 'I hope Giles is okay.'

'Thank you.' She said no more. Perhaps she was worried in case he was guilty, or covering for Hal.

Eve got up, feeling she'd outstayed her welcome. 'And thank you for talking to me. I'll see you on Thursday.'

She strode across the room swiftly to open the door, Gus on her heels.

In that split second as she entered the hall, she knew someone had been listening in. There was a change in the light levels, as though someone or something had moved. She'd heard a creak too. Shifting floorboards.

The hairs on her forearms lifted as she reached for her and Gus's coats and got them back on. 'Come along, Gus. Back home.'

She walked down the gravel path, past the clipped box, now heavy with snow, wondering if anyone was watching her. Like Hal, she had a sense someone was. Was it just paranoia? She turned suddenly. If she could catch them at it...

Sure enough, a stocky figure ducked behind a yew.

Theo Osborne, she was sure of it. Either his meet-up with his daughter had been remarkably short, or he'd lied to Tabitha and never left. Eve was betting on the latter.

15

———

On her way home, Eve's mind was full of Theo Osborne. She bet he had listened in to her interview with Tabitha, but why? He might think Tabitha was guilty, of course, after the way he'd harangued her in the kitchen. Or perhaps he was responsible, and full of fear, wondering if she'd guessed. Either way, he'd lied about going to see Dora, and that was seriously odd. Eve didn't know what to make of it.

She dialled his mobile number, but there was no reply. After that, she sent a text, asking if she might interview him, but she had a hunch he wouldn't play ball. He'd been at daggers drawn with Anthony. Even if he had nothing to hide, he probably wouldn't rush to help. She messaged the gang WhatsApp group, explaining she wanted to track him down.

If anyone spots him, please let me know.

She was perfectly happy to intercept him if required.

Back at Elizabeth's Cottage, Eve warmed up with a bowl of delicious parsnip soup and her thoughts turned to Robin. She was longing to text to ask if he was okay, but what if she distracted him, and he let his guard down? She hoped he'd make contact soon. The morning had worked as a distraction, but her shift at Monty's would give her the chance to think.

She wasn't due there until later, though, and she needed to make the intervening time count.

'Fancy another outing, Gus?'

He looked at her from under his bushy, wire-haired dachshund eyebrows.

Eve glanced at her watch. 'We've just got time to nip into Blyworth. I'm going to try Dora's house again, and if I draw a blank, I'll move on to her neighbours.'

Forty minutes later, after driving gingerly through the snow along narrow country lanes, Eve was staring at the same pile of junk mail as before, Gus sniffing at the doorway on the end of his leash. Her knocking hadn't yielded a response, and there'd been no footprints in the snow before she and Gus arrived.

Eve tried Dora's neighbour as planned.

A woman answered. 'We don't see much of each other.' She'd only opened her door a crack. 'Different schedules.' She sniffed. 'Police were here for her early this morning. They knocked on my door too, but I couldn't tell them anything.'

If Dora had seen the news, she must realise they'd want to talk to her. Eve had heard the appeal for her to come forward on local radio. Yet it looked as though the authorities were struggling to track her down. She wondered what their theory was: second victim, or killer? As for Theo telling Tabitha they were in touch, that lie wouldn't hold for long. The police must be pushing him for information. But from what he'd said to Anthony, he didn't know where Dora was either.

Eve explained her concern to the neighbour. 'I've called her mobile repeatedly but there's no answer. Is there anyone who might know where she is?'

The neighbour frowned. 'I saw her chatting with a woman who works in the lighting department at Parker's. Tall and slender with long, dark hair. I got the impression they were friends. She might know something.'

The department store was close by and Eve felt a spark of hope. 'Thanks.'

Parker's was dog friendly, so Eve and Gus cut through a park to the town centre, past half-timbered stores, looking beautiful in the snow, their frontages full of Christmas displays, from festive hampers to artisan gifts.

At last, they reached the department store with its *Nutcracker* ballet-inspired display. Dancing mice filled the window, dressed in deep greens, reds and gleaming bronze. It made Eve feel like a child again, that automatic prick of excitement, despite everything that was going on.

The blessed warmth of Parker's welcomed them in. Eve enjoyed the cheerful lights and wafts of scent from the perfume counters. On the third floor, she made for the glow of the lighting department. She could imagine Dora befriending someone here, given her job as an interior designer. Eve would love to splash out on some extra table lamps for Elizabeth's Cottage. It still had some dark corners.

The woman serving matched the neighbour's description and seemed faintly familiar. As Eve tried to place her, she went for it. 'I'm sorry to bother you. I've been trying to track down Dora Osborne, and I'm starting to get worried.' She claimed it was only Anthony's obituary which had sent her in Dora's direction, and how her neighbour had helped. 'Have you heard from her recently? I know she and Anthony broke up, so things might have been tough.'

The woman nodded. 'She went very quiet after the split.'

She stopped. She might feel she was oversharing, but Eve could see she was anxious, and anxious people often wanted to offload. Eve sympathised, and she needed the information, so she waited.

'I called at first,' the woman went on at last, 'but she didn't want to talk. She stopped picking up after she'd fobbed me off twice.' Her look of hurt switched to guilt. 'I should have carried on trying. Perhaps you could ask one of her clients. I presume she's picking up for them.'

Eve doubted it, but it was worth a try. 'Do you know who she's working for now?'

'I do, as a matter of fact. She was about to start a job for a woman called Jamieson, in a huge old pile on the north edge of town – Blackthorn House. I assume she'll be turning up there. She'd already bought a lot of lights for the project. But if you want fond memories of Anthony, Dora's not a good choice.'

Eve took a deep breath. 'Obituaries aren't about airbrushing the subject's life. I want to paint an honest picture. It's part of the reason I hoped to talk to her.' That and to solve the mystery of Anthony's death and her disappearance. Eve paused again, wondering how far she should go. 'I got a hint she was the one who broke up with him.' That was entirely invented, but it might jolt Dora's friend into telling what she knew.

'I did too, but it was Anthony's fault, from what I hear.'

Eve waited, hoping more silence would reap rewards.

'He slept with someone else, apparently, right under Dora's nose.'

Right. It was probably anger and upset that had loosened her tongue this time. Eve could hear both in her voice.

'Dora told you?'

The woman shook her head. 'She'd have been too upset. Once I found out, I could see why she hadn't wanted to talk.'

Eve remembered the humiliation when she'd found out her

first husband had cheated on her. It felt like she'd been the last person to know. No wonder Theo had been angry with Anthony. As for Dora, it gave her a motive. She and Ada could have collaborated, if they were closer than Hal thought. 'How did you hear about Anthony's affair?'

'Some mutual friends told me. I live in the same village as Anthony did, so it was a hot topic, I'm afraid.'

'Saxford? Oh, same here. I'm Eve, by the way. Eve Mallow.'

The woman smiled for a moment. 'I'm Jade Cooper. I thought you looked familiar.' She peered down at Gus, 'And you. I never forget a dachshund.'

Gus did a little skip. Slightly undignified, but forgivable under the circumstances.

'Well, thanks for your help. I'll try the woman at Blackthorn House, and are there any other friends I could check with?'

The woman shrugged. 'The ones who know about the affair haven't heard from her. She talked a lot about someone called Maeve, though. I got the impression they were close, but I don't have a surname.'

'Well, if *you* hear from Dora, would you let me know?' Eve handed her a card. 'And I'd love to talk to the friends who told you about Anthony's affair too. They might help me find the woman he was seeing; she'd be a key interviewee. I'd be discreet, of course. I want to tell the truth while protecting everyone's feelings. Please check out my work if you're in any doubt.'

Jade paused a moment but then nodded. 'I trust you. I'll text you next time we meet in the Cross Keys, so you can nip in and ask them.'

'That sounds perfect. Thank you.'

It was essential to identify the woman, assuming the rumours were true. She could be another suspect, especially if it turned out she knew Ada. Eve needed to work out which of the possible killers had had secret dealings with Anthony's sister. It felt like the best way of homing in on someone.

And finding Dora was crucial, of course, especially with her newly identified motive. As she and Gus left Parker's, Eve wished she had more time before her shift at Monty's. Ideally, she'd visit Blackthorn House right now.

16

___

Eve let Gus back into the warmth of Elizabeth's Cottage, then called Greg to tell him where Dora Osborne was meant to be working. She'd have preferred to visit Blackthorn House herself, but there was no time and the lead was too important not to pass on. One of the closest contacts of a recently murdered man was nowhere to be found – whichever way you looked at it, it wasn't good. Eve would never forgive herself if Dora was harmed or in danger. But she could be the killer.

After that, Eve marched through the snow to Monty's, entering the fug of the teashop, which smelled gloriously of sloe-gin spice cakes, mince pies, Earl Grey and Darjeeling.

Astoundingly, Viv hadn't rushed through to greet her and demand news. When Eve nipped through to the kitchen to stow her coat in the office, she was leaning over her phone and jumped, switching off her screen and stuffing it in her pocket. She wasn't looking sweaty any more, but her cheeks were pink.

Eve raised an eyebrow. 'Something you want to tell me?'

'What? No!' She blinked but recovered herself a moment later. 'No, you're meant to be telling *me* things! I was right about needing a distraction. One of Gwen Harris's lot has already complained about the mismatched crockery.'

She must be from out of town. It was a trademark of Monty's, and stylishly done. Eve had loved the aesthetic the first time she'd set foot in the teashop.

Viv's nostrils flared slightly. 'I didn't point out that her foundation was mismatched with her face, but I might, if she says anything else.'

It sounded as though Eve had arrived just in time. 'Leave them to me.'

'Yes, you always keep your temper.' Viv looked mildly resentful. 'You do realise it makes you slightly like a robot, don't you?'

'Gee, thanks.'

Back in the tearoom, Gwen waved her over and Eve prepared to be charming. Secretly, she enjoyed the challenge. If she smiled sweetly enough, and continued to be polite, she usually won the Gwens of this world over. It gave her a weird sense of triumph. As she took the order for another pot of tea, Eve wondered why Viv had looked so sheepish as she'd entered the kitchen. Playing on her phone was allowed – Viv was her own boss.

'Gwen's party really is taking the mick,' Viv said, half an hour later. One of her cronies had complained that her candied peel cake was 'too full of fruit', but only after she'd eaten nine tenths of it. Viv had replaced it with some chocolate layer cake, but only under sufferance. She looked at Eve dolefully. 'Come on, cheer me up. What have you found out?'

Eve explained the lead she'd got for Dora Osborne. 'But something tells me the police won't find her at Blackthorn House. I suspect Theo has no idea where she is either. If she'd disappeared after Anthony's death, I'd guess he was protecting her, but she went before, so that's not enough to explain it. I need to track her down.'

Viv nodded. 'I agree, it's frightening. And what about the other stuff? How did you get on with Hal? Where are we with Simon's boat?'

Eve described his state that morning. 'I'm not sure even he knows whether he was responsible for the leak. As for killing Anthony, it's possible. He looks like he's falling to pieces and he was certainly desperate to keep his job and his reputation. Even if Ada makes him redundant, that will be intact. Unless the eavesdropper speaks out.' It was one of the key puzzles for Eve: who had listened in, and why? 'It feels significant that Hal was meant to be at the boatyard when Anthony died. If Giles is lying for him, it might explain why *he's* so cut up too.' Eve explained about Dr Wincup's visit. 'But Hal collaborating with Ada is where I come unstuck. I don't think he even likes her.'

Viv rolled her eyes. 'No surprises there.'

After that, Eve told her about Theo accusing Tabitha of reacting too coolly to Anthony's death.

Viv sighed. 'That's just plain weird.'

It was, but there must be an explanation. Eventually, when Eve knew it all, the puzzle pieces would fall into place.

Suddenly, Viv grabbed Eve's arm, which would have been fine if she hadn't been holding a spatula covered in red velvet cake dough. A blob of it landed on Eve's new nubuck boots.

Viv grabbed some kitchen paper and bent to wipe it off.

Eve looked at the boot, with its now larger (though admittedly flatter) doughy residue.

Viv righted herself again. 'Sorry, but I just saw Hal and Ada through the window. I think they're coming here!'

'Hal said they were due to meet to talk business.' Eve hoped he was in a better state then he'd been that morning. It was excellent that they'd chosen Monty's as a venue. It would be a prime opportunity for Eve to watch them interact. Her gut told her Hal wouldn't have conspired with Ada, but she might be wrong.

She dashed back to the tearoom so she could be the one to serve them. It meant ignoring Gwen's raised hand, but one of their regular servers, Allie, went instead.

Ada smiled when Eve appeared, but as before, it didn't meet her eyes. 'I didn't realise you worked here on top of your journalism.'

Eve smiled back, but hers was just as false. 'I'd never see anyone otherwise.'

Ada did the ordering, opting for the winter selection. Hal still looked a bit grey, though better than he had earlier. The smell of alcohol and the shakes had gone, and he'd put on a clean shirt.

Eve watched them through the kitchen door as she prepared their cake selection. She was so engrossed, she hadn't noticed Viv peering as well, until she reversed into her.

'What do you think?' Viv asked, in a stage whisper.

'It's weird.' Ada was being bubbly with Hal, but it looked fake. 'It's like she's putting on a charm offensive, but why would she? She holds all the cards. She's not the sort to be nice for the sake of it, so I'd guess she wants something. But what?'

'Maybe she's trying to keep him onside, if he's her accomplice,' Viv said, not quietly enough. 'She might worry he'll turn nasty and bump her off too, because she's a loose end.'

Viv watched a lot of TV thrillers.

'Except he looks like a mouse facing a snake,' Eve murmured.

'Hmm. Yes, there is that.'

Eve carried their order by hand rather than using a tray, so she could make multiple visits to their table. The more she heard of their conversation, the better.

'I won't hear of you resigning,' Ada was saying, as Eve deposited the winter selection on its retro cake stand. 'I won't be able to run the yard without your expertise. You know that.' She leaned forward and touched his sleeve. It was almost a caress. 'You will stay, won't you?'

Hal seemed mesmerised, but at last he blinked and spoke. 'Yes.' He cleared his throat. 'Yes, I'd like to stay on.'

Ada gave a sigh of pleasure, which sounded rehearsed. 'That's great news.'

She was very beautiful, and clearly determined to win Hal over. Eve couldn't fathom her motivation at all. It wasn't as though she lacked the skills to keep the yard going herself, by the sound of it. She'd been doing jobs for various boat owners in the vicinity, undercutting Anthony. And she had a whole crew of casual workers at her disposal. If she and Hal *had* collaborated, Eve could understand her wanting to keep things cordial, but they'd be on an equal footing. Instead, it was more like Ada was putting in the work. Buttering him up.

Yet she didn't seem tense. She was doing most of the eating, which suggested she felt relaxed and in control. She might be scheming, but she seemed confident it would work.

Hal, by contrast, hadn't finished the spiced ginger cake he'd started with. Ada was just taking the last cake from the stand when Tabitha came through Monty's door, flakes of snow landing on the mat, the bell jangling.

'Oh, hello, you two,' she said to Ada and Hal. 'Don't mind me.'

'We weren't going to,' Ada said. 'What a shame I won't be working for you any longer, Tabitha, but there it is.'

She gave a cat-like smile and Tabitha flushed. *Heck.* Eve would be glad to see the back of her if she was Tabitha. It made her wonder why she'd kept Ada on.

Hal was blushing, and opened his mouth. Eve guessed he was about to apologise on his new boss's behalf, but Ada put her hand on his arm again. 'We need to talk money. I don't know what Anthony was paying you, but he always was a skinflint, I expect I can do better.' She asked Eve for the bill, and they were out of Monty's three minutes later.

Eve looked after them. Hal had seemed scared and cautious. She couldn't imagine him knowingly entering into a murder plot with such a loose cannon. And if Ada knew he was guilty, surely the balance of power would be different? Her hunch told her they weren't the correct pairing.

Tabitha sighed as Eve took her order. 'I expect Ada realised I was snooping. I decided to come in when I saw them through the window. Though Monty's wares are always tempting, of course.' She smiled at Eve.

'She's changed her tune,' Eve said. 'She told me she'd be sad to leave you when we first spoke.'

'It must have served her purpose at the time. She pretended that working for me was her life's ambition before she signed her employment contract.'

'You only found out what she was like after you'd taken her on?'

Tabitha gave a mirthless laugh. 'That's right. When I finally realised, it felt as though the devil had managed to con its way into our midst.'

'What did she do?'

'Tiny little poisonous things.' Tabitha paused, her eyes far away. 'They gradually chipped away at the happy atmosphere in the workshop. She came to see me one day and accused me of bullying her, loud enough for the other staff to hear. I had to listen, of course. A boss must be willing to take criticism. But what she described as "bullying" was simply me asking her to do things that fell within her remit, and encouraging her to meet deadlines. I'd swear she was simply stirring up trouble. I've a good relationship with my other workers, but it made them look at me in a different way. It was as though they were re-evaluating everything I said, and asking themselves if I was bullying them, too. And I felt stuck. If I took disciplinary action against her, it could have looked as though I was stopping her from speaking out.'

'It does sound tricky.' Eve couldn't see Tabitha bullying anyone for a minute, but she could imagine the damage Ada had done.

'It wasn't just me she targeted,' Tabitha went on. 'She spread rumours about Giles, how he couldn't keep control at the market garden, and she goaded Theo, like a child poking a dog until it snaps. She spotted everyone's weak points. As for Hal, she implied he was lazy and stupid. And all these things stick, Eve, that's the worst of it. Rumours smoulder and catch fire.'

Eve could believe it. 'Though she was being very pally with Hal just now.'

Tabitha nodded. 'Exactly. And that's worrying.'

Despite the afternoon at Monty's being significantly more distracting than Eve had expected, her mind still strayed frequently to Robin. She felt a huge wave of relief when he texted.

Sorry not to message before. Very busy and some unexpected developments, but all good. Bruise now a horrible yellow. Glad you can't see me. xxx

But Eve wished she could, and the feeling lasted into the evening.

To distract herself, she wrote up her notes from that day's interviews, as well as the interactions she'd witnessed at the teashop. She glanced at her phone. Dora still hadn't called, and Theo hadn't replied to her text either. She rang both numbers again, and left messages, but she didn't hold out much hope. She'd probably have to get creative if she wanted to talk to Theo.

To try to switch off for the night, she found the candy canes Robin had bought and began to tie them to the greenery around the house. She was sufficiently absorbed to jump out of her skin when there was a knock at the door.

Gus, who'd been dozing in his dog bed, leaped up and barked.

Eve opened up cautiously. It was late, below freezing outside and she felt deeply unsettled after the revelations of the day.

She breathed a sigh of relief at the sight of a familiar face.

'Tabitha! Are you all right? Come on in out of the cold.'

Tabitha smiled sheepishly. 'Thank you. I'm sorry to call so late, but I've just had a rather disturbing talk with Hal, and I had the urge to let you know.'

What on earth was coming? Eve closed the door against the night. 'It's no problem.'

A moment later, Gus was snuggling up to Tabitha's ankles and she bent to stroke him.

Eve made hot chocolate and put another log on the fire as Gus pottered back to bed. 'So, what's happened?' She set their drinks on the coffee table.

'I'm afraid Hal had a few too many drinks again tonight.' She met Eve's eye. 'He's not usually like that. Truly. I think it's the strain, and after what he told me this evening, I can see why. Ada's his boss now, but he's not comfortable with it.' She shuddered. 'I'd hate to work under her, I must say. Anyway, he started to talk about the old days, when he, Anthony, Ada and Dora were kids.' She sipped her drink. 'Back then, Arthur's Yard almost went under. You know about that?'

Eve remembered reading about it at some point. 'Wasn't there a fire?'

Tabitha nodded. 'It was before I moved here, but it sounded awful. The place nearly burned to the ground and they lost multiple boats. The story went round that Ada and Anthony's parents had mucked up their insurance, so there was no payout.'

What a terrible situation. Eve couldn't imagine their

despair. 'Had they missed a payment or something?' It puzzled her. They must have been organised to keep the yard going so successfully before that.

Tabitha shrugged. 'I always assumed it was something like that. But Hal told me the truth this evening. The story of the insurance cock-up was a lie.'

Eve held her breath.

'Hal says Ada started the fire, and her dad knew it. That was why there was no proper investigation, and hence no insurance claim.'

'Wow.' Eve sipped her drink. 'How did Hal know?'

'He and Dora saw her do it. They told her dad, in confidence. They asked their grandpa's advice first, but he said they must tell. Otherwise there'd be an investigation and Ada might be arrested. The families went back decades, as you probably know, and Hal said his grandad wanted to protect them. Mr and Mrs Mottram moved from their large house to a tiny one, to help cover the costs, and Hal's grandpa loaned them the rest, so they managed to start over. He and the Mottrams made Hal and Dora swear not to tell. They said Ada would never be able to put the mistake behind her if word got around. So Anthony wasn't aware, and even Giles doesn't know. He's always been fragile; Hal wouldn't have wanted to worry him.'

'It was generous of Giles's parents to loan the cash.'

Tabitha nodded. 'But they were like family. And they could afford it.'

Eve thought of Mistletoe Place and all its land. It figured.

'Giles doesn't know the truth, but he knew about the loan,' Tabitha added. 'His dad maintained he took pity on the family because of the insurance error.'

'Did Hal say why Ada started the fire?'

Tabitha nodded. 'It's not pretty, I'm afraid. It was after a massive row at home. She'd wanted to go to some party with a thirty-year-old guy she'd met.' She snorted. 'She was only sixteen, so her dad said no. Setting the fire was her retaliation. Hal says her dad had been planning to work late in the yard that evening. It was only chance he wasn't trapped there.'

Eve wondered if Ada had intended to kill him.

Tabitha's gaze was back on Eve. 'I think he knew she was unstable. He wanted the yard to go to Anthony, and the fire explains why. But for all that, he was soft on her. She got their house, and now – thanks to the instructions he gave Anthony – she's got the business too.'

Eve wished Hal hadn't been sworn to secrecy. If Anthony had known, he might never have left Ada the boatyard, whatever his dad wanted.

The story focused Eve's mind on Ada's possible guilt. She'd had lots to gain from her brother's death, and, but for luck, she might have become a killer the night she'd set the fire. Then, as now, if she was guilty, she'd used an indirect method. Igniting a building and leaving her dad to his fate echoed calling Anthony before stepping back. Her willingness to take a life and the similarity in approach made her guilt believable. It was interesting that Hal had chosen to speak up now, assuming Tabitha was telling the truth, and she'd only just heard. It wasn't impossible that one of them had engineered the timing to focus attention on Ada and away from themselves, though Tabitha had no motive, as far as Eve knew. She stored the thought away.

Tabitha was shaking her head. 'I know Ada's got an alibi for Anthony's murder, but I also know you're piecing things together. We're all aware you've worked with the police before, so I thought you should know.'

Eve went into damage-limitation mode. The last thing she wanted was to have everyone on their guard. 'It always gets exaggerated. If new information falls at my feet, I pass it on. The police don't take much notice.' Or DI Palmer didn't, anyway. He despised Eve, and the feeling was mutual.

'I understand. And I'm sure they'll ignore this when I tell

them, because Ada can't be guilty. But I'd rather you knew. It's made me realise just how ruthless she can be.' She sighed. 'I hate the idea of Hal working for her, and that's nothing to what Giles would feel, if he knew about the fire. I don't think I can tell him when his nerves are so frayed. I'm sure Ada hated Anthony for getting the yard. And Hal thinks she resents us Osbornes too, because it was Hal and Dora who told on her, and because of our patronage.' She heaved a sigh. 'It probably sheds some light on the way she treated us all when she came to work for me. Perhaps she only took the job to needle us.'

Eve felt chilled to her core. 'Ada knew they told on her?'

Tabitha nodded. 'I suppose her dad must have let it slip when he tackled her about it.'

And now, one of the people who'd told had disappeared, and Hal was a sitting duck.

18

After Tabitha left, Eve's mind was full of Ada, coldly setting fire to the boatyard, perhaps imagining her father inside. Tabitha was right – she couldn't have killed Anthony herself, but Eve was convinced she'd lured him to the boatyard. But who on earth would collaborate with her? She'd already decided that Hal felt unlikely, and now Dora fell into the same category. Ada must hate her for telling about the fire. It made the alliance seem implausible, despite Dora's motive. She sighed. That still left Giles and Theo... though they'd had run-ins with Ada too. Eve would need to dig deeper.

Before bed, she had one last check of the local news sites. There was nothing fresh. The police were still appealing for Dora to get in touch.

Eve's plan the following day was to hound Theo Osborne, and track down Giles, too. She called Theo's number again. He'd know it was her, thanks to her text. She hoped he might give in and answer if he knew she wouldn't give up. She sighed as the call went to voicemail once more and turned her attention to Giles.

Talking to him had been out of the question the day before, when he'd been in bed. Eve messaged Hal to see if he might be well enough now, but he claimed he was still 'indisposed'. Once again, Eve wondered if Giles was guilty, or thought Hal was. His extreme reaction might suggest the former, and it would explain him hiding away too, making the interview even more urgent. She needed to know the secret he'd been keeping from his son, if it had been worth killing for, and what dealings he might have had with Ada.

If Giles was avoiding Eve, she could guess where he might go. It was the market garden which had provided solace when he'd given up his London gallery; it might bring comfort now too. It was bitter outside, but she knew farmers kept going in all weathers. She was familiar with the old outbuildings which had been converted into the firm's offices. If she were Giles, feeling cold, worn and scared, she'd hide out there, turn on the radiator and close the door.

She'd seek him out. But first she needed more milk, and the latest dose of gossip from Moira. Specifically, she wanted to ask about Giles and Anthony's relationship. If they'd been close, Giles's reaction the day before could be grief, but if not, then he might have been coming to terms with killing a man.

'Ah, Eve dear.' Moira leaned forward, deely boppers still firmly in place. It was impossible to take her seriously. 'Tell me, what news?'

'I'll bet you know more than me.' Eve smiled brightly. 'People put their trust in you.'

Thankfully, Moira was too egotistical to realise she was being buttered up. 'Well, I suppose that's true.' The boppers wobbled as she nodded. 'And everyone's been full of the latest news this morning, of course.'

Eve was glad she'd come in. 'What news is that?'

Moira looked delighted by her ignorance. 'Well, you know that empty vodka bottle the Harrises found in their boat? It turns out it was *Anthony* who had a drink problem! The other bottle they found and the dodgy repairs were all down to him! Gwen tells me Simon's craft almost sank, Eve. You never said!' She shot Eve an accusatory look.

Eve was still reeling from the fake news. It took her a moment to respond. 'Ah, well, Simon didn't want it spread around.' What the heck made Gwen so sure she'd found the culprit? 'Are you certain it was Anthony?' It was convenient he was no longer around to defend himself. 'I don't see how Gwen could know for sure.'

'Gwen heard it from Ada, who heard it from Hal, apparently,' Moira said eagerly. 'Ada was terribly apologetic. She said she'd no idea Anthony had a problem.' She sighed heavily, as though she'd remembered it might be seemly to show some sympathy. 'I suppose one never knows what someone else is going through.' The bopper reindeers grinned inanely.

Wow. If Hal was really spreading that rumour, it was a fairly outrageous lie. Eve needed to ask him about it... but she mustn't forget the main reason she'd come in.

'Moira, on another topic, do you know if Anthony and Giles Osborne got on?'

The storekeeper frowned. 'Now, it's interesting you should ask that, Eve. Anthony was always very polite to Giles, that I will say. As though he was trying to win him over. But Giles wasn't having any of it. He avoided him, in fact. If he ever found him in here, he'd walk straight out again. And I heard him badmouth Anthony, too. He told people they shouldn't trust him.'

Hmm. Eve doubted his extreme reaction was down to grief, then. 'I wonder why.'

Moira shook her head and looked wistful. 'I've never been able to find out. When I asked him, he clammed up.'

'Thanks. That's really useful.' Why would Giles make a claim like that, then fail to back it up? Eve guessed he had no evidence, and had other reasons – emotional or practical – for making the claim.

'I always want to do my bit, Eve. You know that.'

Yeah, right. Eve smiled and left the store.

The take-home point was that Giles's reaction to Anthony's death was out of all proportion, given he hadn't even liked him. It nudged him up the suspect list. If she could prove he'd been having quiet words with Ada, he'd move to the top.

Back at home, Eve got Gus into his blue tartan coat, then walked him through the snow on the village green as she continued to ponder Moira's news. The business about Anthony drinking seemed all but certain to be a lie. Eve doubted he'd have been able to keep it from Hal, and if Hal knew, he'd surely have accused Anthony of hypocrisy when they'd argued at the party.

What's more, Eve had never seen Anthony drunk, whereas Hal had been the worse for wear on various occasions. So, either Ada was lying, or Hal was. Eve needed to work out who. She suspected it would satisfy Ada emotionally to muddy Anthony's name, but Hal might also do it to protect his reputation, if someone had suggested he was the secret drinker. They both had something to gain.

Back at home, she wrote some notes, and vowed to find out more. But for now, it was time to find Giles.

Eve left Gus in the warm after his morning walk, and strolled along the lanes towards Giles's market garden. The gardens were a mix of open fields and more enclosed areas, where the produce was sheltered by worn red-brick walls. Eve had visited in the autumn, when the espaliered apple trees were heavy with fruit. She knew Giles supplied the Cross Keys, and Moira's store, as well as various places in Blyworth. And there were veg boxes for delivery too.

Eve was still some way from the gardens when she heard a woman's voice, clear in the still, cold air.

'And whereabouts in Blyworth is it?' It was Tabitha. She paused for a moment then spoke again. She must be on the phone.

'No, no, I like that area. And it's got that lovely little coffee shop just around the corner. Imagine being able to stumble out of bed and be there in five minutes. It sounds idyllic. Let's arrange a viewing.' Then she paused. 'No, that time might be tricky. Giles and I are usually together. Can we make it later? I'll be able to slip away without him noticing.'

After one more pause, she added, 'I know, but I can't tell him yet. It's bound to come as a bombshell. It would be too cruel.'

Eve was in shock. Tabitha had said how much she loved Giles, and bemoaned Theo's lack of trust in her, but it seemed that had all been for show. She thought of the day before, when Giles had sent a message via Dr Wincup asking Tabitha to go and see him. He'd got the doctor to check up on her and Hal too. Tabitha had seemed irritated by his fussing. Perhaps the relationship was too cloying and was falling apart. It certainly sounded as though she was secretly investing in a place of her own and she wanted the person on the phone to be there. Could it be a lover? Eve could barely imagine Theo's reaction if he found out. She'd lose the use of his lovely house, rent-free, to run her business. It was a lot to risk, and a big decision if she planned to walk out.

Heck, it made her another possible suspect for Anthony's murder, if he'd known and threatened to tell. Tabitha had implied she'd break the news to Giles at some stage, but was she being honest? She might have said it to placate her lover, if that's who she was talking to. It was another query to add to

Eve's list. But as with Hal and Dora, Eve couldn't imagine her collaborating with Ada. She'd seemed to detest her, and Eve could understand why.

Eve had reached the market garden now, its red-brick walls topped with snow. Just before she walked through the arched entrance, she saw a team of Osborne employees picking kale, celeriac, turnips and sprouts. It wouldn't be long before the vegetables sat, roasted and delicious, on a multitude of Saxford Christmas Day tables. It must be cold, hard work, but they were going about it with determination, and she could hear their banter too. It sounded companionable.

Inside the walled area, Eve found a woman in a green branded jacket, harvesting savoy cabbage, and asked if she'd seen Giles.

She straightened up and nodded, pointing to the converted farm buildings. 'He was out here earlier, but you'll find him in his office now.'

Eve thanked her and went over to the block, entering an inner hall, then knocked on a panelled door with Giles's name on it.

When there was no reply, Eve went back outside and approached the office's sash window. Peering into the shadowy interior, she saw Giles at his desk, hunched into his chair, slender and curling in on himself, like an insect playing dead. He was striking, with his iron-grey hair, dark eyebrows, and high cheekbones, but he looked as though he was in pain. As his eyes lifted and met Eve's, he shrank back further, as if he could wish her away.

Eve wouldn't normally push herself forward when someone so clearly didn't want to talk. She didn't want to act like the gutter press. But this was too important. So she stayed where she was and at last, Giles got up and Eve re-entered the office block.

'I'm so sorry to bother you,' she said, standing just outside his hideaway. 'You might remember me? I've been to visit your wife a couple of times, and I was at the party on Saturday night. My name's Eve Mallow and I'm writing Anthony Mottram's obituary for *Suffolk Monthly*. I know the Osbornes and the Mottrams go way back and it's thanks to your mum and dad that Arthur's Yard survived. I'd be so grateful to hear your memories of Anthony, because of the family connection. I can be quick. Or come back later or tomorrow if you'd prefer. Any time.' She wanted him to see their talk as inevitable.

Giles sighed at last. 'Very well. You'd better come in.'

He stood back and she walked into his office. It wasn't large and that gave it a cocooning effect, though in this light, its weathered, whitewashed walls reflected the snow outside.

'It must be tough, keeping the garden going in this season.' Best to kick off with neutral topics. Eve wanted him to relax.

He nodded. 'The team's dedicated and a thick layer of mulch helps stop the soil from freezing. There's stuff in the polytunnels too, of course. But the cold gets into your bones.'

Eve bet it would get into his, in particular. He was so slender. She suspected he might live on his nerves, and never put on fat. 'I gather you ran a London gallery before coming back here. It must be a huge contrast.'

He went paler still, but nodded. 'It's been good to come home. So much of it's down to Theo's generosity, of course. My brother – you know?'

Eve nodded.

'He won't take a penny in rent.' His smile was sad as he pulled his ancient-looking waxed jacket more tightly around him. It struck Eve, because she found the office cosy and warm.

'Your family are known for their generosity, from what I hear.' She waited.

'You're talking about the money my parents loaned the Mottrams to rescue the boatyard after the fire?'

She nodded, and he gave a hesitant smile.

'They were always very giving. They left me money, to compensate for Theo getting the family home, but I'm afraid that all went.' His dark eyes filled with unshed tears, and he blinked. 'My wife, you know. A doctor in America had a revolutionary cure he thought might help her, but it was expensive.'

Eve couldn't begin to imagine what they'd gone through. 'I'm so sorry.'

'My parents went before their time too.'

'It must have been terrible. A boating accident, wasn't it?'

He nodded. 'It put me off the sea. Hal was staying with them, the day they went out. He was supposed to be with them, but he had earache so he stayed behind.'

The narrow escape was chilling, and Eve could tell it still haunted Giles. It was terribly hard to have lost his wife and parents in quick succession too. That was probably the unresolved trauma Tabitha had talked about. 'Did you ever get help, after losing three loved ones so suddenly?'

'Help?' Giles looked as though the entire concept was alien to him.

'Counselling. Therapy. I think I'd have needed it, if it were me.'

He frowned. 'Tabitha suggested it a while back. And maybe Hal too. But we're all different, aren't we? The way we deal with things. I thought my career was the answer, and for years, the gallery was. But then things changed...'

He let the sentence trail off. Eve guessed he'd worked hard to blot out the pain, but in the end, everything had come crashing down.

'This is the right sort of work, in the right place,' Giles said at last.

'I'm glad. I always love visiting. The atmosphere's so nice.'

He gave a faint smile, but he still looked sad.

'What did you think of Anthony?'

And now he was like a rabbit in headlights. His eyes were

scared and there was a long pause before he spoke. 'Well, of course, he was wonderful. He had Hal's back, and I love Hal more than life itself, so he had my undying gratitude for that.'

His reply felt fervent. If Moira was to be believed, he was lying, but it wasn't obvious from his tone.

'Someone mentioned there was a question mark over his honesty.' She watched his face carefully.

Giles shook his head. 'I don't think there was, really.'

Few people liked to speak ill of the dead, of course, but once again, he sounded honest. It was weird. Moira revelled in gossip but Eve had never known her to lie. Eve guessed her impressions now and Moira's before must both be accurate, in which case it looked as though Giles's feelings for Anthony were warmer now he was dead. Eve guessed it made some kind of sense, if Anthony was a threat removed. But had he killed him?

'I always thought he seemed great too,' Eve said. 'Friendly, honest, and capable.' She wanted to test him, to be sure. If she pushed the right buttons, he might crack and contradict her.

But he just nodded and looked sadder still.

'I might have been mistaken, though,' Eve said at last, having given up on goading him. 'There are rumours flying around that he was unreliable at the yard. That he drank, maybe?'

Giles looked shocked and his hand shook slightly as he reached for the water glass on his desk. 'Really? Well, I'm blowed. So I was right all along...'

His feelings towards Anthony seemed to be all over the place. And if he'd been asserting that, why was he so shocked to hear it might be true? It suggested he'd never believed it in the first place, but had been spreading rumours regardless. To discredit him, presumably.

'It would be terrible if he had been drinking,' Giles added. 'People don't realise how dangerous it is in a place like the boatyard. There was a worker just up the coast who died two years ago, slipping off a gangplank. Terrible head injury and there was nothing they could do.' Then he blinked and shook his head. 'But I never *saw* Anthony drunk.'

That proved any assertions he'd made were malicious, not based on fact. 'I hope Hal's all right about working with Ada, anyway,' she said at last. 'I've heard she can be a bit tricky and they'll be in each other's pockets.'

Eve watched his eyes. Could Giles have been in league with her?

His reaction was interesting. He looked almost tearful again, and frightened. If the pair of them had done a deal, she was guessing he regretted it. Or perhaps he was worried that Hal would find out. 'Maybe Hal will change his mind about staying on,' Giles said at last.

'You find her difficult as well?'

Giles hesitated, but at last he nodded. He looked colder than ever, and Eve felt frustrated. She was convinced he was scared of Ada, and Tabitha had said Ada had badmouthed him. Eve's gut said he didn't make a likely collaborator either. Were all her suspects excellent liars, or was she missing something? She was sure Ada's call had sent Anthony to the yard. Ada had been excited that night. Anticipating drama. And Eve had seen Anthony on the phone, then dashing up the river. It had to be cause and effect, even if the police weren't convinced.

'I gather you and Hal were together when Anthony was killed,' Eve tried. 'It's good you were around to comfort each other.'

Giles nodded. 'Yes, we were together the entire time, between nine forty-five and ten thirty. I didn't feel well and Hal kept me company. I feel terrible that I kept him from his duties at the yard. If he'd been on time, the killer might never have struck.'

Eve had the impression he'd rehearsed those lines. The timing he'd given was so precise. She was convinced he and Hal were lying, but she couldn't decide who was protecting whom. And they both seemed scared of Ada, which took her back to square one.

At that moment, Giles's mobile rang, making him jump. It juddered around the wood of the oak desk as it vibrated. The glowing screen said, 'Steve'.

Giles stared at the phone as though it was a snake then snapped out of his trance and shunted the call through to voicemail. Eve would be very interested to know who Steve was. Anthony had wanted Giles to text someone...

'Thanks so much for your time,' she said, getting up. 'I'd better let you get on.' She was just moving towards the door when she spotted a letter sitting in a tray on top of a low filing cabinet. It was mostly obscured by some paperwork on top, but Eve could see the letterhead. The Health and Safety Executive.

In an instant, Eve's mind was back on the gossip Viv had gleaned from Moira. Some health and safety people had done a spot check at Arthur's Yard. What if it was Giles who'd called them in? The inspectors had found nothing, but if Eve was right, Giles had been trying to damage Anthony's reputation before he'd died.

Eve didn't buy Giles joining forces with Ada. Her focus would switch to Theo on that front. But she still needed to see that letter. Though how she'd manage it was another matter.

19

———————

Eve was partway back from the market garden, her toes numb from the cold, when her mobile rang. Simon.

'*I was stretching my legs up by Mistletoe Place and I've just seen Theo Osborne leave. He's walking out of town towards the A12. Are you anywhere near? You might catch him.*'

Eve turned to retrace her steps. 'Simon, you're an angel. I owe you a drink at the Cross Keys.' Springing herself on Theo was probably the only way she'd get to talk to him, and he could have a secret affinity with Ada. She'd crossed everyone else off the list.

She dashed back up the river path, the ground slippery underfoot, the air crisp and so cold it caught at her throat. In no time, she was bustling past Mistletoe Place. It looked serene in the snow, when inside it was anything but. After that, she followed the same route Sylvia and Daphne had taken the night of the party and at last, she could see Theo ahead of her. He was hunched forward, hands in his pockets, shoulders tense. Was he going for a wander, like Simon? Or did he have another plan in mind?

Her question was answered when he paused by the gate to

Anthony's house, Willow Cottage. She pressed herself into the bushes to the left-hand side of the path half a second before he glanced in her direction. He looked furtive, as though he was checking no one was watching. Eve waited until he'd entered Anthony's garden, then carried on in pursuit.

What did he want with Willow Cottage?

Eve crept forward, half hidden behind the hedge that marked its boundary, and peered to see what was going on.

Theo was at a side window, fiddling with something. Sliding it between the window and its frame. Heck, he was trying to break in.

She thought about calling the police, but they'd never make it in time, and if she hung back to contact them she risked missing what he was up to. She took a photo instead to back up what she'd tell them later.

Eve waited with bated breath. In just a moment, he'd managed to get the window open. She watched as he struggled to climb inside, his bulk making the operation difficult. She needed to go and peek, so she could give Greg Boles the whole story.

She felt breathless as she stole up the garden path, keeping close to the shrubs to one side. With any luck, Theo would be intent on his mission and not looking out at the cottage's grounds... All the same, she had 999 keyed into her phone, ready if anything went wrong.

She was level with the cottage now, but the windows were dark. There was no way of finding out more without sneaking up close. She went to the one Theo had forced and risked peering in.

The room was set up as an office, and Theo was searching it. Rifling through drawers, shifting through papers in the desk, scanning a collection of cards on a shelf.

What on earth was he after? Perhaps he was looking for clues. Anything that might tell him where Dora had gone. He'd blamed Anthony for her disappearance – he might be hoping for an address. Somewhere they'd been together, perhaps.

But if Eve was right, and Dora and Ada would never have collaborated, then she very much feared Dora was dead. Why hadn't she come forward otherwise? And Ada had reason to hate her, just as she'd hated her brother. It was Dora and Hal who'd told Ada's dad about the fire, and it was Anthony who'd benefited, in Ada's eyes. He'd got the yard. If Ada had killed Dora and conspired to kill Anthony, Hal could be next... Perhaps Ada had simply bided her time all these years, waiting for her moment.

But Theo couldn't be imagining his daughter dead. He'd surely have gone to the police if he suspected anything so horrific.

Eve crept away from the window, but she didn't return home. She still wanted to talk to Theo in person. Every so often, she glanced back at the house and after a while, she saw him in an upstairs window. He was being thorough.

At last, she heard him leaving Willow Cottage by the front door. She guessed he'd secured the window again to cover his tracks. She caught a glimpse of him, which made her catch her breath. He was in tears. He'd had no luck in his search, she guessed.

Part of her longed to show her face, so he'd know he'd been seen. He'd have to explain then. But it felt too risky. Him not going to the police about Dora left her with too many questions. He might have a lot to hide, and Eve had seen his anger erupt with Anthony. She didn't want to be on the receiving end.

Instead, she dashed a little way up the path so she could pretend to bump into him. By the time he appeared, she'd put some distance between them and gave him a wave. 'Hello there.'

He half turned, and Eve wondered if he'd make a dash for it, but in the end, he let her catch up. He'd wiped away his tears, but his eyes were still red.

'I'm sorry to bother you. You probably got my messages about Anthony. I guess you don't want to discuss him, but I'm keen to hear everyone's memories.' She took a deep breath. 'It matters, you see, to paint an accurate picture. If I only talk to people who loved him, he'll come across as an angel.'

Theo gave a curt nod. 'All right, but it'll need to be quick; I'm heading straight home.' His voice was still thick with emotion. He wanted to be alone and she'd only got until Mistletoe Place to ask her questions. She'd better make it count.

'Thank you.'

'What makes you think Anthony and I didn't get on?' He kept his gaze dead ahead.

'Someone said they'd heard you argue at the party.'

He grunted. 'It was a misunderstanding. He was a hard man to read.' He took an unsteady breath. 'Even now, I'm not sure what to think.' The fury he'd shown previously was gone. He sounded anxious and bewildered.

Perhaps he was starting to doubt Anthony's involvement in Dora's disappearance, if he'd found no evidence for it.

'What was the row about?' Eve knew she was pushing her luck.

Theo's jaw tensed. 'I thought he'd stolen my boat to sell.' The same story he'd told the police. Eve still didn't believe it. 'I'd heard he was short of money.'

'Really?'

'The Mottrams never quite recovered after the fire at Arthur's Yard. But Anthony denied stealing the boat, and we agreed to differ.' Every word was clipped.

Eve thought of his drawn-back fist and the look of fury in his eyes. But he would clearly stick to his lie; she'd have to move the conversation on.

'I hope Hal's all right about working with Ada. I hear she's tricky.' Eve watched Theo carefully. Could he be her accomplice?

'I'm sure Hal can take care of himself,' Theo said, 'if he's allowed to.' He didn't sound bothered about Ada, one way or the other. He certainly hadn't looked shifty when Eve mentioned her. Surely she'd have seen *some* reaction if he'd worked with her to kill a man? He didn't strike her as one of life's natural collaborators in any case. But if it wasn't him, then who?

She ploughed on. 'I'd love to talk to your daughter about Anthony too.'

There was a moment's pause. 'You don't have her number?'

'She hasn't returned my calls.'

'Then I presume she doesn't want to talk to you.'

He was very brusque, but Eve had a hunch he was simply holding in his feelings.

They'd reached the gate to Mistletoe Place and Theo turned to go.

'Thank you for your time. I don't want to get Anthony wrong.'

Theo grunted a reply, and turned his back on her, kicking through the snow to his front door.

Back at Elizabeth's Cottage, Eve gave Gus a cuddle, then put the fan heater on to warm up. As they huddled in front of it, Eve called Greg.

A moment later, she was filling him in on what she'd seen at Willow Cottage. 'I'm sorry I didn't call while he was in there. I thought it would be best to keep watching, to see as much as I could.'

'*You might be right, in fairness,*' Greg said. '*We probably wouldn't have made it in time. We'll follow it up though.*'

There was a danger Theo would guess she was the police's witness. 'I'm convinced he's got no idea where Dora is.'

'*He told us he thought she was at home. When we threatened to get a warrant and access his call log, he admitted they hadn't spoken in over a week – and that he'd been trying to get hold of her.'*

'Why hadn't he involved the police?'

'Palmer thinks he's lying to protect her, and he knows where she's hiding,' Greg added.

'What do you think?'

'It sounds as though she went off the radar several days before Anthony Mottram died. We're checking her mobile records to see if she made calls after that and what base station she was near.'

Eve wouldn't be able to rest until she heard the results of that check.

'We looked into the place where she was meant to be working, by the way. Palmer spoke to Raffaella Jamieson, but it wasn't much help. She had to cancel the job with Osborne for her own reasons. It was a dead end.'

Eve sighed inwardly. Palmer wouldn't have made a decent job of it. Why was the job cancelled when Dora had already bought a lot of lights for it, according to Jade Cooper at Parker's? Eve bet there was more to tell. She'd go and visit Rafaella herself. The quicker she got information, the quicker she or the police might solve the mystery of what had happened to Dora. If she was a second victim, there must be another whole crime scene to investigate. Poor Dora. She might yet be guilty, but her teaming up with Ada seemed impossible. Eve felt horribly afraid for her now.

After she'd ended the call, she sent Greg the photo she'd taken of Theo, then rang Viv to suggest a catch-up at the Cross Keys that evening. Exchanging ideas would help and she needed every boost she could get.

After that, she booted up her laptop and googled Raffaella Jamieson, hoping to find her contact details. She got lucky. Blackthorn House, where Dora was supposed to have been working, was the registered address for Jamieson's Legal

Services, and she found a phone number as well as the full address.

Eve dialled and Raffaella picked up, announcing herself by name.

'I'm sorry to bother you, but I'm after an interior designer and someone mentioned you're using Dora Osborne.' Eve had decided it was best to feign ignorance. 'She's with you now, I gather. What do you think of her?'

'*Ah, actually, there was a change of plan.*' There was something awkward in the woman's tone.

'You decided against her?'

'*Erm. No. Well, not exactly. She's worked for me before and she's great – first class. I'd recommend her one hundred per cent.*' Her tone was effusive, but that didn't help. Eve needed to understand what had gone wrong and why Dora wasn't where she was meant to be.

'Look, I'm sorry to be a nuisance, but I'll be passing your place later. If she's done work for you before, could I possibly pop in and have a look? I can give you my credentials.' Eve provided her name, address and profession, so Raffaella could check her out.

If Eve could only speak to her in person, she might tease out the background to the contract falling through. She was being cagey about it, and that might mean something.

After just a moment's pause, Raffaella launched in, just as enthusiastically as before. '*Yes, of course. Please do come. Then you'll be able to see how good she is.*'

After they'd rung off, Eve looked at Gus. 'That was weird. I expected her to turn me down – who wants a stranger in their house? But she's acting like Dora's agent. There's a tale to tell there.'

20

———

'Raffaella Jamieson.' The woman who'd answered the door of Blackthorn House put out a hand. She had long, dark wavy hair that was in need of a brush. A far cry from the head-and-shoulders portrait Eve had seen on her website, where she'd sported a neat bun and a jacket. She was currently dressed in a long, baggy jumper and jeans, her make-up consisting of a smear of lipstick (as though hastily applied for Eve's benefit). She had dark shadows under her eyes.

'Eve Mallow.' Eve handed over her card. 'Thanks so much for seeing me.' It had to be a bad time – you only had to look at her to see that – yet she'd been so keen on the phone. It seemed odder than ever.

They walked along a hall where a series of hooks hung from a picture rail. There were no prints or paintings, only faint marks where they'd been. Eve assumed this wasn't an example of Dora Osborne's work, unless she specialised in minimalism.

They entered a living room next, with a large, expensive-looking sofa, but not much else. A sizeable cardboard box stood in the corner and the surfaces and walls were bare.

'You're moving? I'm so sorry. This really isn't a good time.'

'It doesn't matter.' Jamieson's voice was bright but brittle. 'You must see what Dora did in the basement. I haven't started packing there.'

She opened a door, revealing a flight of stairs leading down. Eve's comment about bad timing seemed to have given her a fresh injection of energy. 'Here, look!'

The room had little natural light, just some squat windows high up at ground level. But at the flick of a switch, Jamieson brought the place to life. A series of low lamps came on, each highlighting a different area of the room – a vase here, a painting and a bookcase there. The yellow ochre on the walls made everything feel warm and enveloping, despite the cold winter light filtering in from outside. A large corduroy sofa in a beautiful deep blue looked inviting.

'Wow.' Eve was impressed. 'She is good.'

Jamieson turned to look at her, her cheeks flushed. Heck, she was emotional. 'She really is!'

'She's become a friend?'

'Not exactly. But we spent a lot of time together, getting this just how I wanted it. We had a lot of meetings to discuss the new project too – tackling upstairs. She was charming – easy to talk to and so obliging. It's funny, I wasn't sure about her when I met her because she looked so... alternative. A bit of a hippy, you know? But you'd never guess it from her work, truly! She's completely keyed into the personal style of each client. You can see that from her portfolio.'

She was sounding like an agent again. What was going on? 'But ultimately, you decided to move, instead of going ahead with the latest project?' The decision must have been last minute. Dora had bought lights at Parker's.

Suddenly, Jamieson burst into tears. Eve's heart went out to her. She should have seen how close to the edge she was. She looked like she hadn't slept in weeks.

'I'm sorry. I'm so sorry.' Her hands were over her face. She'd turned her back on Eve, then dragged out a tissue, wiping desperately at her tears.

'Please!' Eve put a hand on the woman's shoulder. 'It's me who should be sorry. I'm intruding.'

'But I wanted you to. Dora is excellent and she deserves your custom.'

Eve felt bad now. There'd be no way she could afford Dora's services, even if she wanted to hand her design decisions to someone else. 'I can see that. And you want to help her.' Eve paused, then said gently, 'You didn't want to cancel? The decision to move wasn't yours?' The desire to make amends would explain her behaviour perfectly.

Jamieson's shoulders were shaking.

'Would it help to sit down and talk about it?' Eve stood back so she could get to the sofa.

Eve wanted to offer relief and a listening ear, but of course, she wanted to understand too. It would tell her more about Dora's situation just before she'd gone off the radar.

Jamieson collapsed onto the sofa. 'Please sit too.' She took a fresh tissue from a box on a low coffee table and blew her nose. 'Sorry,' she said again. 'It's all a bit complicated and a long story, so I'll cut it short. I discovered my husband was having an affair with my junior partner at the law practice I run. It's sent my personal *and* professional lives to pieces. I lost my rag, and my colleague took her revenge by muddying my name with our clients. I started losing work, and my husband walked out. On top of all that, it turns out he made some bad investments, so we're in debt.' She gulped. 'I had no idea. And now we have to sell, and I had to cancel Dora at the last minute.' Her hands went over her face again. 'It was awful. We hadn't drawn up a proper contract – we trusted each other, so I guess it hadn't been Dora's priority. When I told her I'd have to cancel, it turned out she'd already bought a lot of the lamps and other bits for the project. I wanted to pay her for them, but I didn't have the money, and of course, I hadn't *asked* her to buy stuff in advance.'

She paused to regain control. 'My husband ended up yelling at her. Telling her it was her fault for not having a contract in place and that she must be a lousy businesswoman.' Tears filled her eyes again. 'She thought she'd got months of work lined up. I left her with goods she couldn't use and no income. She ran out of the house, and I dashed after her but she didn't look back. Just got into her car, crunched the gears and drove off.'

'How long ago was this?'

Jamieson looked as though she'd lost all track of time. 'Three weeks ago, or thereabouts. I've tried ringing multiple times since, but she never picks up.'

Eve patted Jamieson on the shoulder. Poor Dora. What a horrible situation to be in. She might have gone to Theo for help, but perhaps pride had stopped her. He wasn't an easy man, and Tabitha had implied they weren't close. Yet without his support, she might lose her home. And she'd broken up with Anthony too, on the back of his affair.

This put things in a new light. She could have gone to ground of her own accord to start with. Eve could imagine wanting to hide in her shoes. But the situation was just as worrying as ever. Whatever the reason for her disappearing initially, she was nowhere to be seen now, despite the police appeals.

21

———————

Eve made Raffaella Jamieson a cup of tea before she left and promised to spread the word about Dora's services. She didn't explain her worries over what might have happened to her.

In her car, she sent Greg a text, giving him the gist of the new information. She felt a moment of grim satisfaction at finding out more than Palmer had, but it hadn't really got her any further. Dora had been short of cash and desperate, but unless Ada had paid her a large sum to kill Anthony, Eve couldn't see how that might be relevant. And as a theory, Eve found it highly unlikely. Dora would have known she couldn't trust her.

She'd only just got home – to a rapturous welcome from Gus, whose tail wagged so energetically it became a blur – when her mobile rang. Tabitha Osborne.

'We'll go for a walk very soon,' Eve said to the dachshund. 'In a minute.' He knew that phrase. And that it meant anything up to half an hour. Then she picked up. 'Tabitha. How are things going?' She couldn't help thinking of the call she'd over-heard. Had she been to view the property in Blyworth? And was she really intending to come clean and leave Giles?

'*Hello, Eve.*' Tabitha sounded tired, wry and sad, all rolled into one. '*The same as before, really. Hal's still reeling. Ada's sniffing around. She's still on a charm offensive with him. And snider than ever towards me, now I'm no longer her boss. Theo is still like a bear with a sore head and Giles is hiding away, either upstairs or over at his office.*'

Whatever Tabitha was up to, the current situation sounded difficult, and Ada schmoozing Hal continued to make Eve's skin crawl. She was clearly after something, but what? Eve worried she might simply be keeping him close, prior to making him the next victim. 'I'm sorry.'

'*Thanks, but enough of my woes. I'm calling on the back of my visit last night with more information. Have you seen the latest article about the murder in the* Blyworth Advertiser?'

'No.' Eve flipped open her laptop as they spoke, to look it up.

'*They used some photos they took of the yard. They were for an article to mark the centenary.*' She sighed. '*Hal and Anthony were feeling so proud and hopeful when the photographers came.*' She was silent for a moment. '*Anyway, if you look at the photo, just to Anthony's left, in the background, there's a woman's scarf on one of the coat hooks.*'

'Just a second, I've got it open now.' Eve saw what she was talking about. 'Ah, yes, with the flowers.' The photo was black and white.

'*I noticed because it's just like one I own. A beautiful yellow background and the flowers are a deep red. It came from a boutique in Blyworth. Last season's.*'

Tabitha always wore gorgeous scarves which left Eve feeling slightly envious. She'd worn a burnt orange one at the party, but the one in the photo was familiar too. 'You're wondering who it belonged to?'

Perhaps she hadn't heard about Anthony's lover.

'*Exactly. I mean, I can't see one of the photographers taking it off, then leaving it in shot. And there aren't any women working at the yard. As for girlfriends, I can't imagine any visiting the casuals for long enough to hang anything up, and Hal's not seeing anyone, now he and Gabby have broken up.'* She paused for a moment. *'Poor Hal. Which only leaves a connection of Anthony's.'*

Eve felt uncomfortable. 'I'm really sorry, Tabitha, but I think that's quite likely. I hear he was seeing someone behind Dora's back.'

'Oh no! Really?' Her response felt a bit hypocritical considering, but Eve could understand her disappointment. *'Poor Dora,'* Tabitha said at last. *'I knew the scarf couldn't be hers. If it had been tie-dyed or something with a fringe, I might have believed it. But not a designer scarf.'*

It figured. Raffaella Jamieson had called her a hippy.

'Thanks for letting me know, Tabitha. Have you told the police?'

Tabitha assured Eve she'd pass it on, then rang off.

Eve paused for a moment as her thoughts settled. Tabitha was going out of her way to be helpful, and Eve wanted to take it at face value. She'd always liked her, but a tiny warning note was sounding in the back of her mind. Was this meant to distract or divert her?

Still, tracking down Anthony's lover was important. The scarf might help, but information from Jade Cooper's friends would probably be more useful. Jade had texted to say they'd be in the Cross Keys that evening. She'd be ready and waiting. She was due there anyway, for her catch-up with Viv.

She went back to studying the article in the *Blyworth Advertiser*. If it was originally intended as a celebratory piece for the centenary, Ashley Horton, the journalist who'd written it, might have interesting insights into the place, and into Anthony too.

And Ashley had interviewed Eve before. She was friendly

in a nice, rough-and-ready way and Eve had given her an exclusive in the past. One good turn deserved another. She pinged her an email, asking if they could talk, then sighed.

'Right, c'mon, Gus. You've waited long enough for your walk.'

The sun had come out, and the snow was gradually melting as Eve and Gus set out into the fresh, clear air. Eve was still very glad of her chocolate-coloured winter coat and Gus was togged up in his tartan too. They turned right out of the gate, away from the village green, towards Elizabeth's Path, the narrow track that led to the estuary. Like her cottage, the track had been named for the Elizabeth who'd rescued the servant boy in the 1700s. This had been their route to safety; she'd rowed him across the River Sax under cover of darkness. Eve thought of Elizabeth often. She'd been so brave. Someone to look up to and remember, if ever her sinews needed stiffening.

Eve and Gus turned right when they reached the body of brackish water. Reeds rose up before them, with the mudflats stretching beyond, dotted with wading birds searching for food. Eve loved this route heading towards the coast, but you couldn't see far ahead, the meandering path and vegetation saw to that.

It meant that Eve heard Giles Osborne before she saw him.

'I don't know what you mean.' He sounded angry, but scared too.

'Oh, I think you do!' a gruff voice Eve didn't recognise replied. 'If you didn't, you'd tell me to go to hell. I was watching the entire time!'

Giles was silent.

Eve felt a moment of panic. This was a dangerous conversation to overhear. If she was caught listening, either man might want to keep her quiet.

She glanced to her left. It was marshy but if she and Gus ducked into the reeds, there was one solid bit that would hold their weight. She put her finger to her lips, then shovelled Gus onto the outcrop ahead of her. They'd just arranged the reeds around them, Eve ducking slightly, when the two men, only visible as dark shadows, came into view.

Eve couldn't see the second man's face and it was too risky to part the reeds and look. 'Don't think of trying anything,' he said to Giles, 'or bleating to anyone about this. Just do as I say and we can both walk away happy.'

'Happy?' Giles spat the word out. 'You'll never work for me again!'

The other man laughed. 'No kidding!'

As the pair passed beyond Eve and Gus's hiding place, Eve parted the reeds at last. She caught a glimpse of Giles's blackmailer as he turned slightly, and committed his appearance to memory. Wiry and dark-haired, with a straggly beard and a thin face that reminded Eve of a rat.

Dimly, Eve remembered the call that had seemed to scare Giles so badly when she'd visited him in his office. She pictured his mobile, vibrating unanswered on his desk, the name 'Steve' on the screen. Unless Giles felt threatened by multiple people, it was possible she already had the first name of his blackmailer.

22

———————

Back at home, Eve called Greg Boles to tell him what she'd seen and heard. All kinds of new ideas were bubbling up on the back of it, now her adrenaline was calming down. She ordered her thoughts, ready to chew everything over with Viv at the Cross Keys. She was impatient to share ideas, and to question Jade Cooper's friends about Anthony's affair too.

She also felt more focused thanks to a call from Robin to say the day had gone smoothly and they were making progress. He planned to be home for another visit the following night. As she touched up her make-up she felt a bubble of excitement at the thought of seeing him, and a flicker of hope that this job would soon be over. There'd be another one, of course, hot on its heels. His old force clearly missed him. But he was doing what he loved, and what he was good at. Just like her.

As she and Gus left the cottage for the Cross Keys, she could hear faint music which swelled as they approached the village green. Sweet singing. The choir from St Peter's stood near the Christmas tree on the green with its pinprick lights. Each singer held a glowing lantern, and at their head stood Jim Thackeray, the vicar. He was beaming as he sang, his strong tenor voice mingling with the rest. When he saw her and Gus, he waved, and she waved back, caught up with emotion suddenly. It was so beautiful and so homely. Just what the run-up to Christmas should be about – togetherness and celebration, not murder.

At that moment, the carol changed from 'God Rest Ye Merry Gentleman' to 'O Come, O Come, Emmanuel', and Eve froze. She knew what would happen next. Sure enough, Gus began his accompaniment. It was heartfelt and strong, but probably not exactly what the choir members were after.

'Lovely, Gus!' Eve bent to stroke his head. 'But maybe we should get going now.'

As she pulled him gently away, she caught Jim's merry eyes watering in the torchlight. He was managing not to laugh. Just.

When Eve reached the safety of the pub, she found Toby had reserved her and Viv the snug, which was ideal: warm, cosy, and private.

They'd only just got seated after ordering their food when Eve saw Ada Mottram and Hal Osborne come in. Of course, the privacy of the snug worked both ways. She'd be able to watch them through the internal window, but she wouldn't hear what they said.

They settled themselves, and Viv dragged out a notebook, opening it to a page that had cake batter spilled on it.

Eve suppressed a sigh and nodded subtly through the window. 'We should keep an eye on those two. Let's listen to what they're saying when we go to the bar.'

Viv eyed the pair. 'I wouldn't be in Hal's shoes.'

Ada was looking at him like a spider viewing a tempting fly and Eve thought about her starting the fire at the yard. 'Nor me.'

Eve felt she was batting her head against a brick wall. She couldn't imagine Hal or any of the key players wanting to conspire with Ada. And she had a pub full of alibis. Yet Eve was sure she'd been involved; the phone call, her hatred of Anthony and what she'd gained were too much to ignore. There must be an answer, but she couldn't see it.

'So, where are we?' Viv leaned forward, pen poised.

Eve explained what she'd overheard on the estuary path.

'Wow.' Her eyes were like saucers. 'So Giles is definitely guilty of something.'

'Or protecting someone who is. I'm sure he'd shield Hal, and probably Tabitha or Theo too. But if any of them are guilty, then I've got it wrong, and one of them's more closely connected to Ada than I thought. I can't get my head around it. It seems hugely unlikely that any of them did a deal with her, yet I'm sure her call's central to the murder. The timing was precise. He headed to the yard *as* he rang off. Someone going there independently to kill him is way too much of a coincidence.'

But Eve mustn't get hung up on that detail. The only way forward was to dig into every query she had. Hopefully the pieces would fall into place when she knew more.

She refocused. 'I need to find out about the man who's got leverage on Giles. He's clearly an employee. Or rather an ex one, now Giles has fired him. I'll go to the market garden tomorrow and ask around.' Eve had noted the man's description the minute she got home, and done a rough sketch too, though she was no artist. 'I need to find out what he saw.'

Viv pulled a face. 'Tricky.'

'Yes. I'll get as much information on him as I can, then challenge Giles and pretend to know more than I do. Perhaps he'll give something away.'

'Could the blackmailer be the person who eavesdropped on Anthony and Hal, discussing Hal's drink problem?'

Eve thought back to the night of the party, when she'd seen the shadows shift as someone exited the kitchenette. 'It's not impossible. The police already know about Hal's lapses, of course, but it hasn't got out more widely. I could see Giles paying to protect his reputation. But the blackmailer said he was watching, not listening. Perhaps he knows Hal and Giles weren't together when Anthony was killed. Or even that one of them went to Arthur's Yard during that window.' All of the Osborne employees had been invited to the centenary celebration. The ratty man had probably been there. He could have seen.

'The question of the eavesdropper needs answering, though. If it wasn't the man on the estuary path then who was it, and why have they sat on the information? Perhaps there's a second blackmailer, or the eavesdropper wanted to know what was going on for another reason.'

Viv nodded, made a note and underlined it. 'Anything else on Giles?'

'You remember you told me there was a health-and-safety spot check at the yard recently?'

'Yep.'

'He had a paper in his office with Health and Safety Executive letterhead. I wonder if he reported the yard. From what Moira says, he didn't like Anthony, though he'd changed his tune when I interviewed him.' And not speaking ill of the dead didn't quite explain it. People usually gave their resentment away in their tone or body language, but Giles hadn't. It was as though Anthony's being dead had changed his mind. Of course, Giles must have seen him as a threat, and now that threat had been removed.

'I still need to know what Giles was keeping from Hal, and if it was worth killing over, but there's no obvious way to find out. I'll keep digging.'

Toby came in with their food. Game pie for Eve, with rich gravy, roast potatoes and buttered kale. It smelled like heaven. She couldn't wait until she and Robin could come and eat here together, knowing the danger was over.

Gus stirred at her feet and she bent to stroke him.

When they'd thanked Toby, Eve glanced out at Ada and Hal again. 'She's really making up to him.'

Ada had put out a hand and was touching Hal's arm. He looked deeply uncomfortable and it was horrible to watch. Eve knew how desperate he was to keep his job. There was a gross imbalance of power. Eve sensed Ada knew exactly what she was doing and how helpless Hal was.

'What about Hal?' Viv said, her eyes on him and Ada too.

'We still don't know if he was responsible for the empty vodka bottles, but him being drunk at work once is a fact. He'd had too much at the party too, when there were important guests.' Eve checked the timeline she'd created. 'That was at 9.20 p.m. or thereabouts, and Anthony was killed between 9.50 and 10.25. Anthony could have seen Hal staggering about at 9.40, say, shortly before he left for the yard. He'd have known Hal was due there too and they could have fought. I find it hard to believe Hal never went there. Would he really abandon his duties to sit with his dad, when his job was under threat? Wouldn't he be doing his utmost to seem like a reliable employee?'

Viv nodded. 'Good point. But that would make the call from Ada coincidence.'

Eve sighed. 'I know, so that's where I come unstuck. It's not impossible. Not literally. But as well as me seeing Anthony rush up the river path immediately afterwards, Toby saw Ada make the call, and noticed how smug she looked. I'm convinced she sent him to the yard.'

Viv was scribbling away in her notebook. 'Bother. The pen's not taking where I spilled the cake batter. Anything else?'

'Ada's spreading rumours that Anthony was the secret drinker at the boatyard.' Eve looked through the internal window. 'She claims it came from Hal. It might not be relevant, but I'd like to ask him about it and now might be my chance.'

Ada had just nipped off in the direction of the ladies. 'I'll be right back.'

23

Eve eyed Hal as she meandered towards the bar as though she was about to buy more drinks. She turned as she reached his table, as though in surprise.

'Oh, Hal. I only just spotted you there. Look, I'm sorry to bother you when you're out for a meal, but I had one more quick query. I heard a rumour that poor Anthony had a drink problem. I won't mention it in the obituary, obviously, but it might hint at underlying worries and that's relevant. I gather you knew all about it.'

Hal's frown of confusion looked genuine. 'What? No. I've never seen Anthony the worse for drink.'

'But the person I spoke to said they had it from Ada, and that Ada had had it from you.'

Hal tapped his fingers nervously on the table. 'She definitely didn't get it from me.'

'Oh, I must have misunderstood then. I'm sorry.' Eve went back to the snug and relayed their conversation to Viv. 'They both have potential reasons to lie, but Hal looked shocked when I mentioned it. Gut instinct says he's telling the truth and Ada's the real source.'

'Well, we never did trust her,' Viv said.

'True.'

Before they could talk further, Ada herself burst into the snug. 'Hal's just taken me to task for spreading gossip about Anthony. I'm pretty angry about it, to be honest, because he was the one who told me Anthony had a drink problem. I found it very hard to believe, but if it's true, I'd rather people knew the recent issues at the yard were down to him.'

'So you never suspected him of drinking?'

'Never.' For once, Ada sounded honest too.

After she'd left, Eve and Viv's eyes met.

'I believe she doesn't think he drank,' Eve said, 'but that doesn't mean she didn't start the rumours. Character-wise, I'd say she's more likely. She was keen to see Anthony's downfall. She fits.'

After that, Eve explained what she'd found out from Raffaella Jamieson at Blackthorn House. 'I'll keep trying to locate Dora.'

'So we're on to Theo,' Viv said. She was writing sideways in a margin.

Eve tried not to stress. 'I still believe he and Anthony were arguing over Dora, not a boat, though he did have one go missing. He clearly blamed Anthony, and he looked angry enough to kill over it, on Saturday evening. He hasn't admitted as much to the police though, and until they challenged him, he seemed to be covering up Dora's disappearance. I can only think he knew Anthony hadn't harmed her but blamed him for her going off – because she was upset by his affair, presumably. He might have kept quiet because he's too proud to admit she's turned her back on him.'

Viv looked thoughtful. 'That could fit.'

'We've got one possible clue to Anthony's lover's identity.' Eve told Viv about the scarf in the newspaper photo. 'But if this other woman visited him at Arthur's Yard, it feels like a risk.

Hal or any of the casuals might have seen her and told Dora.' Eve felt she was going round in circles and consoled herself with another forkful of pie. 'Perhaps the scarf is a red herring, but we know the lover exists, thanks to Jade Cooper at Parker's and her friends.'

'But until we find them, we're still looking at three suspects?' Viv asked, taking a swig of her Malbec. 'Giles, Hal and Theo, none of whom would be likely to conspire with Ada?'

'That's about the size of it.' It was so frustrating. She told Viv about Tabitha's phone call. 'It looks as though she's preparing to buy or rent a place, possibly with whoever she was talking to – a lover perhaps – and that he was pushing her to tell Giles. She said the time wasn't right, as though she might come clean eventually. But it's hard to believe she will, when living at Mistletoe Place is crucial to her business. Theo would be bound to throw her out if he knew. But that doesn't give her a motive unless Anthony found out what she was up to, and there's no hint he did. And she seems a spectacularly unlikely accomplice for Ada too. Their relationship sounds dire.'

Viv put her head on one side. 'But Theo had a go at Tabitha for being unemotional after the murder. Does that make her look guilty?'

'I'd say the opposite. I can't imagine many people bludgeoning a man to death without batting an eyelid afterwards. You'd think she'd be shaken at the very least, if she'd done it. I'm keeping an open mind, though. I'm due to interview her again on Thursday for the advertorial; I'll see what I can glean.'

'Can I come?' Viv bounced lightly in her seat. 'I love Tabitha's bits and pieces. Maybe she'll give me a freebie, if I play my cards right.'

Part of Eve wanted to go alone. If she needed anything delicate done, Viv's presence wasn't necessarily a bonus. But her eager face made Eve relent. 'All right, I'll ask if it's okay.' Tabitha was bound to say yes. She was that sort.

They glanced outside the snug again. Ada was getting more and more touchy-feely, and Hal looked increasingly uncomfortable, but he didn't push her away. When Eve went to the cloakroom, Ada was leaning forward well into his space. She heard some of her words.

'I keep thinking back to the old days and how blind I was then. I only ever saw you as a friend, almost like a kid brother. I see you properly now.'

Eve felt a shiver of fear. Ada's father might have left Arthur's Yard to her and Anthony jointly, if Hal hadn't told him about the fire. She could be planning her revenge and he looked terrified.

She rushed back to the snug to share her fears, only to find Viv on her phone. She jumped at Eve's sudden reappearance, just like she had in Monty's kitchen, shoving the mobile into her pocket.

'What are you up to?'

Viv smiled brightly. 'Nothing. Tell me what Ada was saying.'

Eve folded her arms. 'Not until you explain. That's twice you've hidden your phone from me. Does this relate to the new foundation?' Viv had looked pleasingly un-sweaty ever since they'd discussed it. She must have gone back to her usual sort.

Viv harrumphed. 'I'm not sure I like having a sleuth as a best friend.'

'You're internet dating, aren't you? And you'd never let me keep that to myself, if our roles were reversed.'

There was an extended silence while Viv pulled faces, as though she was trying to find a way to deny it. At last, she sighed and slumped forward, elbows on the table.

'All right. But you mustn't make judgemental comments and on no account touch my phone screen! You might accidentally match me with Harry Himbo.'

'Who?'

'Oh, just the nickname I've given one of them. He keeps popping up for some reason.' Viv held her phone where Eve could see it and flicked through several profiles. 'What do you think of this one?'

'I thought you didn't want me to judge.'

Viv stuck out her tongue. 'But seriously?'

The guy had so much beard and moustache Eve couldn't really see his face. His profile said he liked whale music and macramé.

'Erm. I'm sure he's lovely.'

Viv eyed her suspiciously. 'You're not.'

'Well, he looks unconventional, just like you. But maybe in a different way.'

Viv sighed. 'I did have my doubts about the whale music.'

Eve was just about to ask to see some more when she saw Jade Cooper had entered the pub with some Saxford friends. It was time to find out what they knew about Anthony's lover. 'This isn't over, Viv. I may have to withhold my case updates if you don't tell me about your dates. That's all I'm saying.'

As Eve left the snug, Viv was back on her phone again.

Eve waved hello to Jade and offered to buy a round, which was always a good precursor to asking for information. She returned with their drinks and joined their group, as Jade made the introductions. Eve explained about Anthony's obituary and how crucial it was to understand his character.

'I promise you I'll be discreet, but it's relevant that he was two-timing Dora Osborne. The woman he was seeing might tell me more about his personality too. I don't have to name names, or even quote anyone directly. How did you find out about the affair?'

A young woman with short brown hair snorted. Part humour, part derision, Eve decided.

'We saw him with her – the idiot. They were at the Swan in Wessingham, sitting in a spot commonly known as lovers' nook, because it's tucked away. I could see Anthony the whole time, but only the back of the woman's head.' She shook hers. 'For a moment, I thought it was Tabitha Osborne – similar hair – so I have to admit I went to get a better look. I was so shocked. I work at her interiors firm, you see.'

In reality, Eve imagined she'd been consumed with curiosity. It wouldn't be unnatural.

'If you go to the ladies, you can view the nook from a different angle,' the woman went on. 'I could see Anthony's bit on the side reflected in the mirror and it wasn't Tabitha, of course. But I did recognise her. She works at a pub in Cressingfield called the Bell. Pretty sure her name's Leah. My boyfriend lives in the village, so we go there a lot.'

Eve noted down the details. 'That's really helpful. Thank you.'

One of her friends pulled an agonised face. 'It was excruciating to watch. Anthony had clearly clocked us. He jumped like a scalded cat when the woman leaned in to kiss him. She avoided us the whole time, looking away, but he popped over to our table on his way out to say it was a business meeting. He was blushing like crazy and I'm not surprised.' She rolled her eyes. 'Talk about a feeble excuse.'

'I was tempted to have it out with Ada at work the next day,' the Tabitha's Interiors employee added. 'Tell her what a pathetic two-timer her brother was. It was so unfair on Dora. But she and Anthony weren't close. She wouldn't have bothered herself with it.'

That figured. Eve thanked them – it was prime information – then headed back towards the snug, feeling thoughtful.

She'd need to verify the story, but it sounded conclusive. Leah could be a suspect. Anyone who'd been so closely and secretly involved with Anthony had to be on the list. As for Dora, it was still hard to imagine her collaborating with Ada, but her motive – jealousy – was alive and kicking.

She found Viv with a happy smile on her face, her phone no longer on the table.

'I've matched with someone. You can't look, in case you disapprove.'

'Hobbies?'

'Rock gigs and a couple of other things.'

Eve waited, but Viv folded her arms. 'Tell me what you've found out!'

Back at home, Eve made plans, then began to enact them immediately with a call to the Bell pub in Cressingfield.

'Hi, sorry to bother you, but will Leah be working tomorrow night? Only I'll be passing and I need to return a top I borrowed from her.'

The man on the end of the line confirmed she was, so she thanked him and rang off.

After that, she texted Robin to ask if he fancied a quick drink in Cressingfield once she'd picked him up from the station. By the time she'd explained why, he sounded as keen as she was.

That night, Eve lay awake in bed. She'd always found her home comforting. The beams in her and Robin's bedroom reached over the bed like protecting arms. Yet now she was filled with anxiety. It was probably the sight of Ada, fawning over Hal, and him looking so helpless. Somehow, she knew before she fell asleep that she'd hear the ghostly footfalls in the lane that night. Echoes of the men who'd run through the village, searching for the young boy who'd hidden under the floorboards in the very house she occupied. She felt his fear, and woke with a start at three in the morning, shaking, the footsteps echoing in her head.

24

———

The following morning, Eve took Gus to Giles's market garden, ostensibly to buy some veg, but really to try to identify his blackmailer.

The snow had gone completely now and it was a crisp, sunny day, with blue skies. Eve enjoyed breathing in the cool, clear air.

The walled part of Giles's outfit was a hive of activity, with staff digging up produce and packing veg boxes. Eve went to admire one, with Gus at her heels. She'd got him on his leash, due to one memorable occasion when he'd disgraced himself and run amok amongst the beetroot.

'Do you have a waiting list for the veg boxes?' Eve asked one of the female employees.

'I think you're in luck. We've got one or two spaces.'

Eve carried on making small talk about the contents of the box, and the vagaries of the weather, then took the plunge. 'It was one of your colleagues who suggested I might like to put in an order. I bumped into him at the boatyard party, but I'm not sure of his name. Dark and wiry with a thin face. About this tall.' She marked his height with her hand. 'I think he might have been called Steve.'

The woman frowned. 'Or Stuart perhaps? Over there?'

But it wasn't him. Stuart wasn't at all rat-like. 'He had a beard. He might have just left – he implied he'd be moving on.'

'Oh.' The woman looked mystified. 'In that case, I'm stumped. We've got three people on the team with beards, but one's grey, one's a red head and one's a lot taller than you said. And no one's left recently.'

Eve sighed inwardly. Perhaps Giles employed someone up at the house. A gardener, maybe? It was Theo's place, but he might do it as a thank-you to his brother. She'd have to ask. 'Thanks anyway.'

Eve bought some carrots and parsnips, and was heading out of the walled garden when she bumped into Tabitha. Once again, she invented a scenario where the bearded rat-like man had recommended Giles's wares.

'He said he worked for Giles, but I haven't seen him here. Perhaps he does something at Mistletoe Place?'

Tabitha shook her head. 'There's a gardener, but Theo employs him. He's been with us for a year now, and they get on like a house on fire, unlike the last one who he booted out after a very acrimonious row about roses. It can't be him though; he was grey-haired and rather bent. There's a cleaner too, who comes in once a week, but he was hired by Theo as well, and he doesn't have a beard. Why don't you come for a cup of tea, now you're here?'

Eve thanked her. It could only help to spend as much time as possible at Mistletoe Place. She took the opportunity to ask if Viv could come along for the advertorial interview the following day too.

'She was fangirling when I told her I was due to visit. She loves your stuff so she's keen to hear about it.'

'Of course.' Tabitha grinned. 'The more the merrier, and

it'll be good to take my mind off things. Everyone's on edge and it's made me feel the same.'

Back at the house, Eve and Tabitha were having tea in the sitting room where Eve had interviewed Hal when one of Tabitha's team came in. As Gus scampered up to say hello, she held out a small, firm cushion in an indigo botanical print.

Tabitha took it and smiled warmly at her employee as she patted it. 'Excellent. Nice and firm for the small of the back. Yes, this is just right. Thank you.'

The team member reached to take the cushion back, but Tabitha paused. 'Actually, leave this one with me, would you?'

The woman nodded and withdrew.

'Theo has back trouble. I'm going to give it to him. He's been incredibly grumpy with me, as you know, but there's been a slight thaw. I don't know why, but I'll give him this and capitalise on it! I'm sure a cushion's as good as an olive branch.'

Eve wondered if Theo knew she was buying a bolthole without Giles's knowledge and quite possibly having an affair. If so, she doubted anything would placate him. Theo clearly looked out for his brother; he'd taken him in when he'd lost the gallery. He wouldn't stop protecting him now.

It was five minutes later that Theo appeared. He looked less than pleased to see Eve, and there was uncertainty in his eyes as he glanced at Tabitha. Gus must have sensed the tension. For once he didn't dash forward and roll over for a tummy tickle.

'Here.' Tabitha stood up and proffered the cushion. 'New design, for the small of the back. I thought it might help.' She reached for a sheet of ivory paper and wrote on it with a flourish, laughing.

To dear Theo, from Tabitha. Hope your back feels better, you grumpy old so and so. xxx

'There you are, you see. You get your own, personal message, not like my regular customers.'

Theo took it from her, then suddenly, he seemed to crumple. His shoulders were still stiff but his eyes were filling and he turned away quickly, marching for the door.

Tabitha was silent. At last, she said, 'That wasn't quite the effect I was hoping for.' She sighed. 'All the same, I'm glad he accepted the cushion.'

Given that he had, Eve guessed he had no idea about Tabitha's secrets.

As she finished her tea, she barely kept up with what Tabitha was saying, her mind was so full of Theo and Giles. She became aware of other voices in the house though. Once she tuned in, she realised it was Ada and Hal, though she couldn't hear what they were saying.

Tabitha paused, as though she'd suddenly become aware of them too. 'You know, Ada seems to be making a very determined play for Hal. She came back with him last night after an evening at the pub, and I'd swear she was angling for him to take her upstairs. In front of all of us too, though maybe that amused her. Poor Hal. It's not ideal. He doesn't have any privacy. He managed to fob her off without causing offence, but I'd like to know what her game is. Believe you me, she never does anything without a cold, hard motive.'

As Eve left Mistletoe Place, Gus scampering ahead, sniffing at something interesting in a flowerbed, she looked back at the house. Something had caught her eye. Movement?

Sure enough, something shifted, which made her look upwards. It was Ada, just visible through a bedroom window. Hal's room? It looked as though she'd got him to take her upstairs after all. That was a bit weird, in a shared house, in the middle of the day.

But a moment later, she saw Hal downstairs, entering the room where Tabitha sat. His body language told Eve he was asking her something. Ada's whereabouts, perhaps? He might not know she'd sneaked upstairs.

Eve was forced to consider a new possibility: that she wasn't after him at all, but something he had in his possession. Her mind flitted to the scrap of paper found between Anthony's dead fingers.

Eve dashed back up the river, dropped Gus at home and went to do a lunchtime shift at Monty's. But she was back at Elizabeth's Cottage that afternoon when the next development took place.

She was sitting in the dining room, writing notes, warmed by the open fire and a mug of tea, with Gus drowsing at her feet. The shadows were lengthening outside, but the sun still shone, belying the throat-catching cold. She was facing the lane side of the house and looked up from her work for a moment, deep in thought. Movement brought her out of her trance. A robin, exploring her hedge. It looked very seasonal, popping in and out, fluttering its wings quickly, then gliding towards another twig.

But then, as she watched, there was movement of a less welcome sort. A police car, driving up the lane towards the estuary path. Its jarring presence on that quiet road, where there was no parking and never any traffic, set Eve on edge. The dream of the footfalls filled her head.

25

———————

All Eve's thoughts were focused on the estuary path. What had happened there? It had to be where the police were making for. And if an attacker was after somewhere to strike, it would be a good choice. A body could be hidden amongst the reeds, and the walk was lonely. If you picked your moment, you wouldn't be seen.

But a killer would have to lure their victim there, meaning the victim would either have to trust them, or be wildly overconfident. Eve's mind was poring over the key players in the case, but she was getting ahead of herself. It might not be anything to do with the Osbornes and the Mottrams. All the same, she got up to look through the window, to a faint protest from Gus, who'd been using her feet as a pillow.

Another car drew up, and an ambulance too. People were dashing to and fro. DI Palmer got out of the car. Eve felt queasy and breathless as the possibilities filled her head. First, Dora had disappeared, and Ada had a grudge against her. Then Anthony had been killed, and the same applied. Hal would complete the trio who'd denied her the yard, either by telling on her, or simply by being the favoured child. Could he be the latest victim? His face haunted her.

She texted Robin to let him know what was going on and to beg him again to be careful. She couldn't help feeling that if disaster had struck here, it might be mirrored where he was. She shook her head. That made no sense.

Eve wondered whether to go to Moira's to see if she had news. But presumably whoever had called the police would be waiting up the estuary path for them to arrive. Moira probably didn't know anything yet.

At last, after waiting for half an hour, unable to focus on anything else, she saw DC Olivia Dawkins, her protective arm around a stooped woman with a long grey plait. Sylvia!

Eve had almost failed to recognise her. Her neighbour's back was normally ramrod straight. She carried her height with pride but now she looked crushed. Daphne was just behind to offer support, thank goodness, her face pinched and anxious.

Daphne said something and Dawkins nodded. A moment later, there was a knock at Eve's door, sending Gus into a frenzy.

Eve opened up to find Sylvia, Daphne and Dawkins on her doorstep. Gus dashed forwards, then clearly realised something was up and drew back, whining.

'Hello, boy! It's all right.'

Good old DC Dawkins. She had all the empathy that Palmer lacked. She looked at Eve. 'I'm afraid there's been a death on the estuary path. We've taken initial statements from your neighbours; they were first on the scene. Perhaps they could come and have a cup of tea while I get back to my colleagues?'

Eve was already ushering them inside. 'If anyone else wants a hot drink, please just knock.' She'd rather pour one over Palmer's head, but she liked his team.

'Thank you.'

Daphne settled Sylvia on one of her couches.

Eve put the kettle on, then joined them again. She took one of Sylvia's cold hands, and one of Daphne's too, crouching to their level. 'I'm so sorry. Let me get you those drinks and then you can talk about it if you want. Or not if you don't.'

They both looked deeply shocked. She fetched the teas and put them down on the coffee table.

'It's Ada Mottram,' Daphne said, her voice cracking. 'I... I didn't even see her body. It was Sylvia who found her. She wouldn't let me look.'

Ada?

The news left Eve reeling. She'd convinced herself it would be Hal. She was sure Ada had the motivation and mentality to punish her enemies and he was one. Eve had read an article about psychopaths once, and Ada fitted the description. Someone who'd been born without empathy. DC Dawkins's polar opposite. And then Eve thought of Ada, sitting in that very room, pretending to have loved her brother, and to think well of Tabitha. And after that, an image of Eve's final sighting of her flashed up, sneaking around upstairs at Mistletoe Place.

'I'm so sorry, Sylvia. That must have been terrible.' Eve pushed the tea towards her, and Sylvia clutched the mug with her long, strong fingers.

'It was.'

Daphne looked concerned. 'I don't want you to try to protect me if it means bottling it up. It's not good for you and I shall only worry more. You'd feel the same, if it were me.'

If it were Daphne, of course, she'd already be telling them, but Eve knew what she meant, and she was right.

There was a long pause. 'All right,' Sylvia said gruffly. 'Eve will need to know everything anyway, for the investigation.'

If it hadn't been for that, Eve suspected Sylvia might have stayed silent.

She sipped her tea again. 'We'd just gone out to enjoy the sunshine before it got dark. I was on the left-hand side of the path, nearest the water, when I saw something down in the reeds. I crouched to look and found it was a pair of sunglasses.'

'I wasn't paying proper attention.' Daphne sighed. 'I'd spotted some snow buntings in the fields.'

'I wish I'd been watching them,' Sylvia said drily. 'Anyway, when I reached for the glasses, I saw something shadowy beyond the reeds. Most of the water was glittering in the sun, but there was one disturbed patch. So I pushed the vegetation aside and that's when I saw her. She was mostly underwater, but part of one arm and her face were at the surface.'

No wonder Sylvia looked so pale.

'There was a red mark around her neck,' Sylvia said. 'I could see it, just under the water. I suppose someone strangled her, then pushed her into the estuary.' She shook her head and said no more, but Eve's imagination took over. She saw Ada's eyes, open but glazed, and tendrils of her hair floating in the salty water.

'I'm so sorry, Sylvia. Both of you.'

'You went through the same thing yourself, at the party,' Daphne said.

'But I was already sure something was wrong. It prepared me for the shock. Did the police give anything away?'

'I don't think so.' Sylvia was staring into space, her eyes still wide. 'Dawkins and Greg Boles were first on the scene and they're a lot more professional than Palmer.'

'I saw Ada myself, this morning, at Mistletoe Place.' Eve explained the circumstances. 'So I know she was alive at around eleven a.m.' It was three o'clock now, so a four-hour window. She'd need to know where everyone had been.

'You'll get news from DS Boles, via Robin, I suppose?' Daphne said quietly.

Eve nodded. 'I expect so. And Robin's due another flying visit tonight. I might just get the updates in person.'

26

After Sylvia and Daphne had gone home, Eve made a note to email her contact at *Suffolk Monthly* once Ada's death was public. She wanted to suggest making her obituary a joint one. It would help when it came to asking questions of the key players, and it would feel weird to write about one sibling and not the other, however unpleasant Ada had been.

Next on her list was telling Viv and Simon what had happened. They hadn't been close to Ada, of course, but Eve still had the urge to let them know in person. She went to Viv first, knowing there'd be hell to pay if she heard it from someone else. She broke the news in Monty's kitchen.

Viv's eyes were wide with shock. 'I mean, I really didn't like her, but it's still awful. And even though she had a multitude of alibis, I was as convinced as you that she was involved in Anthony's death.'

'That's still perfectly possible. Let's go through it all this evening.' Robin had texted, suggesting Eve invite Viv to join them after they'd eaten. 'Eight thirty suit you, for a post-supper drink?'

Viv nodded. 'So it looks like Ada was strangled.'

'Yes. I wonder what they used to do it.' It was horrific to imagine someone holding their grip with steadfast determination as Ada struggled. They must have been utterly possessed by fury or fear.

After Eve had left Viv, she nipped over to pass on the news to Simon, then headed off to Mistletoe Place. It wasn't the family she was after. Quizzing them was crucial, but it would have to wait. They'd be in a state of shock, and the police would be there too. They were bound to interview Hal as a priority, when Ada had been set to be his boss. But if Eve wanted more of a handle on Ada, there was another possible source: her old co-workers at Tabitha's Interiors. You couldn't work alongside someone for months without gleaning some interesting details. With any luck, the police would leave their interviews until tomorrow, so they'd be free to speak to Eve.

As she passed Arthur's Yard in the winter darkness and neared Mistletoe Place, she could see two police cars in the drive, and some press too, lit by an outside lamp. They'd probably pounce on Ada's old colleagues if they got the chance.

But when five o'clock came, she saw three of them, peering outside, clearly aware of the situation.

They exited by some French windows. Eve could see Tabitha, considerate as ever, ushering them out. Then Tabitha spotted Eve and waved, beckoning her over.

'I'm so sorry.' Eve nodded towards the press and the police. 'It must have been a difficult day.'

Tabitha's chest rose and fell. 'Not the best.'

Eve explained she was expanding her interviews, following Ada's death. 'It would feel wrong to focus my obituary solely on Anthony, now that she's dead too, and they were both associated with Arthur's Yard.'

'I can talk to you about her tomorrow,' Tabitha said, 'when you come to discuss the advertorial.'

Eve nodded. 'That sounds great. And I'd love to speak to

you too,' she added, addressing Ada's former co-workers. 'Whenever it's convenient. I could buy you a drink, if you're heading into the village? I won't keep you long.'

The one she'd spoken to previously about Anthony's lover had to leave for a date, but the other two agreed to meet her at the Cross Keys. They headed off on bikes, and Eve went to pick up Gus, then made for the pub.

It was early, and only Wednesday, so the pub wasn't busy, and Eve was lucky enough to get the snug again. She treated the women to glasses of white wine as Gus dashed over to Hetty. The pub schnauzer was the love of his life.

A moment later, Eve got down to business. 'I'd met Ada,' she said. 'She made an instant impression on me.' She watched the pair. Their eyes met and one of them raised an eyebrow. *Good.* They had strong opinions too, Eve was sure.

She sipped her tonic water and carried on. 'But I didn't know her well. She was a longstanding connection of the Osbornes, of course, but Tabitha was her boss. She might have modified her behaviour because of that.' Though not all that much, by the sound of it. 'You'd have seen her in more unguarded moments. If I want to do a decent job with my obituary, I need to give a rounded impression.'

Again, her co-workers' eyes met.

'No one likes speaking ill of the dead,' Eve said at last, 'but I'd never quote you without your permission. If you're happy to help me write something truthful, I can always attribute your contributions to "close connections" or something like that.' Promising anonymity often helped.

At last, one of them sighed. 'I couldn't believe it when I heard Anthony was dead. It was horrific. But when I realised it meant Ada would be leaving, I was so happy. I feel bad about it now.'

'She was hard to work with from the start?'

The woman nodded. 'Resentful. It was so weird. She

seemed to hate Tabitha, yet she'd gone to her for a job. I heard a rumour that the Osbornes had helped the Mottrams out financially at one point. Reading between the lines, I don't think she liked being beholden to them.'

So it was definitely odd that she'd approached Tabitha for work. Perhaps she'd been short on options, but Eve suspected there'd been an ulterior motive. She'd seen her upstairs at Mistletoe Place that morning. She'd clearly wanted access to someone's room – Hal's most probably. But that couldn't have been her goal; she wouldn't have left it until after she'd resigned. Sneaking around that day must have been triggered by something recent. Anthony's murder, at a guess. She must have had another reason to want to work for Tabitha. Of course, it gave her an excuse to be close to the boatyard, day in, day out. That might be relevant.

'How long was she with the firm?'

The second woman gave a hollow laugh. 'Not long. Three months? But it felt like forever. Of course, we didn't know the end was in sight.'

'Did you ever see her making up to Hal?'

They both looked confused. 'No.'

Then one said, 'She behaved as though he was beneath her notice. I'm sure I heard her call him lazy once.'

That agreed with what Tabitha had said. So the charm offensive had only begun very recently. Again, probably since the murder. It looked as though she'd needed something from him as a result of Anthony's death.

'And did you see Ada interact with Anthony much? I guess he must have visited Mistletoe Place sometimes, given he was so close to Hal.'

The first woman nodded. 'He was in and out. Ada was nice as pie about him if anyone asked but you could tell she wasn't sincere.'

'Was there anyone in the household she seemed to get on

better with? If so, I should interview them, to get a balanced view.' In reality, Eve still wanted to know who Ada might have teamed up with.

But the women shook their heads, so Eve remained stuck.

She needed to go back to basics. To the evidence. Ada's sole focus had been on Hal since Anthony's death, and now Ada was dead too. And Eve was convinced Ada had searched Hal's room. Whatever their past relationship, that made Hal more suspicious than the others.

She refocused on her questioning. 'Incidentally, I got chatting to an employee of Giles's recently.' She thought back to the man who'd been blackmailing him. 'A thin-faced guy with dark hair and a beard. About five ten. I'd like to track him down again.' They looked surprised, so she embellished her back story. 'He had some interesting things to say about Ada. Do you know the man I mean? I want to say he was called Steve, but I might have got that wrong.'

But neither of them had any insights on him, either. Who the heck was he?

27

Eve thanked Tabitha's employees and handed over her card in case they thought of anything else. After that, it was time to fetch Robin from the station. She couldn't wait to see him.

It was such a relief to see his face less swollen and bruised, half an hour later. The Christmas decorations at the station no longer seemed jarring, but a promise of what was to come: a time when Robin would be home properly for the holidays, ready to make merry and meet up with family and friends. She pictured him, her twins and their partners filling Elizabeth's Cottage with laughter, chat and companionship.

As Robin reached her side of the barrier, she clung on to him, then felt embarrassed. She was behaving like a love-struck teenager. He was grinning at her though; she guessed he didn't mind. They walked to the station car park arm in arm, Gus leaping about giddily at their feet.

Eve gave Robin's arm a squeeze. 'Any nearer catching the brute who dared to beat you up? Want me to come and join in, give him his comeuppance?'

Robin laughed. 'You've got your own bad guys to deal with.

And I think in the interests of safety, we should each aim for a clean collar, rather than a fight.'

That was precisely what Eve was hoping for in both their cases. The alternative was high in her mind though, despite her light words. She couldn't bear it if anything happened to Robin.

'We're still gathering intelligence,' he went on. 'Trying to get key people onside. That way they won't know we're coming, and we'll go in well prepared.'

He made it all sound so easy, but 'going in' had to be hazardous. Images of all the police raids she'd ever seen on TV filled her head. Usually with added guns and unexpected consequences. 'Please, please be careful.'

He smiled. 'I will. So, what about this trip to the Bell then? Let's go and find Anthony's lover.'

Eve drove them straight to the village of Cressingfield, a short way south of Blyworth, and they entered the Bell, an old half-timbered inn, its lights glowing cosily through leaded windows.

Eve went up to the bar with Robin at her side and ordered warm drinks: a mulled wine for him, and the winter-spiced apple juice for her. It was a man who served her, but at the other end of the counter she saw a woman with shoulder-length dark hair, wearing a chunky jumper and gold bangles.

As soon as she'd paid, she approached her. 'Leah?'

The woman frowned. 'Yes.'

'Hi. Eve Mallow. I'm sorry, I don't know your surname.'

'Mason.' Leah seemed to answer on autopilot, then looked doubtful, as though she'd given too much away.

Eve had relied on people's automatic desire to be polite. It was amazing how well it worked. She handed over her business card as Robin took their drinks and went to find them a table. 'I'm writing Anthony Mottram's obituary for *Suffolk Monthly*.'

Leah opened her mouth, then closed it again. She looked anxious, that was for sure.

'I'm so sorry for your loss. This is a bit delicate, and I'm certainly not planning to mention your name in the article – unless you want me to – but it would be invaluable to talk to you about him. I understand you were seeing each other.'

'I—' The woman seemed lost for words. 'No. Not at all. We weren't involved.'

'Please don't worry. I'll be very discreet. But you were seen together at the Swan in Wessingham.' In the lovers' nook.

'But... but that was just a meeting.'

Yeah, right. Eve thought of what her informant had seen. Leah leaning in to kiss Anthony. But she'd have to coax her if she wanted to find out more. 'Ah, I see. What kind of meeting?'

Leah was blushing so deeply that Eve knew to expect a lie in response. 'I, er, I inherited some money recently from my grandad. I— well, I was considering investing it in the boatyard Anthony owned.'

It sounded like baloney. 'So I guess his business partner Hal will know all about this?'

The blush deepened. 'Actually, I asked Anthony not to say anything until I'd made up my mind, so he might not.'

Very convenient.

'I just want to say how sorry I am, Leah. It must hurt, losing him.'

'But we really were just business contacts.' She failed to meet Eve's eye, and when she looked up again, her face was etched with fear. 'Are you thinking I had something to do with his murder? Is that it? I mean, you are a journalist after all.' Anger mingled with the anxiety in her expression now. 'Well, I was working here all night when he was killed.' She called across to the guy who'd served Eve. 'Wasn't I here all evening last Saturday, Dave?'

'Dave' looked perplexed. 'What? Why?' But then he shook his head. 'Yes, of course you were. We were on till closing.'

Eve would relay all of this to Greg Boles and he'd check, but she reckoned Leah was out of it. Proof of her existence made her focus on Dora again though. She *could* have come back to Saxford and killed Anthony out of jealousy, but if so, the timing would need explaining. From what Jade Cooper said, she'd broken up with him well before that. All the same, it was monumentally odd that she hadn't come forward. Unless she was dead…

Eve pushed the horrible thought away and rushed to smooth Leah's ruffled feathers. 'I'm not that sort of journalist. I just wanted to make sure I spoke to you, in case you had thoughts on Anthony you wanted to share. If you don't then I'll leave you in peace and I'm sorry to have troubled you. Before I go though, do you own a scarf like this?' Eve showed her the photograph from the *Blyworth Advertiser*. She'd zoomed in close on her phone so Leah wouldn't see the context.

'What? I—' She seemed lost for words again. Eve was fairly sure she recognised it. She probably couldn't work out whether to admit it or not. 'No,' she said at last. 'That's not mine.'

Eve went to join Robin and filled him in. They sat, their hands cupped round their warm drinks, discussing the implications of what Leah had said in low voices. Eve breathed in the scent of apple, cloves and cinnamon. She was mid-sentence when she spotted a short woman of around sixty with curly hair approaching their table.

The woman leaned in and hissed, 'I heard you talking to Leah up at the bar.' Her look was sour. 'I'm her neighbour. Plays her music till all hours, she does.'

She had a grudge, clearly, but her information might be useful. 'Please, have a seat, Ms—'

'Mrs Lisa Bryant.'

'Can I get you a drink?'

But she shook her head, nodding to another table occupied by a stout woman with grey hair. 'I'm all right, ta. Left mine over there. I just couldn't keep quiet, when I'm sure Leah's spinning you a pack of lies. Inheritance from her grandad?' Lisa Bryant let out a tactlessly loud hoot. 'Inheritance my foot. Her car was repossessed three days ago. She overspent, as per. What about that scarf you asked her about?'

Eve showed her the photograph.

Mrs Bryant looked triumphant. 'Oh yes, I saw her wearing that when she left on an evening out a few weeks back. I remember it because it looked expensive.' She snorted. 'Either she nicked it, or bought it from a charity shop.'

'Have you ever seen her stealing?' It wasn't really relevant, but Mrs Bryant was starting to annoy Eve. She was fairly sure she was telling the truth, but the level of vitriol was unpleasant.

Bryant blinked. 'Hm. No, to be fair, a charity shop's more likely. If you want more information, here's how you can reach me.' She wrote down her name, address and phone number on the back of a supermarket receipt.

'Charming woman,' Robin muttered as they left.

But useful. So it seemed Leah must be the owner of the mystery scarf, and that she told untruths. But why lie about her relationship with Anthony when she had an alibi for his murder? It might make sense if she thought Dora had killed him in revenge for the affair, and she was in danger too. But the news about Ada's death was out now as well. Leah must see that pointed to a different motive.

And why deny all knowledge of the scarf?

Did she just see Eve's questions as an invasion of privacy? Eve could understand that, but Leah had seemed almost scared, perhaps of what would happen if she came clean, which meant there was an extra layer to this that Eve didn't yet understand.

. . .

Back at home, Eve called Greg Boles to let him know about Leah, then she and Robin had a nice, quiet supper, talking over his case and hers. At eight thirty, Viv arrived and the house went from its peaceful, cocooned state to a flurry of energy and Vivervescence. Gus scampered around her ankles, with a skip here and there.

Eve got them all glasses of mulled cider and they sat on the couches, warming themselves by the inglenook fireplace.

'You look a bit better.' Viv was peering at Robin, her head on one side. She took out her phone and opened the notepad app.

'No paper?' It was a point of concern. Viv's thumb typing was terrible and she left the words to whatever autocorrect dictated, assuming she'd remember the gist later. That and the fact that her mind worked faster than her fingers meant she also left words out. Recently, she'd forwarded Eve a shopping list for the cash and carry that included requests for 'selfie flower' and 'vicar of soda'. Eve had worked it out, but the case notes would be less predictable.

'I think I must have put my notebook somewhere funny,' Viv replied vaguely.

Regretfully, Eve reached for one of her pristine new pads from the drawer in the side table. 'Here you go.'

'Ooh! I like it! Thanks!'

Eve was starting to wonder if Viv was playing her. She clearly had a soft spot for nice stationery.

Viv grinned. 'So, what news from Greg Boles?'

Eve had been through it all with Robin during supper, but she was looking forward to hashing over it again. The more she reviewed the facts, the more likely she was to see connections and anomalies.

Robin checked his notes. 'The pathologist says Ada died between midday and two p.m. There'll be a post-mortem, but it's thought she was strangled before she went into the water.

The doc thinks the killer might have used a scarf, so it's impossible to tell if it was premeditated or spur of the moment.'

Everyone had been bundled up against the cold lately. It would certainly have been a readily available weapon.

'Presumably Ada had no idea this person was a danger when she agreed to walk with them,' Robin went on.

Eve didn't think that ruled anyone out. 'I don't believe Ada was the sort to feel vulnerable. I suspect she'd been running rings around people for so long, she'd convinced herself she was invincible.'

'Do any of the key players have alibis?' Viv asked. Eve could see she'd already doodled a picture of Bugs Bunny across one of the precious pages of her notebook.

Robin sighed. 'I'm afraid not. Hal was in and out of the boatyard, keeping an eye on things. He says he was there between one and two, but the casual workers had gone for lunch, so they can't vouch for him. After that, he claims he returned to Mistletoe Place, and went to his room, but again, there was no one to see. Tabitha's in a similar boat. She was in her design room while her team worked at their sewing machines. They can't confirm she didn't leave. In fact, she told them she wasn't to be disturbed, which Palmer finds suspicious.'

That was Palmer all over. 'She's working on her new collection, to be fair.'

'Giles was at the market garden, but in his office. A witness confirms seeing him shortly after twelve, and someone else thinks they glimpsed him before two, but they're not sure, and he'd have had time, anyway.

'As for Theo, he's renowned for being a loner, I gather. True to form, no one can vouch for him, though he says he was about the house at first, then went for a walk. What might be of interest is who benefits.'

Viv leaned forward. Eve couldn't wait to see her reaction.

'As you already know, Anthony's dad left Arthur's Yard to

him, on the proviso that he'd leave it to Ada, if he died childless. But Anthony's will states that if Ada predeceases him, or dies before the estate is settled, then Hal gets it.'

'Wow.' Viv's eyes were wide. 'I'm guessing he'll be pleased about that.'

Eve imagined she was right. 'Yes. He was desperate to stay on when we overheard him talking to Anthony. He called it his passport to freedom, remember?'

Viv nodded. 'But his role was under threat from Anthony.'

'And then Anthony died.' Eve sipped her drink for comfort. 'And although Ada said she wanted to keep Hal on, I'm sure she had an ulterior motive. If he knew that, he probably guessed she'd get rid of him once she'd fulfilled it. Now, he gets to run the show.' If he'd wanted to keep his job, killing Ada could have felt essential. She'd all but written him off, but her thoughts had shifted now.

Viv chewed the end of her pen for a moment. 'But we both saw how frightened he looked with Ada in the pub. Would he have been brave and ruthless enough to corner her and kill her?'

'Before, I wouldn't have said so, but protecting his job and gaining the yard is quite a prize. He might have hankered after that security, and told himself it was just one hurdle away. And other circumstances could have compounded his motive too. The timing of the latest killing is interesting, so soon after I saw Ada upstairs at Mistletoe Place. Perhaps there's an element of cause and effect.'

'Go on.' Viv's frown deepened.

'Maybe Hal had kept evidence that she was involved in Anthony's death as an insurance policy, to use against her if needs be. She could have gone to remove that, after which, she might have been planning to report him and let him take the rap. Or similarly, she could have known or hoped he had something that would prove he'd done the actual killing.' If they'd worked together, she'd want to ensure she kept control and proof would give her that power.

'Wouldn't it be risky to report Hal to the police if she was involved?' Viv said.

Eve agreed. 'I doubt most people would go for it, but she was supremely confident. Hal would accuse her of having had a hand in it no doubt, but if she knew his evidence was circumstantial, I doubt she'd have worried. No one can prove what she said on that call, for instance. The upshot is, if he'd been tempted to kill Ada for the yard, and she'd become a threat to his freedom too, it could have tipped the balance.'

Viv was scribbling away. 'So we're saying Hal could have killed Anthony as well as Ada?'

'Well, we know he had a motive. And we also know some kind of document or letter's likely to be key. The police found a tiny scrap of paper between Anthony's fingers, remember? Perhaps Hal had the rest of it.' Eve needed to work out what it might have been.

'So what about Ada and Hal collaborating?' Viv said. 'We didn't think they would before.'

'No, I know. But I went through each of the suspects and none of them seemed likely. Unless the call was irrelevant, which I can't believe, that means I need to think again. I can see it from Ada's point of view – if I'm right, then she got rid of her brother without getting her hands dirty. As for Hal, it's still hard to imagine him relying on her, but we know he was staggering drunk at the party, and perhaps the arrangement was last minute. Ada could have suggested it when he was desperate. Perhaps Anthony had decided to sack him after all, after seeing him so out of it.'

Viv whistled. 'It sounds possible.'

'Of course, there's still Dora. She's an anomaly we can't ignore.'

'And she also had a motive for Anthony,' Robin said.

Eve nodded. 'It's like we thought before. She was Anthony's ex. He'd betrayed her, so she was bound to be angry. And we now know she needed money badly when she disappeared too. But I find it very hard to imagine her being both desperate and angry enough to agree to kill Anthony in exchange for payment from Ada. She knew Ada of old. I doubt she'd trust her. And although Anthony's affair must have hurt, time had already passed since she'd discovered it. Would she have gone in cold and bludgeoned him to death?'

'Though we don't know it all yet,' Robin put in. 'Especially in her case, since you've never met her. Something new might have pushed her over the edge.'

'True. But there's one more thing to bear in mind. Hal was due to be at the yard on Saturday night, and it's more than possible Ada knew that. She was on the spot, and if she was plotting the killing with an outsider, she'd have been watching his and Anthony's routine. She'd have wanted to avoid any nasty surprises.'

Robin nodded. 'It's true, it would have been a risk to send Dora or anyone else there when Hal would likely be on site too. All the same, we shouldn't ignore the others.'

'Okay.' Viv smoothed out Eve's pad. Not that it was hers any more, obviously. 'So hit me with Theo and Giles's motives for Ada.'

Eve sighed. 'Either of them could have killed her if she was their accomplice, and they realised she was a loose cannon.'

'Did the police ask Theo what he was doing, breaking into Anthony's house?' Viv asked.

Eve nodded. 'He admitted he's worried sick about Dora and hoped he'd find clues to her whereabouts inside.' Robin said he'd refused to answer at first, but then it had all come tumbling out. He'd been emotional and they'd let him off with a warning.

Viv took up her pen again. 'So Hal's top of the suspect list now?'

'I think he has to be. There's an outside possibility there are two killers, not one, and it's Giles who's being blackmailed, of course, but I'm sure he'd pay up to protect his son.'

'So what next?' Robin asked.

'I'm missing some key information. I need to fill in the blanks so I can make my case. Trip Hal up, or find a witness.'

'You mean the blackmailer?' Viv said. 'Have the police asked Giles about that?'

Robin nodded.

He'd told Eve all about it over supper. 'Giles came up with some cock-and-bull story about him being a casual worker he'd sacked from the gardens a couple of years ago. He claims he wanted his job back and threatened to tell everyone he was having an affair unless he complied.'

Viv harrumphed.

'Exactly,' Eve said. 'And to cap it all, he told the police he'd sent him packing and couldn't remember his name. Their conversation made it clear he was an employee, of course, so that fits, but it sounded as though he'd been working for Giles right up until he turned to blackmail. Perhaps Giles was paying him to do something secret and Anthony had found out. It could explain their conversation, the evening Anthony died.'

'And maybe it was this unknown guy who listened in to Hal and Anthony's conversation too,' Viv said.

Eve nodded. 'Finding him is crucial.' It filled Eve with indignation that he'd keep whatever he knew about Anthony's death to himself to make some money. 'The trouble is, no one recognises my description, and I didn't see him at the party. It's like he's a ghost.'

28

___

The next morning, Eve had to drop Robin at the railway station again. There was nothing sweet about the parting. It was 100 per cent sorrow. She couldn't stop thinking about the moment when he and his team would descend on the gang they wanted to bring down. A thousand worries filled her head. Would they be outnumbered or outgunned? What if the people Robin were 'getting onside' betrayed him? But she kept quiet about her fears and simply hugged him very tightly before he went through the barriers, telling him to take care and promising she would too.

She visualised Christmas lunch all the way home, Robin carving the turkey, candles twinkling on the table, holly and ivy, mistletoe and berries. Her family around her. That was the vision to hang on to.

Viv came to meet her and Gus when they parked by the village green, just as she had before. 'He'll be okay. It'll be over before you know it.'

Eve took a deep breath. 'Thanks. You're right.' Say it enough times and she might believe it. 'I'll come and call for you soon, to go to Tabitha's.'

Viv nodded and let her go.

. . .

Back at the cottage, preparations for her open house vied with the urgent need to solve Anthony and Ada's murders. She settled down to decorate her wreath base, theories doing battle in her head. After that, she checked the baking ingredients she needed for the umpteenth time. Viv had suggested leaving them at Monty's but Eve had been too anxious about them getting mixed up with the general supplies. Everything was in order. (Of course. She'd known it had been already. Why did she always have to check?) After that, she ran through her thoughts on the case as she pinned her Christmas cards to cheerful red ribbon suspended from the beams, then put delicate frosted wreaths around the candles she'd placed on high shelves. They were exquisitely pretty – handmade by a local craftswoman with a stall on Blyworth Market.

She'd almost finished when her mobile rang. Ashley from the *Blyworth Advertiser*, calling her back.

Eve was smiling as she sat on the couch to chat with her. 'Ashley! Thanks so much for ringing.'

'*Anything for you, Eve.*' Her journalist friend's voice was warm. '*That exclusive you gave me got me my last promotion and I've applied for a job at a national. Keep your fingers crossed for me!*'

'I will.' Ashley deserved it.

'*So, you want the lowdown on my interview with Anthony Mottram for the centenary piece? Shame I had to reformulate it into such a sad article.*'

'I know. Tragic. But yes please. Your inside knowledge could be invaluable.'

'*I love being flattered!*' Eve pictured her wide grin and dark bouncy curls. '*So, what d'you want to know?*'

'You did the interview the same day your photographer visited?'

'Yep.'

Eve was sure Leah Mason was the owner of the scarf now, but it was worth cross-checking. 'I don't suppose you saw a woman there, did you?'

Ashley sighed. 'No, *but the place smelled of perfume, if that's any help.*'

It triggered a memory. The police said they'd smelled perfume when they'd arrived at the scene of Anthony's murder too, only Eve hadn't noticed it.

'I don't suppose you know the brand?'

Ashley chuckled. '*Something well out of my price range, I'd guess. I'm more of a body-spray person.*'

The perfume was odd – particularly the smell of it at the crime scene. Two out of the four women involved in the case – Ada and Leah – had cast-iron alibis for Anthony's death. Dora was an unknown quantity, but everyone said she was a hippy. Pricy perfume didn't sound like her style. That left Tabitha, but she of all people felt highly unlikely as an Ada collaborator. And there was no hint Anthony had known about her plans to leave Giles, and possible affair.

'And how did you find Anthony and Hal?' Eve went on.

'*Cheerful.*' Ashley sighed. '*Though there was a moment of tension when I mentioned a visit they'd had from the Health and Safety Executive. Someone tipped me off, so I had to ask. They had no idea who'd reported them, or why, but it wasn't the first time it had happened. Reading between the lines, I reckon Anthony thought his sister Ada might have been responsible. No love lost there. But I gather she can't have killed him.*'

'That's right. Did he say why he suspected her?'

'*No, but I knew there was bad blood between them. I heard rumours a while back, when Anthony's dad died and he inherited the yard.*'

'I understand she was left the house.'

Ashley tutted. '*Maybe, but from what I hear, she thought she should have got half the business too. I suppose Arthur's Yard runs in their veins. She's good with boats, apparently, and Ada questioned why Anthony had hired Hal as his second in command, not her.'*

Eve thought of the fire Ada had started. Anthony didn't know about it, but he'd clearly got the measure of her, nonetheless. It hadn't taken Eve long to pick up on her nastiness. 'You asked Anthony about it?'

'That's right. He told me he would have hired Ada like a shot if she'd been around, but Hal got there first. It's all in the article. I didn't believe him, though. Ada was away travelling for a bit, but he could have called her back. From what I can see, Anthony was in a great hurry to promote Hal before she reappeared and started pressuring him to take her on instead. Hal was already working at the yard, of course.' She paused for a moment. *'There was something in Anthony's eye when he talked about her. I think working with her was the very last thing he wanted.'*

And it was his childhood friend, Hal, who'd benefitted. Ada had had multiple reasons to get back at him. Eve could imagine her pushing him to kill her brother. It would amuse her. Especially if she intended to make sure he paid for it too.

Twenty minutes after Eve had thanked Ashley and rung off, she took Gus to meet Viv by the village green, ready to visit Tabitha. Gus bounded up to another dachshund wearing a red Christmas coat and Eve had the ridiculous feeling she'd let him down by only providing his standard tartan.

'Tell me you're kidding,' Viv said, when Eve explained. 'In any case, Gus would look far too frivolous in a Christmas coat. I put my Santa earrings in earlier, without thinking, but I took them out again. In fact, I feel a bit weird, tagging along, now Ada's died. It doesn't seem right to show a keen interest in interiors in the aftermath of a second murder. Still, I can help you observe and look for clues.'

Eve instantly felt anxious. Viv was bound to make it obvious.

Gus scampered ahead along the river path out of town, excited to be off his leash, and Eve tried to relax and appreciate her surroundings. Everything was laced with frost today, glittering in the winter sun.

'How's the internet dating going?'

Viv gave a secret smile. 'I'm heading into the world of actual meet-ups!'

'This is with the guy who likes rock gigs?'

Viv nodded. 'Tonight!'

'You will meet somewhere public, won't you?'

She rolled her eyes. 'I know you're more grown-up than me, Eve, but I do have a brain. We're meeting at a place called More Magic in Blyworth.'

'Is that the one with all the purple wall hangings that smells of joss sticks?'

'Possibly.' Viv gave a dignified smile. 'But enough of all that. We need to focus.'

They turned off the river path and into the grounds of Mistletoe Place. The cold air had turbocharged Eve's senses, making her feel alert.

Both police cars and press had left the premises. It looked peaceful and beautiful, the plants in the garden decorated with frosty cobwebs, and the roof iced white. It was only Dr Wincup's car, present once again, which hinted at the recent horrors.

They were just about to round the corner to the front door when they heard Tabitha's voice.

'Theo, they're lovely! Is this in return for the cushion?'

And then came Theo's gruff reply. Eve was pretty sure he was suppressing emotion. 'In a way.' He cleared his throat. 'The truth is, I don't show my appreciation enough. I— Well, you're very good for Giles. I know he doesn't always see things in a balanced way, but he loves you so deeply. And I see you love him back, even when things aren't easy. He'll need you now, of course. More than ever.'

'It's been horrible this morning, seeing him go to pieces.'

Eve and Viv's eyes met. What did Theo mean by 'now more than ever' and what had sent Giles off the rails?

They carried on and found Tabitha close to the front door, holding a pretty bouquet: deep pink hellebores, pittosporum and viburnum. Her cheeks were rosy, which might be down to the cold, but Eve suspected it was emotion. She could be touched, but perhaps guilt was more likely, if she was cheating on Giles.

Theo turned away the minute he saw them. He was a taciturn man, but Eve was still struck by how grumpy he'd been with Tabitha in particular. Taking her to task for not seeming more upset about Anthony was just plain odd when he'd been angry with him himself. Eve wanted to know why. It was a minor query, but Eve wouldn't relax until she understood how everything fitted together.

Tabitha shook hands with Viv and seemed delighted that she was interested enough to come along. She bent down to fuss Gus and looked up at them. 'I'm excited about the new range, of course. It'll take the business to the next level. I'm sorry. I know I should be making a show of being sad about Ada, but she wasn't a nice person. It would feel false.' She got up. 'You don't really want to ask me about her for the obituary, do you, Eve? I mean, you know what I thought.'

They headed inside and Gus sniffed the umbrella stand. Eve was glad to be in the warm. 'I was still curious about why you hired her, and how she approached you.' Ada must have had a goal in mind. Her interest in interior design had clearly been feigned.

Before Tabitha could reply, Dr Wincup appeared. He shook his head. 'Dear oh dear, he's much worse, isn't he? But then he would be, after what you said. I've prescribed some new pills.'

If only she could come straight out and ask what was wrong with Giles, but it wouldn't endear her to anyone here, and she needed to keep them onside. Could he really be that upset about Ada?

Tabitha cocked her head. 'Thank you, Doctor, but we should discuss this another time.'

Viv looked as disappointed as Eve felt.

Tabitha let the doctor out, shut the door behind him and put her shoulders back. 'I'm sorry. Where were we?'

'I was asking how Ada approached you for work. Did you agree to take her on immediately?'

Tabitha looked thoughtful. 'I suppose I did, but that makes me sound rash. We'd bumped into each other a few times around the village, and she'd been charming. Then she suggested a coffee and asked me all about my business. She told me she'd wanted to work in interiors for years, and if I ever had an opening she'd be interested. Even if it was something menial.'

'So you felt you knew her, by the time a vacancy came up?'

'Exactly. And she was Anthony's sister, of course. He always seemed like a decent sort.' Tabitha whistled softly and shook her head. 'But Ada had me fooled. It was only after I'd got her in, contract signed, that I mentioned her appointment to Hal. I could see he was anxious about it. Now I know about the fire, I understand why.'

'Yet he didn't say anything at that point.'

'I suppose he felt it was too late. And he'd promised his grandpa not to tell, of course. Grandpa thought everyone deserved a second chance, I gather, but he didn't know Ada. Sorry.' She closed her eyes for a moment. 'I shouldn't be speaking about her like this when she's just been killed, but she was only out for herself.'

'I'd love to know why she wanted to work for you.'

Tabitha nodded. 'Me too.'

But of course, it had put her close to Anthony and Hal. Two people she hated. She glimpsed Viv, a look of furious concentration on her face.

'Shall we move on to the new collection?' Tabitha said. 'And when we've finished, you must let me give you some tea or coffee too. I'd offer now, only I'm rather precious about my fabrics. They don't mix well with food and drink.'

Viv was very well behaved as Tabitha talked and Eve took notes. She oohed and ahhed in all the right places, at the glorious jewel colours and the intricate designs. And she was similarly absorbed by the prototype soft furnishings too: cushions, throws, pouffes and an ottoman.

It was when they started to discuss more theoretical stuff – prices, and schemes which would show the goods to best advantage – that Viv seemed to lose interest.

Eve was uncomfortably aware of her walking round the room, fiddling with things. She turned away and tried to focus on Tabitha.

At last, when Viv circled the room for the fourth time, Eve did look up. Viv was touching little ornaments sitting on bookcases, a mantelpiece, shelves and a bureau. They looked precious. It wouldn't be great if anything got broken. The pretty Japanese Imari bowl looked especially vulnerable.

Eve tried to turn off her anxiety but gradually, Tabitha picked up on Viv's movements too, despite her excitement over the new collection.

As Tabitha watched, her eyes got wider. And then she looked utterly perplexed. Perhaps she'd never met anyone quite like Viv before.

Eve stood up and grabbed her friend's arm. 'Why not come and sit down again. You're making Gus dizzy.'

Gus took a step back and gave Eve an accusatory look, as though he knew she was using him as an excuse.

'Sorry.' Viv perched on a chair again. 'It's just such a lovely room.'

Tabitha carried on looking at Viv strangely as Eve noted the last details she needed.

'Right, let me make you those drinks,' Tabitha said. 'Tea? Coffee?'

After they'd thanked her and put in their requests, she left the room. 'I'm not sure she's going to offer me a free sample,' Viv muttered.

'I'm not surprised. She was probably too distracted by you touching all her things.'

'It wasn't all of them. I—'

But before Viv could continue, Eve heard a mobile ring, somewhere close by. Tabitha's, probably. Instinct told Eve to listen; she wanted to know as much about her as possible. She wasn't high up the list of suspects, but Eve couldn't rule her out. She stayed absolutely still, straining to hear.

'Just a second,' Tabitha said. And then came the sound of a door closing.

Eve gave Viv an appealing look. 'Would you keep an eye on Gus if I go and listen?' There was no time to argue. The conversation was clearly private and that had to mean something.

29

———

Eve slipped out of her shoes and stole through the quiet, shadowy hallway towards the one closed door. From beyond, she could just make out the murmur of Tabitha's voice. She'd only hear if she put her ear to the wood panelling. And the trouble she'd get into if she was caught didn't bear thinking about.

Eve went for it anyway.

'No, it's still good,' Tabitha was saying. 'Giles is safely tucked up in bed, so I'll come as planned, darling. I can't wait to look over the house. From the pictures it seems perfect. The sort of place where one could relax – and get romantic too. Some real privacy! It's just what I've been hoping for. I'll see you at two!'

Eve tiptoed back to her shoes at speed and slipped through to Tabitha's design room again. She told Viv what she'd heard in a whisper. Tabitha would only just be setting the kettle to boil. It felt safe enough.

Viv gave a low whistle. 'Wow. Definitely a lover then – and they're going for it. What if Anthony found her out? She'd be out on her ear if Theo knew. And she's doing it right under his nose, too.'

'I know. It all feels horribly volatile.' Eve met Viv's eye. 'I still can't imagine her planning the killing with Ada, and we don't know Anthony found out, but I think it'd be worth following her.'

'What? How?'

'I'll have time to catch Hal at the yard first. It's urgent I talk to him as the top suspect. But then I'll sit in my car near the turn-off to this place and wait for her to drive past.'

'Cool,' Viv breathed. 'Can I come?'

'What about Allie?' She wasn't expecting to be running the show at Monty's all afternoon, as well as all morning.

'There are plenty of cakes, and she's much more organised than I am.'

That was a point.

'You're meant to contradict me, Eve.'

But Eve's mind was still on practicalities. 'We should pay her extra and check it's okay.'

'I'll pop in and do the deal while you talk to Hal.'

'She should have more notice, and the option to say no.'

Viv flapped a hand. 'All right, all right. I'll text her now.'

Viv was still thumb-typing when Tabitha re-entered the room with their teas.

After they'd finished their drinks and Viv had left for Monty's, Eve went to find Hal at Arthur's Yard.

As the building came into view, she caught movement. Sudden and quick. Someone ducking out of sight. A red-haired man. He'd been standing just outside the office window. What the heck?

Eve went to look, but it was as though he'd disappeared into thin air. The hairs on the back of her neck lifted; he must be hiding, so he was up to something.

She gave it up and went to knock on the door nearest the admin section. The same door she and Viv had walked through when they'd found Anthony's body. Eve marched straight in afterwards and Hal looked startled by her appearance.

He was holding something that looked like folded material, wrapped in plastic, and instead of greeting her, he turned and slipped into an inner office. Eve could hear him scrabbling about, and the rustle of paper, then he reappeared without the package. He hadn't wanted her to see it.

'Hal.' Eve walked forward and shook his hand, trying to banish all traces of doubt from her expression. 'I'm so sorry about Ada. You must feel totally shocked and disorientated right now.'

He nodded dumbly, fear in his eyes.

'Is it okay for us to talk? Under the circumstances, I'm making the obituary I'm writing a joint one, for Ada and Anthony.' Hal winced at his friend's name. Eve was sure he was grieving his loss, whatever he might have done. 'I wanted to ask you about Ada. And about the person who was following you too.' When he'd mentioned it, Eve had wondered if it was a figment of his imagination but that seemed less likely now. 'Were they red-haired?'

His shoulders tightened. 'I don't know. It's like I told you, I'd just catch a shadow moving, then I'd look up and they'd be gone.'

'Okay, sorry. I just wondered.'

His eyes were haunted. 'Are they out there now?'

'I did see someone, but I think they've gone. It might just have been a passer-by. Shall we go through to your office and talk there?' It was freezing cold where they were standing, and she wanted Hal to relax. She was also hoping she might find out what that package was.

'Okay,' Hal said slowly and led her through the door.

There was a large Jiffy mail bag propped up between a filing cabinet and a desk. Eve was guessing the parcel might be in there, but there was no way of knowing what it was.

'I gather you inherit this place now,' Eve said, nodding through the door at the rest of the yard.

'Yes.' Hal's tone was dull – exhausted. If he'd killed to get it, he was probably overcome by the enormity of what he'd done. Eve sensed he was way out of his depth. 'I'm sure you must know almost as much as Anthony did about running the place,' she went on. 'You worked so closely with him.'

Hal bit his lip, then took a deep breath. 'You're right. I should be able to do it. I mean, I can do it. It's just that everything feels out of control.'

A sliver of doubt worked its way into Eve's mind. Would he really have killed for all this if he didn't feel equal to it? But of course, his worries could have rushed in afterwards, when he was faced with reality.

'It's only natural.' She kept her voice soft. She needed to build a bond. 'And things can't have been easy even before these terrible events. I hear you had a visit from the Health and Safety Executive.'

Hal blushed a deep red. 'It was stressful, but they left happy.'

Ashley had suggested it could have been Ada who'd called them in but Eve's money was still on Hal's dad. If only she could get a look at that letter in his filing tray... 'Was it hard, working here when your dad didn't like Anthony?'

Eve needed to push. She still didn't know what had come between them, and what Giles's secret was. He might not be her top suspect, but it would be cavalier to ignore anything so significant.

Hal started slightly at her question. 'What makes you think Dad didn't get on with Anthony?'

But he sounded as though he was acting. Eve guessed he knew there'd been tensions.

'It seems to be common knowledge in the village.' If Moira knew, everyone did. 'And Anthony knew about a secret Giles was keeping.'

Confusion. Hal had no idea what she was talking about, Eve guessed. 'I can't imagine how he'd know anything about Dad.'

'Because they weren't close?'

There was a long pause. 'No, well, all right. They weren't, but that doesn't mean anything. They're a different generation. Dad had nothing against Anthony. Nothing at all.'

He was protesting too much. Eve figured he knew exactly why they hadn't got on, but was unaware of the secret. The hold Anthony had over Giles couldn't have been the sole reason for their strained relationship, then.

Eve didn't think she'd get any more by pushing in that direction, so she moved the conversation on. 'I suppose you'll need someone as a second in command now.'

Hal nodded. 'It's essential to have two permanent, dedicated individuals to hold things together. One of our casual workers has a lot of good experience and we get on all right. I might take him on, on a trial basis.'

'That sounds good. By the way, someone mentioned Anthony had a dinner meeting recently with a potential investor in the yard.' Eve was already sure that Leah had made all that up, but she always cross-checked everything. If there was any truth in her story, she imagined Anthony would have mentioned it to Hal.

As expected, Hal looked astonished. 'Really? That's the first I've heard about it. I suspect someone's got their wires crossed.'

It was good to have it confirmed, though it didn't take her further forward. Leah might have been Anthony's lover, but she had an alibi, and no obvious motive anyway.

They talked a bit about how the yard was run. Eve wanted him to relax his guard so she could try to catch him out. If he and his dad had lied about being together when Anthony died, breaking that alibi would be a crucial step forward. Hal was supposed to visit the yard on Saturday night and Tabitha said he was normally reliable. Eve's aim was to prove he'd been there. It would explain why his dad was being blackmailed.

At last, she let out a sigh, then paused. 'Sorry. It's eerie being back here after finding Anthony's body. I shouldn't even be mentioning it. It's far more traumatic for you. I keep being thankful he was face down and I didn't see his expression.'

She watched Hal closely and saw his eyes flicker. Just the smallest reaction, but enough to raise suspicion. He knew that wasn't right. Either he'd heard from someone else that Anthony had been found face up, or he'd been there and seen for himself. Either way, he'd know she'd been trying to trip him up.

Eve's mouth went dry. 'Tell me about Ada. How did you feel when you realised you'd be working for her?' She leaned forward. 'She told me you, she and Anthony were like the three musketeers as kids. But I heard on the grapevine that she was difficult.'

'I thought she'd take some getting used to,' Hal said at last. 'But I was glad she was keeping me on.'

'She looked pretty keen on you when I saw you together in the pub on Tuesday.'

Hal looked uncomfortable. 'That's just what she was like.'

But not without good reason, Eve was sure. 'And then I saw she'd sneaked up to your bedroom when I visited Mistletoe Place yesterday morning.' Eve didn't actually know it was his room, but it felt like a reasonable guess.

There was a tic going in Hal's cheek now. 'She was a law unto herself. I noticed she'd disappeared, but I didn't know where to.'

That might be true. But on the other hand, he could have

realised she'd given him the slip and guessed exactly where she'd gone, and why. Stealing the paper torn from Anthony's hand would be quite a prize, if it was Hal who'd taken it. The only query was, why wouldn't he have destroyed it?

'Look,' Hal sighed, 'if you want the truth, I always felt uneasy with Ada. I don't think she liked me, despite her behaviour, and I felt like I was walking on eggshells.'

That all sounded honest, but none of it jarred with her theory.

At that moment, one of the workers at the other end of the indoor unit called out.

'Hal, mate! We've got a problem!'

Hal flushed and dashed out of his seat. He really was anxious. He hadn't excused himself or worried about leaving her alone with the mysterious package. Something going pear-shaped at the yard trumped everything. Anthony had seemed steady and self-assured, but Hal appeared to be the opposite.

Eve hesitated. He might not be gone long, but if she wanted to know what was in that Jiffy bag, this was her chance to find out. She rose and moved to the door, holding her breath as she checked there was no one nearby. Then she darted back again.

Tugging the Jiffy bag open, she removed the plastic-wrapped package inside. *What on earth?* It was a green sweat-shirt. Brand new, by the look of it. She glanced over her shoulder, then turned it over to examine the other side.

The logo on the front said, 'Osborne's Market Garden'. Of course, it was in their brand colour. And just underneath, the embroidered words read, 'Deputy Director'.

30

———

Eve managed to slip Hal's sweatshirt back into its bag without being seen. When he didn't reappear, she went to find him. He was staring worriedly at the hull of a boat as she took her leave.

Half an hour later, she was sitting in the layby in her Mini Clubman with Viv, as cars whizzed past on the A12. They'd been hashing over her interview with Hal. 'He's a bundle of nerves,' Eve said. 'For a moment, I wavered about him being the killer; he seems anxious about being in charge.' She shook her head. 'But if he's guilty, it's no wonder he's het-up, and I'd swear he knew Anthony was found on his back.'

'I can't believe you tested him like that without backup.'

'The place was crawling with his staff.'

'Hmm. Fair enough, I suppose. And what about the sweatshirt?' Viv tucked her berry-red hair behind her ears. 'That's so weird.'

'I can only think that his dad's offered him a swanky position at the market garden, but it's secret. I suppose it might irk Giles's existing employees. It'd look like favouritism when Hal's a boat builder, not a gardener. Maybe he agreed to take the role rather than work with Ada.'

'I wouldn't blame him for that,' said Viv, shuddering.

'It's still odd, though. I had the impression boat building was his be-all and end-all, when he begged Anthony to keep him on.'

'I guess the garden job will be off the agenda now anyway,' Viv said. 'Running the yard without Ada oiling all over him is a different proposition, even if he is nervous.'

'I think you're right. He'll stress over the practicalities, but— Oh, look, it's time to go.'

Tabitha Osborne had just driven past.

Eve and Viv followed her into Blyworth. She parked on a side street to the north of the town centre, and Eve managed to find a space a little further down the road. She was pretty sure they hadn't been spotted. As Eve and Viv sat watching, Tabitha got out and locked up, her car's lights flashing. She strode down the road, past Victorian cottages painted in warm colours with arched sash windows. Very pretty. At last, she paused outside one sporting a 'For Sale' sign and glanced at her watch.

'Think lover boy's about to turn up?' Viv said.

'I hope so.'

Sure enough, a man appeared. He looked a lot closer in age to Tabitha than Giles, his thick, slightly greying hair curling over the collar of a good quality coat. Before he reached Tabitha, someone opened the door to the house and let them in.

'Wish I could be a fly on the wall,' Viv said.

It would be useful, though even watching from a distance was hard to take. The betrayal echoed her own experience with her ex-husband too closely. Eve felt for Giles. He'd had the doctor in attendance each time there'd been a death, and it was more than possible his son was a killer. What effect would Tabitha's desertion have on him? Or maybe she and her lover would just carry on secretly, using this place as their love nest. Tabitha might persuade him it was better that way. She could have her cake and eat it.

'What's the plan?' Viv asked.

'I'd like to hear what they say when they come out. If we're lucky, they might go for a coffee or something. Let's see what they do, and follow them if we can.'

Viv giggled. 'It's like something from a spy movie.'

'You are going to take this seriously, aren't you?'

'Totally.' Viv was fishing in Eve's glove compartment. She found Robin's spare beanie and pulled it down over her eyes.

Eve thought it was probably best to take no notice. She always played the fool when she was excited. Perhaps it was down to that night's date.

It was twenty minutes before Tabitha and her companion reappeared and they looked happy. Tabitha gave him an excited hug, but then her expression turned anxious. Perhaps she was thinking of the risks involved. The flowers Theo had given her filled Eve's head. The way he'd thanked her for being so good to Giles, his baby brother.

Tabitha and her companion walked off towards town, away from where Eve and Viv were parked. 'Right,' Eve said. 'We must go or we'll lose them. Maybe keep the beanie on. You could tuck your hair under it. The red's quite hard to miss.'

Viv looked gratified, and did as Eve suggested.

Tabitha and her plus one had turned the corner now and Eve dashed ahead to see where they were going. Viv was hot on her heels.

'There they go.' They'd disappeared into a café called the Copper Kettle. The question was how to follow them without being noticed.

Eve motioned Viv to stand back, grabbed her own hat from her bag, and pulled it on. There was a menu pasted in the café's window, and Eve pretended to scan it as she surveyed the seating area beyond. Tabitha was bagging a table, then she and her companion went to the counter.

Eve beckoned Viv. 'Quick. If we dash in now, we can get seated while they're still ordering.' Her chest tightened as they made a run for it. If Tabitha turned around and saw them, it would all be very awkward.

They kept their beanies on and sat just round the corner from Tabitha's table. Hopefully they could loiter for a while without the staff noticing. The place was busy.

Tabitha and her man were taking their seats now.

'So what do you think?' the man said.

'I think it's perfect, and that you're a genius for spotting it. Thank you.'

'It'll make a difference, won't it? A proper, private place. Away from Giles.'

She nodded but when she spoke again, she sounded emotional. 'That's right.'

'So go ahead and offer?'

'Yes. Yes, it needs to happen.'

The man leaned forward and squeezed her hand. 'And when are you going to tell him? Better to do it sooner rather than later, don't you think? If it comes at the last minute, out of the blue, it'll be far worse.'

Eve was close enough to hear Tabitha take a deep breath. 'You're right. But things are difficult at the moment. He's already in a terrible state.' She sighed again. 'All the same, the house is too good to miss. I've put it off for long enough. I'll wait another day or two maybe, just in case the police investigation reaches a conclusion. But at that point, I'll break the news, whatever happens.'

She sounded like she meant it, but it might be a hollow promise – something to get her lover to go ahead and buy. In the cold light of day, Eve found it hard to believe she'd sacrifice her business premises. She'd said Tabitha's Interiors was at a crucial stage in its development.

'How's the investigation going?' the man asked.

Tabitha shrugged. 'I don't think the police have the first idea what's going on. They're still trying to trace Theo's daughter, as she's Anthony's ex. Theo says he can't raise her either. I'm starting to suspect he hasn't seen her in weeks, though he was pretending they were in touch until the police questioned him.' She shook her head. 'I'm not sure what he's playing at.'

Eve wasn't either. Or what Dora was up to – whether she couldn't or wouldn't come forward. Eve hoped to goodness she was safe.

As for Giles, it seemed he was living in a fool's paradise. Maybe Tabitha would keep him in blissful ignorance, but if she did confess her affair, her potential motive for killing Anthony went out of the window. Eve would have to watch and wait.

31

———

Eve and Viv managed to sit in the busy café unnoticed by either Tabitha or the staff until she and her companion left again. After that, they treated themselves to cups of tea and some cakes which Viv rated 'uninspiring'.

'What's next?' she asked. 'I'm paying Allie extra, just like you said, and she's happy to manage until I go and help lock up. She says it'll be good for her CV.'

The thought gave Eve a pang of anxiety. She'd be applying for another job before they knew it.

'I'm at your service.' Viv smiled. 'Ready to Watson.'

Eve thought through the options. 'Although Hal's top of my suspect list, there are still plenty of questions about Giles and Theo, and we need to find Dora too. Leaving them aside for a moment, the perfume my friend Ashley smelled at Arthur's Yard is bugging me as well. She noticed it when Leah's scarf was there, but the police also commented on it at Anthony's murder scene. And that can't have been down to Leah. She was miles away, working at the Bell.'

Eve felt like she was banging her head against a brick wall.

'Yes, but what do we do *now*?' Viv asked.

She wanted action, clearly. 'One concrete query is, did Giles put the Health and Safety Executive onto Anthony? I'm guessing it was him, not Ada, but it would be good to know for sure. The inspectors didn't find anything, according to Hal, so the complaint could have been malicious. If I can prove Giles was responsible, I might be able to push him into talking about it and revealing more. It's not just that I want to understand his animosity. Every chance I get to speak with him counts. If he's giving Hal a false alibi, he might slip up.'

'True.'

'But to find out if the letter in his office relates to the spot check at the yard, I'll need to get inside.' The thought was daunting.

'No problem,' Viv said.

'Excuse me?'

'We can go to the garden together, then I'll create a diversion while you slip in.'

Eve felt the gravest misgivings about that plan. 'What kind of diversion?'

'I got some carrots from them a couple of days ago. I'll drill holes in them and say they must have been infested with something.'

Eve wasn't sure what she was more worried about, the incredible awkwardness of the confrontation or sneaking into Giles's office. 'You think Giles will come and deal with you personally, rather than leaving it to a member of staff?'

Viv grinned confidently. 'If I make enough of a fuss, he's sure to. I will "demand to see the manager" in my best Moira voice.'

Hmm. That might do it. But all the same, Giles would surely smell a rat.

'You're very quiet,' Viv said. 'You're not doubting my acting skills, are you?'

'Heaven forbid.'

Viv folded her arms. 'If you've got a better idea then I'm all ears.'

Eve hadn't. 'All right then. Let's give it a go.'

'Excellent. Drop me home first, so I can prepare my iffy root veg.'

Eve drove straight there.

Eve had never seen anyone drill a carrot before. Viv made surprisingly short work of it, and then, encouraged by Eve, smeared some dirt around the tiny fake tunnels. They looked marginally more realistic now. Viv also insisted on dressing up in what she felt would be the most intimidating costume, which consisted of green wellies and a long waxed coat.

'This is exactly how my mother-in-law dresses, and she's one of the scariest people I know.'

Everyone who'd known Viv's late husband said he was a gem, but Eve had met his mother and agreed with Viv. She wasn't sure the hair fitted the ensemble, but she let it go.

After that, they dropped in on Gus and made a fuss of him, then walked over to Osborne's Market Garden.

'Right,' Viv said. 'You hover near Giles's office then dive in the moment he leaves.'

'Good luck.' Eve felt slightly queasy. She watched as Viv marched over to the far side of the walled garden, and approached a male member of staff a foot taller than her.

Eve approved of her tactics. If Giles did go to help, he'd have to walk to the far side of the huge garden, leaving his office unoccupied for the maximum amount of time. Viv was upon the staff member now. Eve couldn't hear what she was saying, but she was proffering the carrots and shaking them at the employee. The next minute, she stamped her foot, reminding Eve powerfully of her twins when they were at the tantrum stage. Eve was worried she was over-egging it, but it seemed to be doing the trick.

The man was gesturing at Giles's office, but Viv stood her ground, saying something, then folding her arms. Eve guessed she'd just refused to visit the admin block and demanded that someone come to her.

At last, the poor beleaguered employee jogged over to Giles's office himself.

'Sorry, Giles,' Eve heard the employee say, 'but there's this weird woman kicking off about her carrots. She says she won't leave without speaking to the manager.'

'Oh dear.' Giles followed him out.

Bingo. Now, Eve had to hope that Viv would keep him talking while she completed her mission.

She glanced surreptitiously over her shoulder, and when no one was watching, she opened the door and slipped inside.

She was unpleasantly conscious of her heart thudding and her mouth going dry as she crossed the hall. Thank goodness the tray with the letter was only just inside the door. She spotted it in seconds and pulled it out carefully.

Dear Mr Osborne,

Thank you for registering your concerns about Arthur's Yard online. We have now completed our site visit, but once again, we found no cause for concern. Although, as you say, there are hazards present, we found Mr Mottram had the correct procedures in place to mitigate the risks. If you have any further queries or concerns, please contact us so we can discuss them and determine whether any follow-up visit is necessary.

Eve didn't read the closing niceties. She placed the letter back in its original position in the tray and made for the door.

As she let herself out, she glanced over at Viv and caught her eye. It was still several minutes before she allowed herself to be placated though. Eve suspected she was enjoying herself.

'How did you get on?' Viv asked as she rejoined her, replacement carrots in hand. Giles and his staff probably figured they were a small price to pay to be shot of her. 'Was it worth it?'

'It certainly makes Giles's antagonism towards Anthony seem significant. He called the Health and Safety Executive in more than once. I think they were probably getting a bit fed up with him; they might have suspected it was malicious. We need to know what went wrong between Giles and Anthony. And we still don't know the secret Giles is keeping from Hal either – perhaps Anthony realised he was trying to get the yard shut down and wanted him to back off. It might not be relevant, but it's part of the puzzle.'

Viv dashed off to help Allie close Monty's, leaving Eve at the market garden. She went and bought a selection of winter vegetables out of guilt, then began her journey back towards home. She'd just got onto the river path when movement caught her eye. Someone was hanging around Arthur's Yard again.

Instead of turning towards the village, Eve paused in her tracks and ducked close to the hedge. It was the red-haired guy, slipping around the side of the building, as quick and furtive as before.

A moment later, Hal let himself out of the office and locked up. If everyone else had left for the day, the red-haired guy had to be there for him. Eve held her breath. Was he out to harm him? She could call the police, but they'd never get there in time. She put down her bag of veg, her hand on her mobile.

As she watched, the red-haired man followed Hal in the direction of Mistletoe Place. Eve picked up her bag and followed too, still primed to call the emergency services. But when Hal disappeared through the gate, the red-haired man let him go.

Eve waited and so did Hal's pursuer. She couldn't guess what he'd do next, but if he turned in her direction, she didn't want to meet him head-on. She went back to the market garden's entrance and hovered there, sighing with relief at her foresight when he pivoted towards her. She hid behind a bush until he'd gone by, then followed him at a distance. Presumably he'd given up watching Hal once he was inside the house, but what was he after, and when would he make a move? She must find out.

The journey back to Saxford was slow going, thanks to Eve's caution. She couldn't risk him turning again and seeing her. But at last, she reached the steps up to the Old Toll Road. She was in time to see the man make his way onto Love Lane and into the Cross Keys.

Eve dashed up Haunted Lane at speed. She couldn't leave Gus any longer. The poor dog needed sustenance. She made a fuss of him, then called Toby at the pub as she dished out his supper.

'*A red-haired guy who's just come in?*' Toby said, in answer to her query. '*Yes, I see him. He's bagged himself a table.*'

'Is he familiar?'

'*No. Want me to ask Matt?*'

'Please.' Between them, Toby and his brother knew all the locals. 'I'll be over in just a minute.' Gus was making short work of his food. 'If Matt doesn't know him, then it's a cheek to ask, but when he comes to the bar, could you try to get his name?' Toby was quietly friendly, and good with the customers. 'There's an excellent reason, I promise.'

Toby chuckled. '*I trust you, and it'll liven things up a bit. You're on.*'

Not long after, Eve dashed around the corner with Gus, the breeze strong and chilling, and made her way into the warm, welcoming embrace of the Cross Keys, where a log fire was blazing brightly and delicious smells were emanating from the kitchen.

As Gus made a beeline for Hetty, Eve spotted the red-haired guy nursing a pint at a table tucked in a corner. She went up to Toby at the bar.

'A mulled wine please, Toby, and whatever you're having.'

He grinned. 'Payment for services rendered?'

She smiled back. 'How can you suggest such a thing? Joking apart though, any luck?'

He nodded. 'We chatted enough for me to introduce myself and he replied in kind. Jackson Smith.'

'Hmm. Sounds like a film star or something.'

Toby poured her mulled wine and a low-alcohol beer for himself. 'He said he'd had to hang around outside a lot this afternoon, so he was keen to warm up. I expected him to sit by the fire, but he's squirrelled himself away.'

No surprises there.

Toby raised an eyebrow. 'What do you want him for?'

'He's been following Hal Osborne.'

Toby frowned. 'That doesn't sound good.'

'I'll let you know what I find out.'

Eve sat near the fire herself and got to work on her phone. Moments later she'd found Jackson Smith.

Very interesting indeed.

32

___

Eve kept her seat by the fire for a moment longer as she considered her approach to Jackson Smith. Gus was happy with Hetty, so Eve had a free hand. Going in quickly and surprising Smith to knock him off balance seemed like the best route. He'd probably been in the pub just long enough to warm up and start to relax. It almost felt cruel to disturb him, but discovering the truth was essential.

She strode to his table, taking her drink with her, and pulled out a chair as she spoke: 'Jackson Smith?'

The man jumped and reddened instantly. 'Erm, how did you know?'

Eve silently thanked Toby and the internet. 'I recognise a private investigator when I see one. Who hired you to follow Hal Osborne?' If he'd been at it long enough, he might have seen something the night Anthony was murdered. Or maybe someone hired him afterwards, to search for proof that he was guilty.

Smith was stuttering now. 'I–I, well, I'm not meant to say. Investigator–client privilege.'

No kidding! 'Is this your first assignment?' He seemed terribly nervous.

He pulled himself up. 'No!'

Hmm. If not first, then second, Eve guessed.

'Are you a PI too?' Smith went on, his blush still present. 'You must be a professional to have spotted me.'

It seemed too cruel to say she'd seen him twice in one day. 'No, I'm not a PI. I'm a journalist.'

'Ah, there you are then!' Smith forced a laugh. 'We're birds of a feather.'

Even the notion... Eve had managed to follow Tabitha without being seen. And she'd never have done it in the first place if the stakes weren't so high. 'I usually write obituaries. I'm working on Anthony and Ada Mottram's currently. But I'm not about to publicise our conversation. This is personal, not professional. Hal's a friend.' That was stretching a point, but allowable, under the circumstances. 'Please, tell me who hired you. I'll find out sooner or later.'

Smith stared at his lap, his false good humour gone. He looked utterly miserable.

'Look, here's an easier question.' People were so relieved to avoid the tricky one that they often just answered. '*When* were you hired?'

'Just yesterday.' The words came out quickly, the pitch high.

A few days *after* Anthony's murder. Perhaps the person who'd listened in to Hal and Anthony's conversation had brought him in, having got suspicious.

Eve sighed. 'I'm sorry, but I really do need to know who hired you. It might be relevant to something else I'm pursuing. If you won't tell me, I'll have to start asking around and let everyone know I spotted you.' She didn't want to make his life a misery – clearly the guy was no grizzled gumshoe from a hard-boiled novel – but this was too important.

'Oh, please don't,' Smith said. 'This isn't my first job, but

I'm still building my business. If the person who hired me hears you sussed me, I'll be out on my ear. And I could really do with the work. It's a good, solid, contract. The guy who did it before me was on it for months.'

'Months?' *Heck.* It couldn't be anything to do with the murder then. 'What happened to the last guy?'

But before he could answer, Eve suddenly saw the truth. It had been staring her in the face. Who had recently lost an employee whom Eve had failed to identify?

'It's all right. I know who took you on. It was Giles Osborne.' Eve remembered their acrimonious discussion on the estuary path. The previous PI – the man called Steve, most probably – really had seen something damning, she guessed.

For a second, Eve wondered why Giles would hire someone to follow his own son, but as Gus pottered over to join them, his feet tapping on the Cross Keys' well-worn floor, disparate facts drew together to provide an answer.

Giles's wife had died very young and he'd lost his parents in a boating accident. It was only luck that Hal hadn't been with them. Giles had lived with him in London, but feared for him when his nanny was mugged. So he'd sent Hal to the country, then worried about him having too much freedom. Boarding school had followed, but in the end that had felt too risky too. He didn't like his son riding or sailing. He'd talked worriedly to Eve about a fatal accident at a boatyard nearby and he'd called the Health and Safety Executive to Arthur's Yard at least twice. Tabitha had said Giles had seemed less anxious when they'd met. She'd helped to distract him. But now Eve thought about it, it must have been around the time Hal became independent, with a job at the yard, that Giles had lost control at the gallery. She guessed his fears for his son were simply too great to ignore. Things had gone south in London and ultimately, Giles had followed Hal to Suffolk, with Tabitha in tow, where he could keep a proper eye on him.

And after each of the murders he'd been so anxious he'd been bedridden. That might be because he knew or guessed Hal was guilty, but there were other possible reasons too. Anthony's death meant upheaval and Hal working with Ada, whom everyone thought was trouble. Cue more anxiety. Then Ada's death put Hal in charge. The very last thing Giles would want.

He'd probably hoped Hal might go to work at Osborne's Market Garden, hence the sweatshirt in Hal's office. Eve was sure he'd have loved to install him in a nice, quiet managerial post right under his nose. He'd decided his current profession was dangerous. If the swanky job title and sweatshirt had been intended to tempt him, Eve guessed Hal had hidden it out of embarrassment. He was a grown man who should control his own destiny.

Ada's death must have dashed Giles's hopes utterly. He'd have known Hal would never leave the yard now he was in charge. Eve imagined both Tabitha and Theo understood why he was so devastated – that was what they'd been talking about when Dr Wincup was in the house.

And then Eve thought of Hal's many ex-girlfriends. 'Unlucky in love,' Simon had said, but what was the betting Giles had put a spanner in the works? He wouldn't want to lose Hal, and she bet no one was ever good enough for him. It would explain Hal's feelings of inevitability and despair when he'd broken up with his latest, Gabby.

She turned to Smith again. 'It must be nice work. You just have to watch Hal and ensure he comes to no harm?'

The rookie PI nodded at last. 'If I see him doing anything risky, I have to report it immediately and try to stop whatever it is.' His anxious eyes met hers. 'I haven't had to do that yet. I'm not quite sure how it'll work. Please don't tell anyone about this.'

But Eve couldn't make that promise. 'I definitely won't write about it, at least.'

She went back to her table, with Gus at her heels, and bent to stroke his head as he settled himself by her feet. This had to be the secret that Anthony had discovered. No wonder he'd confronted Giles about it. It was a horrible invasion of privacy, and it had put Anthony in a difficult position. How could he not tell his best friend?

Eve had seen the anxiety etched into Giles's face, but spying on his son wasn't the answer. He could do with some counselling instead. But it sounded as though he'd rejected help, and he'd refused to cancel the PI when Anthony asked. He couldn't bear to. Yet the alternative was Anthony telling Hal. Eve could only imagine how claustrophobic and angry Hal might have felt if that had happened. It sounded as though Giles had been curtailing his freedom for years. Eve pictured Giles attempting to reason with Anthony at the yard, then panicking and lashing out when he'd stood firm. And Giles must have resented him for years. It was Anthony who'd offered Hal the position at the yard (a very risky role in Giles's eyes), and as a child, he'd helped Hal sneak away from his nanny's clutches to do 'dangerous' things. Giles probably hoped the Health and Safety Executive would shut Arthur's Yard down. Except Anthony had operated safely. The threat was in Giles's mind.

It explained other anomalies too. The way Giles had been kind about Anthony once he was dead, for instance. His grudge against him was over. It wasn't him keeping Hal at the yard any more, it was Ada. And now Ada was dead too... If Giles had killed her, he might have had no idea Hal would inherit the yard next.

And then Eve thought of Giles's surprise when Eve had shared the rumours about Anthony drinking. 'Well, I'm blowed. So I was right all along...' It seemed he'd been asserting the same thing, without actually believing it. Now Eve could guess why. He'd wanted to muddy Anthony's name. If the business went under, Hal couldn't work there any more.

The take-home point was that Giles's first PI was now blackmailing him. Up until now, Eve had imagined it was Hal who was guilty, but she might be wrong. Giles and Ada had had a shared interest in getting rid of Anthony, and like Hal, Giles had been panicking the night of the party. It might even have been his and Tabitha's room Ada was searching.

33

At home that evening, Eve called Robin.

'How's the face?' she asked when he picked up.

'Almost back to normal. Bruises barely discernible. I look as though I need a good wash.'

She breathed a sigh of relief and told him what had been happening in Saxford.

'I can't decide whether to confront Giles. It's not right to let him carry on spying on Hal, but even if I give him an ultimatum, he probably won't act on it.'

'And look what happened to Anthony when he did that,' Robin said. *'I think you should hold fire until you know more. Besides, from what you say, Hal will catch the PI at it before long anyway.'*

'You have a point. You could teach him a thing or two.'

Robin laughed softly. *'Not a job I'd fancy. I was intending to ring you too, by the way. Greg was in touch a short while ago.'*

'Oh, anything interesting?'

'They interviewed Leah Mason earlier today. She gave them the same story she gave you. Greg agrees it sounds like rubbish, but they've confirmed her alibi. The upshot is, they've got no

excuse to dig further. I'll bet if they checked her accounts, they'd find the story of the inheritance is a lie, but spinning a yarn's not unnatural if she's trying to cover up her and Anthony's affair.

'On the upside, it means they're alert to the possibility of jealousy as a motive. But whether Dora Osborne would or could have come out of hiding to kill Anthony is another matter.' He paused. *'Eve, they've got her mobile records now and I'm afraid it doesn't look great. She last had her phone switched on in Blyworth a week before Anthony was killed. There's no record of her using a cash machine or mobile banking since then either.'*

Eve's heart sank. Not many people would go nearly two weeks without leaving an electronic trace. It made her think again of how precarious life was. 'You will take care, won't you?' she said for the umpteenth time before she rang off.

'I promise,' he replied. *'You too.'*

Eve took a deep breath and went to cook herself some pea and mushroom risotto with parmesan. She relaxed enough to wonder how Viv was doing with the rock fan in the joss-stick bar.

After supper, she sat at the kitchen table, Gus warming her toes, and wrote up her notes from the day. She let thoughts circle in her head, her mind crawling over everything.

Hal was still her top suspect, just because he'd spent the most time with Ada, and it was likely he who Giles's PI had seen entering Arthur's Yard the night of the first murder. It was Hal he was meant to be tailing, after all. And Hal who'd flinched when Eve lied about the position Anthony had been found in.

But Giles's motive was much sharper in her mind now. She could imagine his desperation.

She was happy to keep the others further down the list. She'd seen Theo's fury with Anthony, but it was way harder to imagine him conspiring with Ada. He seemed far less vulnerable than his brother and nephew. It was the same for Tabitha. She was self-possessed and knew Ada's games well.

Her mind moved on to anomalies. The perfume the police had smelled at the yard when Anthony died – which Ashley had also noticed, the day Leah's scarf was there – and the person who'd listened in on Anthony and Hal's conversation.

As Eve got into bed that night, Hal loomed large in her thoughts. Giles's love for him was so cloying, so all-consuming. And if Anthony had sacked him, his feelings of claustrophobia would have got worse. Giles would have pushed Hal to work at the market garden and he might have been forced to agree, with no other income. He'd have been under his dad's eye every hour of the day. The thought would have left him desperate, and desperate men killed.

When at last Eve fell asleep, confused dreams filled her head, vivid each time she came to the surface. During the third or fourth one, she was back in Monty's, listening to Viv describe Hal's determination to get Theo to talk to him, the night Anthony died. As she woke, the imagined scene filled her head. Viv said Hal had avoided Theo's eyes. Instead, he'd wandered around Tabitha's design room, touching various objects. A nervous habit? Like someone touching something for luck?

She dozed again, then woke up suddenly with a clear image in her head. One of Viv, also touching a series of objects in Tabitha's design room, as Eve and Tabitha talked.

Eve remembered the ornaments in question. Antiques, including a pretty Japanese Imari bowl. Tabitha had looked surprised and confused when she'd noticed what Viv was up to. But then Viv tended to elicit that sort of reaction.

Eve had taken Viv to task for 'touching all her things'.

Viv had said hotly that it 'wasn't all of them'. She'd been about to add something, but Tabitha had come back and interrupted.

So Hal and Viv had both touched objects in the same room.

Was that significant? Could it be why Viv had said, 'not all'? Had she been absent-mindedly mimicking Hal? And could that explain Tabitha's look of astonishment?

Eve lay awake after that, waiting for morning so she could call Viv and check.

Two hours later, Viv answered her phone with a yawn, and something unintelligible.

'Say it again.'

The huff was easy to understand. '*Do you have any idea what time it is? I mean, I get you want to hear about my date, but I was up until all hours.*'

Eve did a mental facepalm. She'd been so taken up with her theory that she'd forgotten what Viv had been up to the night before. 'It went well, then?'

She groaned. '*He was an utter bore. I drank too many cocktails to pass the time and now I'm paying for it. He was going on and on about a band I'd never heard of called Elemental Melon. Or Felon. Something like that. I couldn't get a word in edgeways.*'

'Why didn't you make an excuse and leave?'

Viv went quiet for a moment, then mumbled something.

'Excuse me?'

'*I said if you must know, I fancied one of the barmen. We're meeting up soon.*'

'Fast work.'

'*My time is precious.*'

'I know. Speaking of which, haven't you got baking to do? I thought you'd be up and at it.'

She yawned. '*Monty's is only next door, Eve. Everything's under control.*'

'Good, because I have to confess, I didn't just call about

your date.' Eve explained the dreams that had bothered her in the night. 'So were you touching the things Hal touched?'

'*I suppose I was.*' Viv sounded marginally more awake. '*It was only when I got up to walk around the room that I realised I could remember. Why? What does it matter?*'

'Tabitha looked at you very strangely when you were doing your circuits.'

'*It didn't make you wonder at the time?*'

'I just thought she was surprised your attention span was so short.'

'*Ha ha.*'

'I'm going to talk to her about it.'

'*Bah. I wish I could come. Report back, won't you?*'

Eve assured her she would, and rang off.

It was five minutes after that that Robin texted.

Interesting update with ref to Leah Mason. Greg just messaged to say she had the local bobbies out twice last night, once around midnight and a second time at 4 a.m. Claims she heard an intruder but no sign. Seemed upset and frightened. xxx

Eve replied, then sat there, staring at the message. What did it mean? She could only think that Leah was scared and that something – quite possibly Eve's visit or the police interview – had put her on high alert. Eve went back to her previous theory: that Leah thought Dora had killed Anthony and would come for her next. But she'd already dismissed the idea. Ada's death didn't fit that premise, and Leah must realise that. Eve shook her head. Her fear had to be driven by something else, but what?

As soon as it was a reasonable hour, Eve called Tabitha and asked if she could drop in.

Fifty minutes later, she was back in the cosy design room, enjoying a cup of tea as Gus investigated a shadowy corner. Eve wanted answers about the objects Hal and Viv had touched, but as she looked at Tabitha, her mind went back to the house she was buying in Blyworth and her agreement to break the news of her affair to Giles. If Giles was as cloying with her as he was with Hal, she could understand it becoming too much, but it was still a massive step.

Eve sighed and pushed it from her mind. 'How's everyone bearing up?'

'Hal's living on the edge of his nerves now he knows the boatyard's going to him, and Giles... well, he's never liked change, least of all anything sudden.'

Tabitha's shoulders were tense as she sipped her tea. 'Theo has been kinder to me of late though, so that's something. The killings were horrific, but perhaps they've brought us together.'

All that would count for nothing if he found out about the affair.

'Did you ever track down Anthony's other woman?' Tabitha went on.

Eve nodded. 'And had it confirmed she owns the scarf you saw.'

Tabitha turned her palms upward and sighed. 'I'd never have guessed he was cheating on Dora. Ah, well. How can I help, anyway?'

Eve reminded her of Viv's behaviour the day before.

'I noticed you looked astonished and curious when she walked around the room, touching some of your ornaments. You didn't say anything at the time, but it came back to me in the middle of the night, and I wished I'd asked. Is there something special about those objects?'

Tabitha was silent for a long moment. At last, she said, 'They disappeared, two or three weeks ago now. I didn't say anything immediately, or call the police, because there'd been no break-in. It had to be a member of staff, the family, or a visitor to the household. I mentioned it casually to my workers, to see if I got a reaction, but there wasn't a flicker.' She raised an eyebrow. 'I kept an especially close eye on Ada, but she looked bored.'

'But you got them back?' The story was even more intriguing than she'd imagined.

Tabitha nodded. 'Yes, some of them were replaced when my back was turned, but not all.'

'So some pieces are still missing?'

'That's right. A very pretty silver card case, a George IV snuff box and an enamel clock. I kept them and the other antiques in here for inspiration. They're beautiful designs, but they're not mine. They belong to Theo, the same as the furniture. They were in here when he offered us house space and he didn't mind them staying.'

She really would lose a lot if she moved out. But love was a powerful motivator.

'And the mystery of who took them's still not solved?'

Tabitha shook her head. 'They reappeared after a drinks party, attended by family, friends, staff, you name it. So I've no idea. I realise your friend Viv had nothing to do with it, obviously, but that was why I was astonished she fixated on those specific pieces. I assumed it had to be a coincidence.'

Eve strongly suspected Hal knew the answer. She wondered whether to tell Tabitha, but decided to hold off in the end. She needed time to think.

Eve's mind pushed and pulled at what she knew. Hal had wanted to talk to Theo and at last, he'd convinced him to go into Tabitha's design room, where Viv had watched them from the door. He'd walked around the room, touching the ornaments which had gone missing. They must surely have been the topic of the conversation. Viv said that Theo had looked angry at first. Presumably he hadn't liked what Hal was saying. But then his expression had changed and he'd looked sad. Suddenly, Eve had a feeling she knew why.

34

———

Eve turned to Tabitha, a plan forming in her head.

'Is Theo around? Do you think he'd speak to me?'

'I think he was in the small sitting room.' Tabitha got up from her chair.

'Don't worry.' Eve remembered the way. It was where she'd interviewed Hal that first time. 'I'll find him.' It would make it harder for him to escape, and this was important.

Eve slipped through the shadowy house, knocked on the door of the sitting room and walked in.

Theo scowled at her, his bushy eyebrows quivering, his dark eyes fierce. 'What are you doing here?'

'I came to speak to Tabitha, but something she said made me want to talk to you.' Eve was going to have to chance her arm and pretend to know more than she did. Theo would cut her short otherwise; he was no pushover. 'My friend Viv saw you and Hal talking the night Anthony died. Hal was touching some of your ornaments in Tabitha's design room. The ones Dora stole and returned.'

She could tell she'd struck gold the moment the words were out. Theo's jaw dropped and his eyes widened.

'How the devil do you know that?'

Eve explained Tabitha's reaction when Viv had touched the same objects in front of her. 'It made sense that it was Dora who was responsible. I bumped into one of her clients.' Admitting she'd tracked her down would be counterproductive. 'I gather Dora thought she had months of guaranteed work ahead of her. She'd spent out on the project, but the client let her down at the last minute. I expect she panicked. She probably had a large credit card bill and the rent to pay and no way of meeting her debts.'

Theo's face darkened at her words. 'It was monumentally stupid of her!' He thumped the occasional table in front of him with his clenched fist, making it wobble and Gus whine. 'I'd told her a hundred times not to spend money until her customers signed a contract!'

Eve waited until he'd calmed down. 'If it had happened sooner, before the break-up with Anthony, she might have moved in with him, I guess, even if it was only temporary. But that had gone wrong too. So in desperation, she stole from you. She realised she'd made a mistake, and replaced some of the items, but not before she'd sold the card case, the snuff box and the clock.'

Theo sank heavily into one of the squashy sofas. His eyes were glistening now, all traces of anger gone from his expression. 'And I haven't seen her since.'

'You thought she'd disappeared because of something Anthony had done?' Eve wasn't sure if he knew about the affair, though it seemed likely.

'I heard rumours he was seeing another woman behind Dora's back.'

It explained his anger, the night of the party. 'But Hal told you what she'd done?'

He nodded at last. 'And Dora wrote to him, too. He's got no

idea where she is – or so he says – but she told him she was okay and that she'd left because she was ashamed. It was nothing to do with Anthony. By the time she wrote, she'd decided the rumours of the affair were rubbish and Hal agreed. He said Anthony would never cheat.'

Eve kept quiet, her mind full of the scene Jade Cooper's friends had witnessed in the Swan at Wessingham, and Leah Mason's guilty blushes.

Theo's head was in his hands, his elbows on his knees.

'How did Hal know Dora had been stealing?'

'He and Anthony saw her. They were both loyal enough not to say anything. Hal only spoke out when he realised I'd got the wrong end of the stick about Anthony.'

It had been brave of Anthony to keep quiet, even when Theo was about to thump him. He might have been seeing another woman, but he still felt for Dora, clearly. He'd refused to give her away to her dad.

'I was going to apologise to Anthony.' Theo paused for a moment. 'I'd laid into him, earlier that evening. I was convinced it was his fault Dora had disappeared, and that he could probably guess where she was. But after Hal spoke to me, I realised *I* was to blame. She was too scared to confide in me. Too determined not to come home.' He looked up at Eve. 'What kind of dad am I, that she'd prefer to steal than to have her old room back? But I never got the chance to say sorry to Anthony and now it's too late. And I still have no idea where Dora is.'

Eve could understand him pretending he and Dora were still in touch now. It was pride. Just like his daughter, he was too ashamed to face the truth. Eve felt a stab of sympathy.

'Even if she went off of her own accord,' Theo said, 'I'm worried sick about her. The police say—' He broke off for a moment. 'The police say she hasn't used her bank account or her mobile phone.'

'Do you think she took your boat?'

He nodded slowly. 'I've visited every secluded inlet I can think of, up and down the coast. I thought it might give me a clue where she'd gone, but I haven't found it. I'm worried I'll never see her again.'

'I'm so sorry.' Eve had the urge to pat his shoulder, but she didn't think he'd welcome it. 'Thank you for telling me. I'll see myself out.'

As Eve left the room, her mind was on the implications of all this. Theo had been a suspect, after the violent way he'd treated Anthony the night he was killed, but that looked shaky now. Everything he'd just told her rang true, and it all fitted with what Viv had seen and Tabitha had said. If Hal confirmed it, then Theo had realised he'd been wrong about Anthony by the time he was killed. And Theo certainly sounded devastated. It might explain his odd reaction to Tabitha's coolness after the death too. He'd have been consumed with guilt at doubting Anthony, and wanting everyone to mourn him properly.

Eve dropped in on Hal at the boatyard, looking out for Jackson Smith as she did so. She didn't see him this time. Perhaps he'd upped his game.

When Eve explained what she knew, Hal's eyes opened wide.

'I won't write about any of this,' Eve said. 'You have my word. I don't want to give Dora away, any more than you do. It's a family matter. But it makes a difference to the overall impression I have of Anthony, and that will affect the obituary.'

Hal nodded at last. 'All right, then. In confidence, it's true. I ended up having a quiet word with Dora about it. It must have been the night she put some of the things back. She was cringing inside, I could see that.'

'And she'd sold some of the pieces?'

Hal nodded. 'The ones she took first, before Anthony and I

spotted her. I think she was too ashamed to carry on, once she knew she'd been found out.'

'She didn't feel she could go to Theo for help?'

Hal sighed. 'He loves her to bits – I know that. But he's strict and irascible. He would have blamed her.' Eve had seen evidence of that herself. 'He misses her, and he'd have been happy to have her home, but when they were under the same roof, sparks flew. She wouldn't have wanted to come back. He's worried sick now, of course. I wish we could find her, but at least I got the letter saying she's okay. I only hope that's still true.'

'Thanks for explaining, Hal. I'm sorry, but I have another question, and this one's even more delicate. I've heard rumours that Anthony was seeing another woman, before he broke up with Dora.' Theo said Hal didn't believe it, and Anthony would have kept it secret of course, but Eve needed to be sure he knew nothing.

'I'm certain that's rubbish,' Hal said. 'I knew him. He wouldn't.'

'And you saw no sign of it?' She was thinking of the scarf, hanging up at the yard.

'Absolutely none.'

'It looks as though this other woman visited here, though. A journalist friend of mine said she smelled perfume when she came to interview you and Anthony, and there was a woman's scarf hanging on your hooks that day.'

Hal frowned. 'I assumed that was Tabitha's – she's got one like it. Though now you mention it, she doesn't normally come to the yard.' The worry lines on his forehead deepened, but then he took a deep breath. 'All the same, Anthony wouldn't. I'm sure of it.' He sounded as though he was trying to convince himself.

As Eve left him, thoughts of Leah Mason swirled in her head. She'd got more than one contact who'd seen her and

Anthony at the Swan and witnessed the tell-tale aborted kiss. That and her behaviour when Eve interviewed her was strong evidence that they were involved. And her neighbour had seen her wearing the scarf too. So far so good.

But if she'd been at the yard, surely someone would have noticed? And why be so careless with her scarf?

There had to be something Eve was missing.

Eve arrived for her shift at Monty's full of news, but Viv hadn't heard her come in. She was on her phone again, messaging.

Eve hadn't intended to creep up on her. Well, not exactly. But approaching quietly meant she saw what was on her screen. A selfie of a man with a goatee beard, wearing a black top hat with a feather in it.

'Ooh, is this the barman you were talking about?'

Viv jumped out of her skin and blushed.

Eve smiled. 'If you want me and Robin to join you for a double date, just say the word.'

'I don't want to risk putting him off so early on.'

'Hmm. Thanks.'

'How are you feeling about the open house tomorrow?'

Despite everything that was going on, the question made Eve's stomach tense. She'd bring the ingredients for her bakes back to Monty's that evening, and she and Viv would get stuck in. 'Fine.'

'Liar,' Viv said. 'It'll be great. It always is.'

It was true, it always had been, but there was so much to

contend with at the moment. Eve wasn't devoting attention to it like she normally would and that made her nervous.

She wandered from the kitchen to the tearoom, thoughts of Viv's new love interest gradually replacing her worries. She hoped this guy wasn't all outré style without the tender kindness Viv deserved. If he led her a dance... But she shook herself. Viv was an adult. Eve mustn't treat her like one of her children. Though they were adults too, of course. It was just hard to switch off the protectiveness.

She snapped out of her anxiety when she spotted some leaflets in Monty's window: 'The Hawthorns'. They were offering wellness and recuperation courses and therapies.

'What are these pamphlets doing in the window?' she asked Viv, when she returned to the kitchen to bake some sloe-gin spice cakes. The paperchain Viv had suspended from the ceiling fell down again, tapping her lightly on the head.

Eve groaned, got a chair and climbed up to sort it out. Again. 'We might need to rethink the decorations.'

Viv, who was on chocolate brownie detail, glanced up. 'Sorry. It's fine most of the time. It's just when it gets too warm.'

Which in a room with more than one oven, happened a lot.

'And the pamphlets on the windowsill?'

Viv slapped her forehead, depositing cocoa powder there. 'Ah, I meant to say. A very young hippyish person came in and asked if we could display them. You're not going to tell me off about that too, are you?'

Viv was a soft touch. It wasn't that Eve objected, she just wanted due diligence done first. 'Have you googled the place to check it looks okay? Because people will judge us if they go there and find it isn't.'

Viv did a mock pout. 'Yes, I do remember you making that point before. It's on my list. Honestly.'

After she'd finished gazing at Mr Top Hat, presumably.

'But the woman who brought them round was really friend-ly,' Viv said. 'She wore tie-dye.'

Viv had a soft spot for tie-dye too.

'Anyway, never mind about boring things like leaflets, tell me everything!'

Eve obliged.

'Wow. So where does that leave us?'

'Theo's looking much less likely now. He seems so crest-fallen about the way he behaved towards Anthony, and he knew he was mistaken in him before he died.

'He seems to have mellowed in other ways too, since Antho-ny's death. He bought those flowers for Tabitha, after berating her for not mourning Anthony properly. Maybe he realises he's been too harsh all round, and that building bridges is the way forward. It might not be too late for him and Dora, if only she's still alive.' Tension twisted her stomach. What were the chances of that, when she hadn't used her mobile or spent any money since she dropped off the radar? It was heartbreaking to think Theo might have missed his chance. 'I need to keep searching for her.'

'What about Tabitha?'

'Well, she's keeping a big secret, but it only gives her a motive if Anthony found out and threatened to tell Giles. There's no reason to suppose he knew. It's not as though he lived at Mistletoe Place. And even if he did, I'm not sure he'd hold it over her like that. Plus, she's told her lover she's set on telling Giles. If she follows through, her potential motive's gone, just like Theo's. She'd never have killed to keep her secret for an extra week. And on top of all that, she and Theo seem least likely to have collaborated with Ada. They're both much stronger characters than Giles and Hal.'

Viv had cocoa on her nose now too, but at least most of it was in the mixing bowl. How was it that she could crack eggs into flour without even looking, yet anything powdery went everywhere? For Eve, it was the other way about. 'That all sounds right,' Viv was saying. 'So, what about Giles and Hal, then?'

'The PI Giles previously hired to watch Hal is blackmailing him. Given his role, I guess it's more likely he saw Hal do something incriminating, and it was Hal who spent the most time with Ada too. Plus, Hal's inherited the boatyard. Living in the same house as his dad must be oppressive. The two deaths should give him his freedom.

'That said, Giles still had a good motive, assuming I'm right, and Anthony knew he was spying on Hal.'

'So Hal's still top of the pile, Giles is nipping at his heels, and Theo and Tabitha are well down the list?'

Eve nodded. 'I think so.'

'What about next steps?'

'I need to be bolder. Talk to Giles about the blackmail. Pretend I know the PI saw Hal do something incriminating. He might give the game away.'

'Sounds dangerous. Have you discussed it with Robin?'

Eve had thought about it, but decided against. 'I can't bother him with it now. You saw how he looked after he was attacked. He's remarkably cool about it, outwardly, but it must be affecting him. I don't want to give him sleepless nights on top of everything else.'

'You could leave it to pea-brained Palmer.'

'He doesn't take anything I suggest seriously and we'll only get one shot. I have a feeling I might sound more convincing. After all, I heard the blackmailer first hand.'

'In that case, we should go en masse. A deputation: me, you, Sylvia and Daphne. Simon won't want to; he'll think it's "too awkward".' She mimicked his voice.

'I couldn't possibly ask it of any of you.'

'He can hardly kill the lot of us to keep us quiet. And I'll bet they'll be up for it.'

Daphne would be less gung-ho about it than Sylvia, but she'd say yes out of loyalty.

'I'm going to call them and ask now,' Viv said, abandoning her brownie batter and shutting herself in the office before Eve could stop her.

'They're coming,' she said, when she reappeared two minutes later. 'Sylvia's going to bring her shooting stick. She says it's got a good point on it, just in case.'

Eve closed her eyes. 'I don't even think that's legal.' Wasn't it all about intent, when it came to improvised weapons?

'It's too late,' Viv said. 'It's all arranged. You can buy us drinks in the Cross Keys next time we're in as a thank you. I've already promised Sylvia.'

'There you are, you see. Who said you're not good at forward planning?'

Viv stuck out her tongue.

After Emily, another of Monty's servers, arrived to do her shift, and Allie assured them she could cope, Eve walked over to Haunted Lane to pick up Sylvia and Daphne. She was nearing their cottage when a text came in from Robin.

All well this end. Update from Greg – he says they've inter-viewed Leah Mason's neighbours and no one saw the intruders she thought she heard. Including a woman who was up half the night with a small baby. No signs of footprints or trampled flowerbeds either. Dawkins told Greg that Mason seemed very jittery. Privately they think there was no intruder.

That was a relief, but her previous question remained. Assuming it had been Eve's visit that triggered Leah's nerves, it looked like she was scared about her and Anthony's relationship getting out, but why? If Eve's thinking was right, Ada dying still left her feeling like a target.

There had to be a pattern where she'd be the next logical victim after the Mottram siblings.

It was a perplexing thought. Eve tried to make Hal fit as the killer with her latest theory in mind. He was a shoo-in for Anthony and Ada, but she couldn't imagine why he'd want to kill Leah. But of course, no one *had* killed her. The danger might be in her head.

Eve replied to thank Robin for the update, then knocked on Sylvia and Daphne's door. Minutes later, they met Viv by the low back gate which led from Monty's garden onto the river path.

'I can't believe we're doing this to the poor man,' Daphne said, looking anxious.

Sylvia laughed. 'I enjoy a good show of force.'

Eve would have been a lot more relaxed if she'd been alone. As it was, the situation felt out of control. She kept wondering why she'd gone along with it, but of course, the others were right. If Giles knew several people had guessed the truth, any danger became negligible, and deep down, she wondered if the pure surprise induced by the four of them marching in might shock him into being honest. The trouble was, he'd already got his excuse worked out, having talked to the police. She explained the problem to the others.

'I'll have to go in tough. Pretend I know he's lying.'

'He must have known how thin his excuse sounded,' Sylvia said. 'Talk about clutching at straws.'

When they arrived at the admin block of the gardens, Eve took a deep breath and walked straight into Giles's office. She knew he was there. She'd seen him through the window.

'I—' Giles's attractive, careworn face contorted. The rude way they'd barged in would be enough to tell him something was wrong. 'What's going on?'

Eve sat down opposite him, and Sylvia took a second chair as Viv crowded him by walking to his side of the desk. Daphne hung back.

Giles looked especially anxious about Viv, Eve noticed, which wasn't surprising, given the way she'd harangued him about her holey carrots the day before.

'I'm sorry to arrive without making an appointment,' Eve said. 'But it's really important, and I'm anxious. We know you're being blackmailed, and we know why. You and Hal lied about being together when Anthony was killed – probably with the best of intentions.' She had to make him feel they were on his side. 'You love Hal to bits. He's your son. But I know he was at Arthur's Yard around the time of the murder.'

'But—' There was acute pain in Giles's dark eyes. 'How can you possibly know?'

'When I told Hal Anthony was lying face down at the murder scene, I saw him react. He knew Anthony had been face up. It's a plain fact.' Eve had to present it as one, or Giles would wriggle out of it.

'But...' Giles said again.

Even as Eve watched him, she realised he was pulling back, giving himself time to think. She needed to throw him off guard again and another shock would do that. 'The man who's blackmailing you is a PI you hired to keep an eye on Hal.'

It had worked, she could see. His mind was in a spin again. 'How— I mean, what? Does Hal know?' He leaned forward, his shoulders hunched, jaw taut. 'Have you spoken to him about it?'

'You need to tell the police the truth. We're sorry for what you've been through, but sooner or later, they'll work out what happened. It'll be so much better if it comes from you.'

Sylvia nodded. 'It will.' She was holding her shooting stick, tapping its top. 'We know that Anthony had discovered you were having your son followed. Very awkward for you.'

Sylvia was doing a good job at keeping the pressure on, but

once again, Eve could see Giles was rowing back mentally. 'Hal can't have killed Anthony. He loved him like a brother. They grew up together.' Then he blinked quickly. 'And in any case, he was with me.' He shook his head. 'You must have misread his look when you told him how Anthony was lying. And no one's blackmailing me over his death. The man you're talking about was an old casual worker who knows we're under pressure. He thought he could use that to his advantage by threatening to circulate an invented scandal.'

Eve felt deflated. She was in no doubt that the dark ratty man by the estuary was the PI Jackson Smith had replaced. Giles hadn't denied it immediately; he'd been thrown into a panic about Hal finding out. But the visit had achieved nothing. She was sorely tempted to give Smith away too, but she felt sorry for him. His reputation would be shot if Giles discovered he'd not only been spotted, but had shared confidential information too.

She got up to go. 'I hate to think what you're going through. Please consider what we've said. If we've worked it out, the police will too, and we'll have to pass on what we know in any case.'

As she and Sylvia got up and they turned to go, Eve caught sight of a green sweatshirt, flung untidily on a side table, 'Deputy Director' embroidered just under Giles's business logo.

'Hal didn't want to take your job offer,' Eve said, glancing back at Giles, then nodding at the jumper.

'It's not the right time,' Giles said. He looked as though he was holding back tears.

36

———

'What do you think?' Viv asked, as they started their walk back towards Saxford.

Now Eve's head was clearing, she realised there were conclusions to be drawn from the meeting. Important ones, too. 'Giles sounded as though he was trying to convince himself that Hal couldn't be guilty. If that's the case, it means he doesn't know for sure, one way or the other.'

'And therefore Giles has to be innocent?' Sylvia said.

'Yes, assuming I'm right.'

'That's the way it sounded to me,' Daphne put in.

'So he goes down the list, along with Theo and Tabitha,' Viv said, 'leaving Hal in the hot seat. That's progress. So what's next?'

'I might have to put my cards on the table with Hal himself. Instinct tells me to go now, before Giles has a chance to tell him about our visit. And I think I should go alone. He's not the most confident of people; I suspect he'll clam up if we all appear. I need the chance to work on him, one to one.'

Viv eyed her beadily. 'And what would your beloved say, if he knew you were operating solo? I insist on "doing a Robin".'

'A what?'

'The open-call thing.'

If Eve had a potentially dangerous interview planned, Robin would hang around nearby and listen in, ready to intervene if necessary. Viv's idea to copy him was kindly meant, but it left Eve even more anxious about the encounter. Viv was a lot less disciplined than Robin, and it was important to keep quiet when listening in.

Eve reminded her of the fact.

'Oh ye of little faith. I can do quiet.'

Eve saw Daphne and Sylvia exchange a glance.

'I can!' Viv must have seen them too.

'Can we help?' Sylvia asked.

'It should be fine, thanks. If I do run into trouble, Viv making a racket outside the boatyard should get Hal to back off. There'll probably be other workers on site anyway.'

So Sylvia and Daphne walked back along the river towards Saxford as Eve and Viv made for the yard. They set up the call and Eve left Viv outside, phone to her ear, shoulders hunched against the cold.

'I'll try not to be long.'

As with Giles, Eve marched straight into Hal's office the moment she'd knocked. He was there, luckily, peering at something on his computer screen, his eyes anxious. That expression intensified when he saw it was her.

'Hal, I'm sorry. I wouldn't bother you if it wasn't important. Something urgent and delicate's cropped up.'

He looked even more nervous now. 'Oh.' He walked round to close the door, which sent a tiny flicker of concern through Eve. But Viv was just outside and multiple workers were chatting in the main part of the building. Hal retook his seat and motioned Eve to a chair too. 'What is it?'

'I should have admitted it sooner, but I know you came here

the evening Anthony was killed – right around the time he died, in fact.'

All the colour drained from his face. She was right then; he really had seen the body first hand. Either he was the killer, or he'd kept quiet about it for other reasons.

Hal's mouth opened, but it took several seconds before he said anything. 'How do you know?'

'You were seen. Not by me.' She wanted her evidence to sound more concrete than it was. It was in a good cause, after all. And she was almost certain it was true, and that the ratty PI had seen him here.

Hal shivered. 'The person who's been following me? I only spotted them in the last couple of days, but it made me wonder how long they'd been at it.'

'Do you know who they are?' She needed to know how much *he* knew.

Hal shook his head. 'I've got no idea.' He leaned forward, elbows on the desk, head in hands. 'Everything's going wrong. From Gabby breaking up with me, to stuff here at the yard. The leaky valve and the vodka bottles. I messed up, but at least Anthony didn't sack me. But then he was killed, and Ada too, and now this!'

He wasn't talking like a murderer. 'What happened that night? I know Giles lied for you, obviously. He'd do anything to protect you.'

Hal slumped lower in his seat. 'He does that too much. He didn't have to vouch for me, but he wades in at every step. I don't know what to do. Poor Dad. But it's absolutely suffocating. Gabby wasn't good enough for him. We might still be together if he hadn't interfered!'

Very faintly, Eve heard Viv's voice through the phone in her pocket. 'Whoops!' and then a thud.

Eve felt the colour rise in her cheeks.

'What did you say?' Hal looked at her, jolted out of his misery for a second.

'I'm so sorry. I hiccupped.' Eve coughed for good measure, in case her excuse made Viv laugh. Words would be had later. 'Would it help to talk about it?'

Hal sighed. 'Will you tell the police?'

'I think they'll work it out anyway, whether I do or I don't.'

Hal clenched his fists and screwed up his face, but at last he looked at her again. She could tell he wanted to offload. 'It's true. Dad lied for me. I was due to come here at around the time Anthony died to check on a boat we're treating for osmosis problems, but I was delayed.'

She couldn't believe she'd finally get the truth. Everything felt as though it was on a knife edge. 'What held you up?'

Hal groaned. 'I felt strange. As though I was drunk, though I'd only had a small amount. Truly.' He must have read Eve's look. 'But I was off balance. Swaying.'

Just as Daphne had said. 'This was after you went to Willow Cottage to get the papers Anthony wanted?'

He nodded. 'I knew if Anthony saw me, he'd assume I'd had a skinful and go ballistic. The press were there, the great and the good. It would have looked as though I was taking the mick.'

Especially after their conversation earlier in the evening, when Hal had assured Anthony he didn't have a problem.

'I realised there was no way I could go and tend to the boat in that state. I went to grab a coffee and as much water as I could find, then hid for a few minutes until I felt better. But you're right. After that, I came to the yard to get on with the job. I was scared, the moment I got near. The lights were on, but I couldn't see anyone inside. And when I got through the door, there was Anthony.'

He closed his eyes again.

'Why didn't you call the police?'

'He'd been supportive when Gabby and I split up, but me

being drunk at work soured things. It was a one-off, but it led to several angry exchanges. I could tell Anthony doubted my drinking was under control. The casual workers heard us at it, so I was terrified. I thought everyone would assume I was guilty. And of course I was desperately upset too. Not thinking straight. I could see Ant was beyond help, so I ran off. I bumped into Dad and I was shaking, feeling sick. All over the place. He knew there was something wrong and I... well, I ended up telling him. He said he'd tell the police we were together. Nothing would change his mind. He said if I told a different story, it would make him look like a liar, and was that what I wanted?'

Emotional blackmail. *Nice.*

'Look, Hal, you've clearly been dealing with an awful lot, but please, you need to tell the police what happened. Trust them to sort it out.' Her gut was telling her he wasn't guilty, but the information had to be relevant.

'They'd never believe me.'

Eve winced inwardly. Knowing Palmer, that was probably true, though Greg might be a voice of reason. 'I hope they will. Either way, it's a serious handicap if they're missing such crucial information. Maybe you saw something that might help them identify the killer.'

Hal shook his head fiercely. 'I'm sure I didn't.'

'You didn't touch anything at the scene?'

'No.'

'But just the same, you need to come clean. For your dad's sake if nothing else.'

'My dad?'

'The man who saw you enter the yard is blackmailing him. If you tell the truth, it'll put an end to his power.'

'But Dad and I will both get charged with perverting the course of justice. We'll be jailed.'

Eve couldn't help but feel sorry for them. Giles was probably about to have a marriage breakup too, though he didn't yet know it. But speaking up was the right thing to do.

'I know you've helped the police before,' Hal was saying. 'Do you have any idea who's guilty? If you could catch them, that would be another way to put a stop to all this.'

He was right.

He went on: 'What about if I promise to go to the police by this time tomorrow, if the case isn't solved?'

Eve had grave misgivings about agreeing. Officially, Hal and Giles both deserved jail for misleading the authorities so badly, but the idea of them being put away felt cruel. Hal hadn't wanted to lie, and Giles's sense of priorities was way off balance, due to the knocks he'd had.

She only hoped she wouldn't live to regret it, but the word was out before she could change her mind. 'Okay.'

Eve heard a gasp from the mobile inside her pocket.

37

Eve felt Viv's eyes on her as she exited Arthur's Yard.

'Don't say it,' she said, pulling her hat on and turning up her collar against the cold.

'Even if I don't, you know what I'm thinking. You always play by the rules.'

'I felt sorry for him.' She tried not to consider what Robin would say about it.

'It makes you seem almost human.'

'Thanks.'

At last, Viv patted her shoulder. 'It's all right. I'm human through and through myself, so I understand. I was totally hooked by the call, by the way. It was better than *The Archers*. What do you think of Hal saying he was staggering when he'd only had a small amount to drink? Could Giles have spiked him, and planted the vodka bottles too, to push Anthony into giving him the sack? If you're right, he hated him working there.'

The same thought had crossed Eve's mind, but on reflection, none of it fitted. 'I don't think so. Giles is scared for Hal's safety. I doubt he'd drug him when he was due to visit the yard.'

'Hmm.' Viv frowned. 'Perhaps not.'

'As for the vodka bottles, they might have prompted Anthony to let Hal go, and I'm sure that would have pleased Giles. But think of the impact on Hal's reputation if word got out. Giles's raison d'être is to protect his son from hurt and harm. I'm not sure he'd risk that either.'

'Okay. You have a point.' Viv grimaced. 'Hal could be lying, but I suppose he could be ill too.'

It was another possibility that had crossed Eve's mind. She very much hoped he wasn't. The moment she and Viv stopped swapping theories, Eve went back to feeling conflicted about waiting a day before going to the police. In her gut, she truly believed Hal was innocent. She suspected he didn't have it in him to lie so convincingly, and the story he'd told rang true. But holding back something so fundamental went against all her law-abiding, rule-adhering instincts.

She carried on feeling miserable all the way back to Monty's and was only distracted as she cut through the teashop to make for home. It was the wellness retreat leaflets that pulled her from her thoughts. Eve remembered Viv describing the woman who'd dropped them off. Hippyish, wearing tie-dye. She looked at them more closely, and the faintest flicker of connection sparked in her mind.

Was it the sunset-coloured background of oranges and purples? Or their logo? Something was nagging at her. Had she heard of the Hawthorns before?

'What is it?' Viv came over to her. 'I thought you were leaving.'

'Just a minute.' Eve closed her eyes. And then suddenly, she had it. The junk mail on Dora Osborne's mat. There'd been a letter from the Hawthorns near the top of the pile – Eve had been able to see the logo but not the name.

And a letter felt more significant than a flyer.

Eve pointed to the leaflets. 'Did you ever look them up to check we're happy to support them?'

Viv bit her lip. 'So sorry, I forgot.'

Eve stood to one side to let a customer out and googled. The outfit was just up the coast, next to a body of water called St Botolph's Creek. From the photos, the place looked down-at-heel. Not the sort of company who could afford large mailshots. So was the letter to Dora targeted? Perhaps she'd been a previous client.

'What is it?' Viv knocked heads with Eve as she tried to get a look.

But Eve was distracted. She was thinking of a conversation she'd had with Tabitha about Dora and the mysterious scarf. Tabitha had instantly concluded it wasn't hers. 'If it had been tie-dyed or something with a fringe, I might have believed it,' she'd said.

The Hawthorns might be just Dora's bag. And it was close to an inlet where she could have taken her dad's boat...

Eve found the retreat's contact details. The manager was a woman called Maeve. She took a deep breath. That was the name Jade Cooper had given Eve at Parker's, when Eve had asked about Dora's contacts!

She explained it all to Viv before she could explode with curiosity. 'It's the best lead we've had to date.'

After that, she went home to make a fuss of Gus, then fetched her car from the village green, and set off for the Hawthorns. She needed to be back in time to begin her and Viv's mammoth baking session, but she couldn't possibly delay this trip. Hope had seized her. If Dora had gone to the retreat, there was a chance she was okay after all. Perhaps they discouraged the use of mobile phones. And maybe her friend Maeve had looked after her, so she hadn't needed money.

But then Eve made herself pull back. If Dora was hiding, not dead, where did that leave her in relation to Anthony's murder? Eve had all but discounted Hal and Giles now, but *someone* had killed the Mottram siblings. Anthony had betrayed

Dora and he'd seen her steal too. Eve had doubted she'd conspire with Ada, but that felt cavalier. It was as Robin had said: she'd never even met the woman. She had no idea of her character. Eve was wandering into a potentially dangerous situation. She took a deep breath. She could turn back. But the retreat would likely have other staff and guests. If it seemed deserted, she could change plan.

Of course, if Dora was hiding, she wouldn't want to see Eve any more than she wanted to talk to the police. And if Maeve was protecting her, she'd want to send Eve packing too. It might be best to try to find evidence that Dora was there first. If Eve could prove she knew, it would be harder for Maeve to turn her away.

She parked her Clubman by the creek. Dora must have hidden Theo's boat somewhere. He'd searched, but he'd been trying to scan the whole coast – needle in a haystack stuff. Now Eve had narrowed it down, she could look properly. It was almost completely dark already, but on the upside, the gloom disguised Eve's snooping and she had her phone torch.

It was boggy around the creek and Eve wished she'd worn wellingtons, but it was worth it. There were three boathouses that might be hiding Theo's missing craft, the *Lady Mary*. They were all attached to houses, which would explain Theo overlooking them.

She'd already tried two and was losing hope when she stepped cautiously along the bank of the creek to the third, a black wooden affair with windows almost opaque with dirt. Beyond it stood a house in darkness. Eve couldn't see any curtains at the windows and guessed it might be unoccupied.

Her heart rate quickened. The boathouse of an empty home was definitely promising...

She pressed her face to the glass and peered in. There, in front of her, was a small but beautiful old boat. And on its side was its name, the *Lady Mary*.

It wasn't much, but being armed with that information could help. For a moment, Eve debated calling the police. But if Palmer came in, all guns blazing, hungry for an arrest, he'd never give Dora a fair hearing. As for coaxing out the truth, it would be a non-starter. She'd bide her time, see how things played out, and call the minute it seemed like the best or only safe option.

So she made her way to the retreat's reception, which was set in a wooden shack at the head of a long drive. It was completely dark now, and the woman behind the counter was clearly cold, though her smile was warm. She wore a beanie, coat and fingerless gloves and was clutching a mug. Fairy lights twinkled around her.

'Maeve?' Eve recognised her from the photo on the outfit's website.

The woman looked curious. 'Yes. Can I help you?' She didn't put the hot drink down and Eve didn't blame her.

'I'm here for Dora,' Eve said.

Maeve opened her mouth, but Eve cut in before she could reply. 'I know she came here after her latest job fell through. I suppose she feels she can't face anyone.' Eve mustn't give any hint that she suspected her of murder. Her sole focus needed to be on her financial troubles and her shame at stealing from her dad. 'I wanted to let her know her family love her. They're worried, and everyone will understand why she did what she did. It was a moment of desperation.' Maeve probably knew the whole story. And if Dora was a killer, she might know that too.

'She's not here,' Maeve said. But Eve could hear the uncertainty in her voice.

'When will she be back? I don't mind waiting.'

'No, I mean—'

Eve cut in gently. 'I've seen the boat she arrived in. I know she's staying here. Please. I might be able to help. I'm writing

Anthony Mottram's obituary. She can look me up if she likes. Would you at least give her my card?'

But Maeve's face had fallen, her jaw slack. 'Anthony's dead?'

Eve was completely wrong-footed. They were only just down the coast. How could she possibly not have heard? 'He died last weekend.'

Maeve sank down on a stool behind the desk.

'The death has been all over the papers. The internet. Everyone in Saxford's talking about it.' Maeve couldn't know about Ada's death either. Or that they'd both been murdered.

'I've got a dumb phone, not a smart one,' Maeve said. 'I listen to the news headlines in the morning on Radio 4 when I can bear to, and that's about it. Our veg comes in from south of here, towards Ipswich, and none of our visitors are local right now.' She sighed. 'In fact, we don't have that many takers, this time of year.'

Hence the flyers, Eve guessed. 'But Dora has a mobile.' Except the police said it hadn't been switched on in the last couple of weeks.

Maeve shook her head. 'She doesn't know. Take it from me.'

Eve would need to relay all of this to the police, but the call no longer felt urgent, or necessary for her safety. Maeve's shock was transparently genuine, and Eve guessed she was right and Dora had no idea either. The poor, poor woman.

She must have cut herself off entirely, too depressed to check for messages or raise her head above the parapet.

Maeve put her hands over her face. 'I can't believe we'll have to tell her. She'll be devastated. They'd split up, but Dora regretted it. They argued over him seeing another woman, but after a while she decided she'd been mistaken. She said he wouldn't do it to her.' She shook her head.

Eve thought of Leah Mason and felt sad.

Maeve sighed. 'I can tell from your expression that you

know different. I didn't know him well, but I must admit, I was worried she'd put too much faith in him. My opinions don't matter though. She'll be shattered at the news.'

Eve felt her pain. It was too awful. But she knew what Robin would say. 'I'm really sorry, but we shouldn't be the ones to tell her. The police have been looking for her ever since the death.' Eve might think she was innocent, but it wasn't her call.

Maeve's jaw dropped. 'The police? The death wasn't natural?'

'I'm afraid not. I know some nice members of the local team. I'll call them now and explain. But Maeve, please can you tell Dora her dad knows about the missing ornaments and he's blaming himself? He's mortified that she didn't feel able to turn to him when she ran into trouble. It wasn't Anthony who gave her away. He risked a beating from Theo to keep her secret, but because of that, Hal told him. Things were getting out of hand, with rumours and accusations flying. I think everyone knows what she did was out of character, and she tried to put things right, of course.'

Maeve blew her nose and nodded. 'I'll tell her. She told me all about it. She just wanted to hide and I understood that. She's been working for me to cover her bed and board.'

Eve called Greg Boles then, and explained what had happened. 'I'd like to protect her from DI Palmer if possible.'

'*Don't worry,*' he said. '*The boss is out at the moment. I'll come myself and bring Olivia. I mean, DC Dawkins.*'

It was a weight off Eve's mind. 'Thanks, Greg.'

Greg asked to speak to Maeve next, to reiterate the request to let them break the news. Eve sensed Maeve was relieved. It was a horrible job.

Back at home, Eve spent some time feeling sad, but cuddling Gus helped. She gave him his supper, and had hers early too.

Sustained by sausage casserole with buttered green beans and potatoes, she left for Monty's to begin the grand baking challenge for the following day.

Viv was full of questions, of course, so Eve filled her in. Her eyes were like saucers as she put on her apron and hairnet. 'Well done, Eve! I'm so glad you found her. And that it looks as though she's innocent. Right. Let's get this show on the road.'

Within an hour, Monty's kitchens were smelling of brandy-soaked fruit and baking dough and pastry. Viv had brought a bottle of sloe gin with her, and although Eve had worried it might impede their progress, she'd joined in with a festive glass. 'Fairytale of New York' was playing on the radio, and Viv was 'testing' her first batch of mince pies when Robin called.

'How are things?'

'Good.' Robin sounded slightly hesitant. '*We're ready to confront our bad guys now, but we need to catch them in the act. They'll never go down for it otherwise. We'll go ahead tomorrow.*'

Eve's stomach dropped. 'Oh, Robin. I know you'll take care, but please, please—'

'*Take care?*' He laughed. '*You can bet on it, don't worry. We've got a large team. I can't see us being outnumbered. I might even make it back for the open house!*'

'That would be amazing. You're a glutton for punishment.' Eve took a deep breath, trying to hold in her excitement in case it didn't come off. 'I'll be thinking of you, and willing you on.'

'*Thank you. I love you. Did I ever mention that?*'

Viv was making an 'aww' face. She could hear him, clearly. Eve nipped into the office as she replied. 'You may have. The feeling's mutual.'

'*Good news.*' She could hear the smile in his voice. '*Greg's texted, by the way, so I know some of your updates. Nice work, finding Dora.*'

Her worry was edged aside for just a moment by a warm glow. 'Thanks.'

'*For what it's worth, he's convinced Maeve was right, and she didn't know Anthony was dead. Same for Ada. She could hardly speak once she heard the full story. What's more, she was with Maeve and another woman when Anthony was killed, so I think she's out of it.*'

Eve debated what to tell him about her other interviews. She felt uneasy to her core, not explaining her arrangement with Hal, but Robin had so much to cope with already. And if she admitted they'd struck a deal to buy him more time, it would put Robin in a horrible position. He was very close to Greg; he'd feel he should be telling him. She didn't want him preoccupied during the raid the following day.

So in the end, she left it and rang off, desperately hoping she'd made the right decision.

Back in the kitchen she relayed Robin's news about Dora.

'So she really is off the list then,' Viv said, starting work on some chocolate orange and cranberry cakes. 'I mean, that's great, obviously, but everyone else kind of is too.'

Viv was right, but one of them must have done it. Eve had missed something.

38

Eve woke the following day feeling twitchy, her stomach in knots. Thoughts of Robin's raid mingled with that evening's open house and the urgent need to find more evidence. She'd have to contact the police once the twenty-four hours she'd given Hal were up. And in the background, worry fizzed. What if she was wrong about him? Or Giles had done it? He'd sounded convincing the day before, but he might just be a good actor. Or Theo? But he'd known Anthony wasn't to blame for Dora's disappearance before the murder. Or if Giles, Hal and Theo were out of it, then could it be Tabitha? But would Anthony really have threatened to reveal her affair? He'd been having one himself, so it would be hypocritical. And would he regard it as his business? He and Giles hadn't been close. Keeping a secret from him wouldn't feel half as problematic as keeping one from Hal, his oldest friend.

As she showered, dressed and walked Gus round the village green, wrapped up against the weather, her soft woollen scarf flying in the stiff breeze, she was preoccupied with Dora too. She wondered if she'd contacted her dad yet. Theo clearly wanted a fresh start. She had the impression he'd try his hardest to see things from Dora's point of view in future. And she could see how much he regretted his fight with Anthony too.

The moment she got back inside her nice, warm cottage, her cheeks stinging slightly from the cold, her phone rang.

Dora Osborne!

She picked up, trying to remove Gus's tartan coat one-handed. 'Dora, it's good to hear from you. I'm so very sorry for what you're going through. It must all be such a shock.'

There was a long pause. Poor Dora. Eve could hear the tears in her voice when she finally managed to speak. '*I still can't believe it. And to think that the last time Anthony and I were in touch, we were talking about my stealing.*'

Eve managed to extract Gus from his coat and sat down on one of her couches. 'He must have understood. He did his utmost to keep your secret, and you were in a terrible fix.'

She sighed. '*There was more to it than that. I was angry as well. Dad and I— Well, we've had our ups and downs. He's got such fixed ideas. I found him so difficult to confide in, because he'd always judge.*'

'It doesn't sound easy. Though having spoken to him, I can see how much he cares for you, deep down. He seems to blame himself too. He knows you should have felt able to turn to him.'

She gave another deep sigh. '*Faults on both sides, I guess. But it's true, I didn't feel I could, and that made me sad, and resentful too. I knew he'd blame me for my work contract falling through. You know about all that?*'

'Yes. I'm sorry.'

'*Don't be. I wasn't calling to moan. And, of course, Dad would have been right. I suppose I was cross with myself, really, but I took it out on him when I stole those things.*' She paused. '*I certainly wasn't trying to get at Tabitha. I just took the orna-ments from there because it was a nice, quiet room where no one would see what I was up to. Or so I thought.*'

'Hal and Anthony spotted you.'

'*Yes. A couple of days later, Anthony called me. He pointed out that it was Tabitha who loved the things I'd taken, not Dad. And that Tabitha hadn't kicked up a fuss about them going missing. That made me feel even worse.*'

'I think Tabitha wanted to minimise the trouble over it.'

'*Yes, she's like that. At first, I ignored what Anthony said. I'd already sold three of the pieces, so I felt stuck. There was no going back. And I was in no mood to listen to him anyway. Several of my friends had told me he'd been seeing another woman, so I was desperately hurt. But deep down, he'd pricked my conscience.*'

'So you sneaked into Mistletoe Place and replaced what was left?'

'*That's right.*' She was crying. '*Tabitha's always been so good to me. Easy to talk to. How can I expect her to understand what I did?*'

'I've a hunch she will. If you feel able to go back, I'm sure she and your dad will welcome you with open arms. I think your dad might have learned his lesson.' He really had sounded desperately sad and worried when she'd spoken to him.

'*That's the stupid thing.*' Eve could hear the anguish in Dora's voice. '*I know he loves me really. He minds about family. Look at Giles. He's so happy to have him at Mistletoe Place. He's looked out for him since he was a kid. It's just that I've always been rebellious and he's always been like a Victorian dad. I could probably face him now, but I can't think how to approach Tabitha, after all she's done for me. Does she know I took the things from her room?*'

'Not unless your dad's told her.'

She sighed. '*He probably hasn't. He'll be too ashamed.*'

'Look, would you like me to go and talk to her? We know each other reasonably well. I could prepare the ground if you like, then call you afterwards?'

'*Oh.*' There was a long pause. '*I shouldn't let you. I should face up to what I've done instead.*'

'I don't mind. Honestly.'

At last, Dora agreed.

Eve was glad of the chance to go and talk to Tabitha. Solving the case was desperately pressing. She had a clock counting down in her head until the deadline she'd agreed with Hal. Visiting Mistletoe Place and interacting with the key players could only help when she needed new leads. None of that was enough to push thoughts of Robin's raid from her mind, though.

As she fed Gus and snatched a quick breakfast herself, she took stock. She kept coming up against the same barriers, each time she circled over the suspects.

Theo had been furious with Anthony the night he died, but Hal had explained the true reason for Dora's absence well before the murder. His mind would have been full of the news of her thieving, and the desire to find her. Meanwhile, Giles and Hal had lied for each other, but Eve was convinced Giles was worried Hal might be guilty. Logically, that meant Giles wasn't. And Hal's account of reaching the boatyard late had sounded convincing. Nothing was guaranteed, but her gut told her he was innocent too. Then Dora had an alibi and seemed knocked for six by the news of Anthony's death, and Leah Mason had been alibied too. None of them looked likely for his murder.

When it came to Ada, Eve still didn't understand the killer's motive. It had to do with the call she'd made to Anthony, just before his death, surely? Eve was still convinced she'd sent him to Arthur's Yard. As before, the logical conclusion was that she was in league with whoever had killed him, and they'd killed her because she was threatening to out them. But if none of them looked likely for Anthony, then none of them looked likely for her either.

So could the phone call and the killing really be unrelated? It felt wildly improbable, but assuming there was a link, she was missing something.

Eve put her breakfast things in the dishwasher, then got her and Gus layered up for the walk up the river to Mistletoe Place. Tabitha's affair still provided a potential motive for Anthony's murder, if he'd decided to tell on her.

If so, then she could have slipped over to the yard after Ada had lured him there. Ada got the boatyard. They might have had a shared interest in killing him. But Tabitha of all people knew what Ada was like. Would she really have committed such a terrible crime to hide an affair, with Ada in on her new, far more dreadful secret? It seemed unthinkable.

'None of my theories make sense,' she said to Gus as she locked up the house.

Eve spent the journey up the river trying to focus on the murders, but her mind kept straying to Robin. Even if the police weren't outnumbered, it only took one mistake, one man with a lethal weapon and— She mustn't think like this. Robin was more than competent, and he wouldn't be happy if he wasn't involved.

She took a deep breath and focused on the bridge-building she wanted to do on Dora's behalf. She was sure Tabitha would forgive her.

But when she and Gus reached Mistletoe Place, she realised she might not have picked the best time to call.

The windows at the house were old. The sort that would rattle in the wind. It meant they leaked sound too, and Eve could hear Tabitha's pleading voice. And Giles, sobbing.

So she hadn't been lying when she'd promised to tell him she was leaving.

39

'Please try and understand,' Tabitha was saying to Giles. She was begging. 'Your protectiveness comes from a good place. I know it does. But it makes you so hard to live with.'

Eve could just see Giles through the window. His agonised face, stretching as his mouth opened. 'Why couldn't you have told me? Why couldn't we have talked about it?'

'Giles, my darling. How many times have we talked about it before? I said you needed to see someone. To get help. But you've never accepted there's a problem. I knew how miserable this would make you and it's the last thing I wanted, but it simply couldn't carry on like this forever.'

'But—'

'I'm going to go and explain to Hal now.'

Eve heard the door shut after her and saw Giles sink into a chair, a look of devastation on his face. It was a horrible situation, but Tabitha was doing the decent thing, albeit later than she should have.

Eve stood there with Gus, uncertain what to do. She only had until that evening to reach a breakthrough and she wasn't likely to get it by retreating from Mistletoe Place. But she couldn't possibly knock now.

As she was havering, full of indecision, she heard a yell.

'What?' It was Hal's voice, angry and upset. 'I can't believe it. What were you thinking?'

She strained to hear Tabitha's reply. '... eventually see it's for the best. Please, Hal. Just give it some time. Let it settle.'

A moment later, Eve heard Tabitha again, more clearly this time. She must have come outside. She let out something between a gasp, a sigh and a sob.

'You told them, then.' That was Theo.

Heck. She must have broken the news to him first. That was brave. But why would she? He didn't sound as angry as Eve would have expected.

'You were right,' Tabitha said at last. 'I should have done it sooner. Prepared the ground. I feel bad I told you first, too. Of course, I'm grateful to you for listening, but you know what I mean.'

'I do. But I'm glad we had that heart to heart.' A heart to heart about an affair? Theo might be mellowing, but there was no way he'd take that lying down. Dora had said how protective he was over Giles. 'It'll be a shock for Hal.'

'Maybe I went too far. But I was desperate to force a change. Somehow.'

Eve felt hot and cold all over. What did it mean? She'd got it wrong. She must have.

She backed away from the house, whispering to Gus to follow. When she'd reached a safe distance, she set to work on her phone. It was Tabitha's Facebook that she went for, searching for her friends. And there was the man she'd looked round the house in Blyworth with. Everything shifted as she realised the truth. He wasn't a lover. He was her brother. And when she googled *his* name, she found he was an estate agent.

So was she buying somewhere to hole up when she needed

a break? But that didn't fit with Theo's comment about Hal. It was a shock for *him*. And then, everything fell into place. Tabitha's words to Giles about his clinginess. It wasn't an excuse to explain her affair, it was to try to make him see that Hal needed his independence. She had to be buying the house for him! No wonder she'd carried on working hard even after Anthony's death; she'd need every penny if she was paying a deposit, and maybe chipping in with the mortgage too.

But for Hal, it had come out of the blue, and in a way it meant she was running his life, just as surely as his dad was trying to. Eve imagined Tabitha had got desperate. If Giles was constantly obsessing over his son, it was bound to have affected their marriage. She probably hoped his fears would ease if she put some distance between them, but Giles was devastated and Hal was angry.

Hal was probably determined to take control himself, after constantly being managed. But Eve sensed that desire for freedom was tempered by a lack of confidence. After a lifetime of Giles worrying over him, doubting his ability to cope, Hal might have started to believe the myth. He was doubting himself when Eve spoke to him after he'd inherited Arthur's Yard. Eve hoped he'd achieve some kind of balance eventually.

As for Tabitha, if she really did intend to buy him a house, it would explain Giles's upset perfectly. He didn't want his son out of his sight, to the extent he'd hired a PI to watch him…

It was a huge thing for Tabitha to have done, and Eve could understand the shock and upset, but she sympathised too. In her shoes, Eve would have been desperate to break the spell somehow.

But none of this got her any closer to solving the murders. Just the opposite, though she was glad Tabitha hadn't cheated on Giles after all.

Eve sighed and crouched down to talk to Gus. 'We'll do a five-minute walk up the river, but then we'll come back. I still need to keep my promise to Dora.' And walking in after a row might throw new things to the surface. Everyone would be off balance.

Eve texted Tabitha to explain she had a message from Dora, and that she'd be passing shortly on a dog walk. It felt too mean to arrive unannounced, under the circumstances. She breathed a sigh of relief when Tabitha replied, saying she'd be glad to see her. She must have decided Dora was more important than anything she was coping with.

40

———

When Eve arrived, Tabitha opened the door then nodded towards the stairs. 'Let's make ourselves scarce. Difficult day, I'm afraid.'

'I'm sorry. It's all right for Gus to come up?'

'Of course.' She bent to fuss him. 'You're always welcome. Yes, you are!'

They followed her up. Eve didn't feel anxious, heading to a quiet part of the house. Giles, Hal and Theo were probably all still there, and Tabitha's motive was out of the window anyway. Eve had always found it difficult to believe in her as a killer.

She took Eve to a comfortable room with a dressing table and wardrobes.

'My dressing room. It's not where I normally receive guests, but no one will disturb us here.'

'It's lovely.' The wallpaper was beautiful – botanical in blues and greens, and the curtains were blue silk, picking out one of the minor colours in the paper design. Eve would never be able to afford anything like it, she was sure, but she could appreciate it all right. Once again, Eve thought how much their tastes overlapped. The perfume they both wore was sitting on the dressing table. It had felt like a bonding experience when Tabitha had recognised the scent when she took Eve's coat the first time they met.

Tabitha smiled. 'So, Dora?'

Eve explained how Dora had come to steal from her design room, how deeply she regretted it, her panic, and her anger at Theo. Her desire to make amends.

'I think she's ready to face her dad now, but she's mortified about taking things that he never really cared for, but which meant a lot to you.'

Tabitha shook her head. 'Truth to tell, when I finally realised Dora had gone to ground, I half wondered if it was her, so it's not a shock. I'm sad that the things she sold are gone, but they're only things. They're not as important as people. I understand why she did it, and I can hardly claim to be the best judge of what to do when. Not after this morning.'

Eve raised an eyebrow, in case Tabitha wanted to offload, but after a moment, she shook her head. 'It doesn't matter. We all make mistakes, that's the thing. If Dora's answering her phone again, I'll ring her myself and tell her how much we've all missed her. Theo will be cock-a-hoop if she comes home. He's been beside himself. I hope he'll carry on being more approachable, though old habits die hard, obviously.' She gave a wry smile.

Eve thanked her and they moved on to talking about Tabitha's work again. She said she was considering branching out into wallpaper. She'd done a lot of fabric design, way back when Giles had featured her work in his gallery.

As they chatted, Eve's gaze fell on Tabitha's perfume once more, and then on the scarf that was a match for the one in the newspaper photograph. It was hanging on an antique hook, mostly hidden by some others. It wasn't this season's colour, so Eve guessed Tabitha had archived it.

Then suddenly, as Tabitha enthused over a design idea, Eve

felt a frisson of fear. Both Ashley from the *Blyworth Advertiser* and the first responders at Anthony's murder scene had smelled perfume at the yard, yet Eve had failed to notice it when she'd found Anthony's body.

Was that because it was the exact same perfume she'd been wearing that night? She was so used to it that it might not have registered. Viv would smell it on her all the time too.

And then Eve thought of the scarf in the photograph again. Leah had one like it, but it didn't follow that the one at the yard was hers. It was Tabitha who'd pointed it out, suggesting Anthony might have a new woman on the scene. But what if it was all a bluff? Eve had met Tabitha several times. She might have worried that Eve would recognise the scarf as hers. Perhaps she'd pointed it out to misdirect her. If so, it had worked well. Eve had never until this moment thought that it could have been hers. And if it was, what had she been doing, visiting Anthony? And had she been there when he died?

'What do you think?' Tabitha was smiling.

Eve sprang to attention. *Heck.* She'd lost focus. She needed to act for all she was worth. The others might be downstairs but Tabitha reading her expression was still a frightening thought.

'I think I should make some extra notes.' She pulled out a pad from her pocket. 'Let's go through everything again from the beginning so I can get it all down in detail.'

It seemed to work, thank goodness. Eve tried to put her thoughts on hold until she'd finished. Note-taking meant she could look at her pad, and hide her expression.

At last, Tabitha took her downstairs again, with Gus hard on her heels. As she left the house, she realised there'd been several minutes when she hadn't been thinking about that night's open house *or* Robin's raid. Still no word from him.

She popped Gus home, then made for Monty's. It was time for a catch-up with Viv.

. . .

Eve wasn't officially on duty at the teashop. She'd set the whole day aside to prepare for the open house, but that wasn't working out well.

She went through to the kitchen to help with the baking as soon as she arrived.

'This is nice,' Viv said, 'but unexpected. Shouldn't you be hoovering your sitting room for the umpteenth time, or dusting your candy canes?'

'I wanted to talk. I've got news.' Eve got cracking on a batch of cinnamon and ginger cakes. Her hands shook slightly as she sifted some flour.

Viv paused in her own preparations. 'I'm making you a cup of tea. You're all over the place. Tell me everything.'

So Eve did. 'Viv, what if Tabitha was having an affair after all, but it was with Anthony? We know he was seeing Leah Mason too, of course, but if he was secretly a womaniser who pulled the wool over everyone's eyes, then why not? Tabitha's a lot younger than Giles, and however much she loves him, he must be hard to live with. I'd guess Anthony was around ten years her junior, but she's elegant and beautiful. I mean it's not totally hard to imagine, is it?'

Viv's eyes were round as she handed Eve her tea. 'No, it's not.'

Eve took a deep breath. 'What if Anthony wanted to take things further? On the face of it, he's starting to seem like a bit of a playboy, but he could have threatened to tell Giles.'

Viv nodded slowly. 'Of course. And then we're back to everything Tabitha had at stake.'

'That's right. The premises for her business and her lovely existence at Mistletoe Place. She might have given in to temptation with Anthony, never meaning for it to be anything more than a fling. She could have assumed he saw it in the same light, especially if she knew he was flighty. She'd have guessed he'd want to keep it secret. It would have ruined his friendship with

Hal if it had come out, after all. I'm sure Hal would hate to see his dad's relationship threatened. He's fond of Giles underneath it all, and the knock-on effects would be terrible too. If Giles lost his second wife on top of his first, his anxiety would only grow. Life would become even more claustrophobic.'

Viv nodded. 'That all makes sense. But if Anthony fell in love, he might not have cared about the consequences.'

'Exactly.'

'So Anthony threatens to tell, and Tabitha grabs the pipe wrench and lashes out in a moment of fear and desperation?'

'Best case scenario. Worst case, it was premeditated, and she and Ada were in it together. It would explain the phone call, though the idea of her and Tabitha collaborating still seems extraordinary.'

Viv had gone back to her cake batter and was stirring succulent pieces of ginger into the mix. 'Can you imagine any way they might?'

Eve let thoughts play in her head. 'Ada worked closely with Tabitha. Perhaps she uncovered the affair with Anthony and blackmailed her into killing him. If she knew Anthony was pressuring Tabitha to tell, she could have presented it as in their shared interest. But Ada being Ada, she'd always want more. She could have gone to Tabitha for money after that, so Tabitha killed her too.'

'That sounds horribly possible. What would Robin say, if he were here?'

'He'd tell me to look for the weaknesses in my argument.'

Viv sneaked a bit of ginger, caught Eve's critical gaze and went to wash her hands. 'Go on, then.'

'Why would Tabitha be so careless as to leave her scarf hanging up in full view when the press went to take photos of Arthur's Yard? They were there by appointment, after all.'

'Hmm. Yes, that's a good one. Anything else?'

'Tabitha was moved by Anthony's death, just like the rest of us, but not deeply upset. Theo picked her up on it.' It had stuck in Eve's mind. He thought she'd been unnaturally cool about the whole thing. 'Surely, if she'd killed him, and he'd been her lover too, she'd show more reaction?'

'Yes.' Viv added some mixed spice to her batter. 'She'd have to be very detached not to. What are you going to do?'

'Run my thoughts past Greg. He could talk to Tabitha again. And in the meantime, I think I'll make sure I'm not alone with her.'

41

―――――

Back at home, Eve started on the hoovering Viv had mentioned. Later on, Viv would come over in Monty's clanky van to unload the bakes and Sylvia and Daphne would join the effort, helping to prepare large vats of mulled wine and spiced apple juice. Eve tried to stay calm about the event at least. That was all under control, but both Robin and the case made it impossible to relax.

There was nothing she could do about developments down in London, so she forced herself to focus on the mystery in Suffolk. Was Tabitha really guilty? Eve still wasn't sure she'd got it right, yet what else would explain the facts?

She refilled Gus's water bowl, checked her phone for the umpteenth time, as though a message from Robin might magically have appeared without making a sound, then settled down to call Greg Boles.

Later, over lunch, Eve took her notes and went through everything she'd learned. She kept coming back to Ada, and her involvement in Anthony's murder. That had been her stumbling block all along: her conviction that her call had lured him to the yard, versus her doubt that anyone would collaborate with her.

She thought of what she knew of Ada and Anthony's dealings in the run-up to the killings. Simon had said she'd been undercutting him and Hal. That suggested she wanted his customers and was prepared to fight dirty to get them. But without a premises and the machinery involved in a full-blown business, she was hamstrung. And killing Anthony with someone's help would give her that.

But Eve had been down this route before, running round in circles, failing to identify a co-conspirator. So what if Ada's aim had been to take over the yard via another method?

Eve rushed back to the timeline she'd created.

What had Ada been up to the evening Anthony died, and how might it fit in?

She searched for each mention of Ada.

Frightening poor Hamish with the champagne cork stood out, of course. That and the timing. It was as Eve had thought before, she and Hal must have only just missed each other at Willow Cottage, after Anthony had sent him there.

Ada had hated Anthony, so in some ways the attack on his dog made sense, but it wouldn't have brought her closer to taking over the yard. 'I wonder if Ada had a less emotional, more practical reason to send poor Hamish to his death?'

Gus, who'd been avoiding her as she hoovered, eyed the vacuum cleaner warily and appeared to ignore what she'd said.

Eve kept coming back to the timing. No one had been at Willow Cottage all evening, but then Hal and Ada had shown up in quick succession. Had that been chance?

And then suddenly, Eve saw another reason for Ada to let Anthony's dog loose: a desire to push Hal out. She'd hated him, just as she'd hated Anthony, but crucially, ousting him would open up a space for her at the yard. Anthony had said publicly that he'd hire her 'like a shot' if it weren't for Hal. Those words had been throwaway, Eve was sure. Easily said to smooth ruffled feathers. But he'd find it hard to row back on them, if it came to the crunch. Ada could create merry hell if he refused.

So what if she'd decided ousting Hal was her way in? She could have heard Anthony ask him to go to Willow Cottage to fetch those papers. And Ada knew her brother had started to doubt Hal's reliability. All she had to do was nip along just after him, send the dog running and leave the door ajar. Anthony would have got home to find Hamish missing and his home unsecured. He'd have blamed it on Hal's drunken carelessness. And if Hamish had died, Eve doubted Anthony would ever have forgiven him.

Heck. Giles didn't fit as the planter of vodka bottles and spiker of drinks, but Ada could have done it. She knew her way around a boat too. Hal couldn't remember if he'd mucked up the valve, but he was sure he'd have done the right things. It would have been second nature. What if Ada had sabotaged his work, hoping Anthony would sack him?

Even if Anthony was forced to hire her, Ada wouldn't have been happy, of course. Not until she was running the joint. But it would be a lot easier to ruin Anthony once she was a permanent presence at the yard.

But if this new theory was right, Ada had never intended Anthony to die. She'd lured him to the yard for another reason. Eve's mind was racing, but she couldn't guess why, or what it meant. She needed to keep going. Piece everything together until it came clear.

'What else, Gus? What else?'

He looked at her uncomprehendingly and she felt goosebumps rise on her arms as a fresh thought struck her. There was an anomaly that she hadn't paid enough attention to. Hal knew Anthony of old, and he was convinced he'd never have cheated on Dora. Ultimately, Dora had come to the same conclusion, and Tabitha had been genuinely shocked at the idea as well. On top of all that, Anthony had still cared enough about Dora to risk a beating from Theo rather than drop her in it.

Eve had thought she'd got evidence of the affair. Jade Cooper's friends had seen Leah Mason lean in to kiss Anthony. But it had been *her* trying to kiss *him*, not the other way about. And Leah had been terrified when first Anthony and then Ada were killed. For whatever reason, she feared she'd be next.

Eve should have seen it. It had to mean Ada was mixed up in *that* business too.

Suddenly, a whole new explanation for Anthony and Leah Mason's meeting sprang to mind. She checked her watch. She might find Leah at the Bell in Cressingfield. And if she didn't, Eve had a rough idea of where she lived, thanks to her nasty neighbour's keenness to dish the dirt on her.

It was time to find out the truth.

42

_____

Eve promised Gus she'd be back soon, then left the house and drove straight to Cressingfield. Moments after she'd parked, she dashed into the Bell, only to find Leah wasn't working that day. She turned tail and put Lisa Bryant's address into her satnav. It was only just around the corner. Eve guessed Mrs Bryant was an immediate neighbour, given her complaints about the noise, which narrowed Leah's possible address down to one of two houses. She got lucky with the first she tried, a down-at-heel-looking end-of-terrace.

Leah clearly remembered her. She looked frightened as she opened the door, but angry too. She was already closing it in Eve's face.

'Please, don't shut me out. I know you're scared, and I understand why.'

It was enough to make Leah pause, the door still ajar.

Eve would have to talk quickly, and bluff. 'Ada Mottram hired you, didn't she?'

Leah was very short of cash. Her car had been repossessed. Mrs Bryant had implied she was often in debt. Eve should have made more of that.

'You needed the money, so you agreed to go along with her plan.' Eve had already thought it through on her way over. 'She got you to call Anthony Mottram and tell him you were interested in investing in the yard. You were to ask to see him, but insist your meeting remain confidential until you'd made up your mind.' Leah had told Eve all this herself. It had come across as fake because that's just what it was. All part of scheming Ada's plan. 'Ada wanted it to look like the pair of you were having an affair. She was doing everything she could to hurt her brother, and Dora Osborne too, for that matter.' Dora had told on Ada for setting the fire along with Hal. She'd be an object of hatred in Ada's eyes. 'I imagine Ada had heard there'd be a gang of Saxford villagers in the Swan at Wessingham that night. She worked with one of them. So she told you what time to book the table, and even where to sit, so you'd look like a couple having a clandestine meet-up. She made you dress up, so you put your hair into a French pleat and wore a smart scarf. Then, when you were sure you'd been seen by the villagers, you were to make up to Anthony. Lean in to kiss him.'

Eve should have understood all this earlier. Of course Anthony had jumped like a 'scalded cat' when Leah made her move. He'd probably been horrified – she'd taken him completely by surprise. And he'd have been scared word would get back to Dora and she'd get the wrong impression. As indeed she had. To start with at least, before reflecting properly and deciding Anthony wouldn't do it to her.

Leah opened her mouth, but her expression told Eve she was right.

'I know it's true.'

At last, Leah opened the door a little wider, tears in her eyes. 'I thought it sounded like fun, and Ada said the man – Anthony – and his current girlfriend had duped her. She wanted to get her own back. So it seemed like an okay thing to do. Ada told me to make sure none of the villagers saw my face.

She didn't want anyone asking me questions, and it helped me feel safe. But then Anthony was killed. And Ada too. And I was scared. I couldn't be sure my identity hadn't got out.' Her breath was hitching in her throat.

'You thought it was Anthony's ex who'd killed him in revenge, then attacked Ada having realised she'd set it all up?'

Leah nodded.

'So then you worried Dora might have got wind of your part in it, and come for you too?'

Leah gulped, her eyes still wide. 'Yes. Is that what you think?'

Eve had the automatic urge to reassure her, despite what she'd done. 'No, I don't think so. But no one knows who killed either of them, or if anyone else is in danger.'

She had to say it. If Leah let her guard down and came to grief she'd never forgive herself.

'Will you tell me, if you hear anything?' Leah looked like a child now, in desperate need of reassurance.

At last, Eve nodded. 'I will. Give me your number.'

As Eve drove home again, she was overwhelmed by what Ada had done. She really took the biscuit. She'd gone to such lengths to make Anthony's life a misery, and Dora and Hal's too.

Eve would have to tell Dora what she'd found out. She needed to have it confirmed that Anthony hadn't been disloyal. She'd feel terrible, knowing Ada had fooled her into breaking up with him. And that they'd parted on bad terms, when Anthony was totally innocent. Eve needed to work out how to pass the information on as sensitively as possible.

Back in Saxford, she parked by the village green and walked back up Haunted Lane towards home.

Inside, as she fussed Gus, she suddenly pulled up short. Yes, Ada had hated Anthony, Hal and Dora, and the fake affair punished all three. But Eve had decided it was the desire to replace Hal at the yard that really drove her, and the arrangement with Leah didn't take her closer to that goal. Hal would have been hurt if he'd found out Anthony was cheating on his cousin, but she doubted he'd have resigned over it.

A tiny background niggle told her she was missing something, but try as she might, she couldn't think what.

She turned her mind back to Hal again. Ada had been pushing forward her plans full throttle, but it must have felt like one step forward, two steps back. Anthony had loved Hal like a brother, and he kept forgiving him. Perhaps it had been Ada who'd listened in to their conversation at the party, as well as Eve and Viv. If so, she must have been on tenterhooks. Anthony was fed up, all right. Angry and anxious. But in the end, he'd let Hal off the hook, all over again.

Eve bet that was it. And Ada hadn't liked to lose, of course. Eve imagined she'd thrown everything at the problem. She could have spiked Hal's drink so Anthony would think the worst. That and the dog. And... And maybe something was supposed to happen between Hal and Anthony at the yard.

Heck, that would fit!

She could have lured Anthony there because Hal was meant to be there too. Eve's mind played over the possibilities. It wouldn't be hard. She could have claimed someone had spotted an intruder there or something. That would have sent him running.

But he didn't meet with Hal as planned, because Hal had delayed going. He was shaky on his feet and terrified that Anthony would see him stumble and think the worst. If Ada had spiked him, she'd overplayed her hand, but that fitted too. She'd been obsessed. The lengths she'd gone to, out of jealousy and spite...

Eve went to boil the kettle for a hot chocolate. Ada could have wanted Hal to kill Anthony, knowing she'd get the yard.

But that felt too far-fetched. It was a lot, to kill someone. And part of Eve suspected she was enjoying seeing Anthony struggle. Eve's best guess was still that she'd hoped to oust Hal, then bring Anthony down from the inside.

Once she was on the team, she could continue her work of sabotage until everyone asked her to do their repairs, not him. She'd have loved rubbing his nose in his failure. All this scheming probably explained her desire for a job with Tabitha at Mistletoe Place too. She could easily have judged when to sneak into the yard, since she'd been so close at hand.

It was a far-reaching conspiracy, but look at the lengths she'd gone to with Leah Mason. Why choose her? Eve wondered. She'd never asked how they'd connected. And once again, the question nagged her: how did the affair take Ada closer to removing Hal and getting his job at the yard?

As Eve made her hot chocolate, her mind strayed to Robin. Still no news. She set her drink on the side until it was cool enough to sip and walked around the house. She wanted to check it was spick and span, and it helped her to think anyway.

'So, if I'm right,' she said to Gus, 'Ada wanted to replace Hal, ruin Anthony's reputation and end up in charge of Arthur's Yard. She wanted to prove them all wrong. It was about revenge and winning.'

Gus looked at her worriedly, following her as she marched to and fro. She bent to pat him.

'I think she eavesdropped on Anthony and Hal and realised Anthony was being way too forgiving, despite all her efforts. So she got Anthony to go to the yard when Hal was meant to be there, and presumably set up a confrontation between them.'

But what? Not more empty vodka bottles, surely? Even Anthony might start to wonder if Hal was being set up.

Eve thought of what she knew. Anthony had been found with a scrap of paper between his fingers. His killer must have torn the rest of it from him. Originally, Eve had assumed it might be evidence of someone's wrongdoing. But what if it was whatever would trigger the argument Anthony and Hal were meant to have? The killer could have taken it because it implicated them, or because it would cause some other kind of harm they wanted to avoid.

Eve was shivering, despite the large radiators pumping out heat. What had been written or printed on that paper?

She couldn't guess.

But in the back of her mind, all her queries, conclusions and niggles mingled. And then suddenly she saw it. Why the heck hadn't she spotted it before? She'd been so shocked by the enormity of Ada's plotting that the more basic facts had failed to pull together.

Thank goodness Leah had given Eve her number. She dialled it now.

'Leah, the scarf you wore when you dined with Anthony. Where did you get it?'

'*Ada gave it to me. She said it would make me look classy.*'

It was just as Eve had thought. 'I suppose she told you to put your hair into a French pleat for the same reason.'

'*That's right.*' Leah's voice was slow now, puzzled.

Eve thanked her and rang off, feeling like a fool. The fake affair *had* been part of Ada's grand plan after all.

It wasn't a coincidence that Leah's scarf was identical to Tabitha's. She'd worn her hair the same way too. And one of Tabitha's employees at the Swan had thought Leah *was* Tabitha, until she'd gone for a closer look.

That was exactly what she'd been meant to think.

Ada must have pinched Tabitha's scarf from her room. After that, she'd left it around to be photographed at Arthur's Yard. Lent it to Leah to wear when she tried to kiss Anthony.

'Heck, Gus. *I* wondered if Tabitha and Anthony had been having an affair when I saw the scent and the scarf in her dressing room. But it's like I said before, not many secret lovers would leave a scarf lying around with the press visiting.' Only someone who *wanted* the scarf to be noticed would have done that.

Ada had been laying a false trail. She must have sprayed Tabitha's scent at the yard the night Anthony was killed too, before she left for the Cross Keys. All to give credence to an affair between them.

That had to be it. After sabotaging Hal's work and planting the vodka bottles had failed, she'd come up with a new plan. It had the added bonus of hurting four people she hated: Anthony, Dora, Hal and Tabitha. She'd hired Leah, not realising later that someone had seen her face and knew she wasn't Tabitha. Eve remembered her colleague saying she'd been tempted to bring the situation up with Ada, as Anthony was her brother, but she knew the pair weren't close. Ada wouldn't be bothered.

Then at the party, Eve guessed Ada planned to make darned sure Hal thought his stepmother was sleeping with his childhood friend.

So she'd put one final bit of evidence in place at the yard, intending Hal to come face to face with Anthony just after he'd seen the fake proof. Because if Hal thought Anthony was cheating with his stepmother, that really would have blown their friendship apart. His dad was so vulnerable, and Hal needed him to get better and stronger. Without that, he'd never be free. Eve bet Ada had wanted a bust-up there'd be no coming back from, even if Hal found out later there was no affair. Terrible words would be said. Hal would walk out – leave his job and never speak to Anthony again. Either that, or Anthony would fire him for what he said or did in the heat of the moment. He'd be furious, because of course he was innocent.

Eve was sure she'd got it right this time, and at last, she thought she could guess what the missing bit of paper was too. She sank down on the couch by her front window as memories flooded her mind. The way Tabitha's employees each wrote notes in her handwriting to go out with every package. And Ada had been one of those employees. She'd been practising Tabitha's handwriting for weeks as part of her job. Faking a love letter would have been easy. She must have come up with the idea once she'd started working for Tabitha. It proved what a shrewd move it had been, getting a job there. She'd put herself at the heart of the family, in pole position to observe them and spot chinks in their armour.

Eve imagined Ada's thought processes as she put her plan into action. She'd have anticipated a huge row. However much Anthony protested his innocence, there'd already been signs there was something going on. Hal would suddenly remember seeing Tabitha's scarf at the yard. It would seem to fit. The affair would have felt undeniable.

Of course, if Hal went to challenge Tabitha, she'd immediately guess one of her team had been making mischief. Ada wouldn't have risked that, but how could she have avoided it? Eve shook her head. She must have written something in the letter that would put Hal off confronting Tabitha with it. She parked the thought.

The point was that whoever had found the note had gone far further than Ada had imagined. They'd been incensed, flown off the handle.

Ada had probably thought Hal was guilty, but she hadn't known for certain. Eve guessed she'd demanded regular updates on the investigation from her because she wanted to confirm her suspicions. And because if her part in it was going to come out, she'd prefer some warning.

Imagining Hal was guilty, she'd kept him close. It explained her desire to keep him at the yard, and all the touchy-feely stuff too. She'd have assumed Hal had the fake note and she'd have wanted it back. He wasn't likely to show it to anyone. It would give him a prime motive for murder. Ada probably hoped he'd destroyed it, but she couldn't be sure. And if it was found by Tabitha, she'd suspect her team immediately. It wouldn't be long before the spotlight would fall on Ada. It would become clear that Anthony had been killed because of her actions. She might be prosecuted, and no one would use Arthur's Yard again. She'd be a pariah. So Ada had searched Hal's room. But had she found anything?

Eve had believed Hal when he said he'd been late getting to the yard. Someone else could have got there first and seen the note. For a second, Eve thought of Giles, but why would he go there?

It had to be someone who'd had a last-minute reason to visit the yard – something that Ada hadn't predicted – and whose fiery temper had ignited the minute they'd seen the fake love letter.

As Eve had the thought, she knew exactly who it had been.

At that moment, there was a knock at the door. It must be Viv with the bakes. Eve went to open up.

43

———

But it wasn't Viv. It was Theo. He stood on Eve's doorstep, smiling in the semi-darkness, the outside light illuminating the large bunch of winter roses he held. Gus was able to act normally, scampering up to meet him, but Eve couldn't control her expression. The realisation of his guilt was too recent, his appearance too sudden and unexpected.

She swallowed. 'Hello. What are you doing here?' Her voice cracked as she spoke. She had to clear her throat and she knew she'd flinched.

'I brought you some flowers. A thank-you for finding Dora.' He knew something was wrong. His words were halting.

He was the man with the short fuse. The elder brother who'd always protected Giles. He'd have gone to find Anthony for a quiet word, because thanks to Hal, he'd finally discovered why his daughter had disappeared, and how Anthony had been protecting her reputation. He'd told her himself that he'd wanted to apologise.

Bulky Theo stood in the doorway, his smile fading. And then he walked forward, forcing Eve back.

Eve was too scared to disguise what she was feeling. She

wanted to override her adrenaline and its effects but it was impossible. He must have found Ada's fake love letter, and decided he'd been right about Anthony all along. He *was* a deceiver. After all the Osbornes had done for the Mottrams, Anthony had used his position at the heart of the family to make up to Tabitha, start an affair and threaten to destroy Giles's peace of mind, once and for all. Or so Theo had thought.

Theo kicked the door shut behind him. 'You know.'

'Know what?' But she knew he wouldn't believe her. And however hard she tried to act normally, her thoughts ran on. Visions of Theo striking Anthony, letting out all the fury he felt. No wonder he'd been so angry with Tabitha in the aftermath of the killing. He couldn't tell her he knew about the supposed affair – it would make him an obvious suspect – but he couldn't hide his fury.

Eve had already suspected he'd listened in to her interview with Tabitha and now she knew why. He was starting to doubt the evidence Ada had faked. Why wasn't Tabitha more upset? He'd even asked her that. Rubbed in the tragedy, waiting for her to give away her true feelings. But she'd remained calm and uncomprehending.

Theo dropped the flowers he'd been carrying and walked towards her, taking up a Maglite torch from the coat stand as he came. Eve had thought before what a good weapon it would make when she'd carried it on dusky walks with Gus.

If only she had some immediate neighbours. Until Viv, Sylvia or Daphne turned up to prep the open house, there was no one to see what went on. Just the quiet winter darkness, the hedgerow, the fields and the estuary.

All the while, thoughts spun in her head: the way Theo had searched Willow Cottage. Only now did she see his excuse made no sense. He'd already known Dora had left of her own accord and written to Hal to say she was safe. He'd never have imagined Anthony would have a note of her whereabouts. Why would he? They'd already broken up, and she'd cut herself off out of shame. No, he'd gone there for another reason. He'd been looking desperately for signs of Anthony and Tabitha's affair. He'd found none and his doubts had increased. He'd been in tears afterwards, she remembered. He was starting to fear he'd killed an innocent man.

When had he finally accepted the truth? Eve recalled Tabitha giving him a cushion for his back. She'd written him a note to go with it, laughing. Eve could remember the words:

To dear Theo, from Tabitha. Hope your back feels better, you grumpy old so and so. xxx

She'd handed it to him, saying: 'You get your own, personal message, not like my regular customers.'

That must have been when the penny dropped. He'd have realised how easily any of her staff could have faked the love letter. He'd seemed to crumple, his eyes filling with tears. Eve imagined he'd lit on Ada as the guilty party almost instantly. She was the one with a grudge, for whom everything about Anthony and the yard was personal.

'I know you were goaded into it,' Eve said. 'Any jury would see that.'

He hadn't raised his hand. His expression was neutral. But he was backing her towards the stairs and Gus whimpered. There was no room to dodge round him.

How must he have felt when he realised he'd been had, and who was responsible? The enormity of killing at all would be hard to bear. The fact that he'd killed an entirely blameless man thanks to Ada's scheming didn't bear thinking about.

He'd have attacked Ada, because in his eyes, she'd turned him into a murderer. Without her toxic plotting, Anthony would still be alive and Theo's conscience would be clear.

'If you tell your story, people will see how Ada played you.' Eve's voice shook.

'I can't go through that,' Theo said. 'I've killed two people. And all because of Ada Mottram.' He swore. 'She made me something I'm not, but things are turning around. Dora's coming home. You must understand, I'll never do anything like this again. It's all over now. Me going to prison won't help anyone.'

He hoped she'd see things his way, but he'd picked up the Maglite. It had seemed almost subconscious but if his temper turned, she'd be faced with a strong man wielding a weapon that could easily kill her.

She could promise to keep quiet, but he'd know she was lying. He'd see it in her eyes.

'If I go to jail, what will happen to Dora?' Theo's tone was still reasonable, but he was backing her up the stairs. 'And to Giles? I never wanted this, any of it. It's just the hand I've been dealt.' Then suddenly his eyes flashed, and she saw that other side of him again. 'You'll never understand!' He was yelling now. 'You've got morality but no compassion!'

The switch was terrifying.

He swiped the torch at the side of her head and she screamed. She couldn't help herself. He'd only just missed her and his eyes were wild. Promising he'd never kill again was easily done, but his fuse was short and his anger, when it blew, was violent.

She reversed up the stairs, trapped and cornered, bracing for the next blow. If only she could get through to him. Bring him back from the place his fury had pushed him.

'You think it's fair to kill me to preserve your bubble? How will you sleep at night?'

'How will I sleep? How will you? You want to destroy me, my daughter and my brother, and all because of that monster Ada Mottram!'

'You're wrong.' Eve's voice shook, but she managed not to shout. She was desperate to calm him, but she needed him to see clearly too. 'You killed an innocent man, but even if he had been sleeping with your sister-in-law, it would still be unforgiveable. What about Dora? What about her feelings for Anthony?'

Theo had raised the torch again, but at her last words, she saw a flicker of emotion in his eyes. She had to capitalise on this tiny moment of vulnerability. It was her only chance.

'Dora loves you, you know. And she knows how duplicitous Ada was. She'll realise you'd never have killed Anthony if it weren't for her. She'd hate you to kill a third time for her sake.'

And at that, Theo seemed to deflate. He sank down where he was on the stairs and sobbed. Eve felt tears prick too – shock, and simple distress. It was all such a mess, and so tragic.

Eve didn't think Theo would turn on her again, but she dashed to the top of the stairs while he cried and opened one of the casement windows. Viv was late with the van, which was nothing new, but Sylvia and Daphne were due to be with her in a few minutes, and they were invariably on time. The frigid evening air hit her, bringing her new determination and clarity of thought.

A second later, her neighbours appeared from their house just up the lane and she called down to let them know what had happened. 'I left my mobile downstairs, but would you call the police? The mulled wine might have to wait.' Eve would be ready for a large glass when the time came. She felt faintly hysterical.

44

A short while later, Elizabeth's Cottage was full of police, Viv, Sylvia and Daphne and a scene of confusion. Umpteen villagers were queuing up in the lane, very determined to get the mince pies and drinks they'd been promised, while a bemused constable tried to keep them at bay. Saxford's residents were a doughty lot and in no mood to be denied. They were standing there with folded arms, a sea of Santa hats and Christmas jumpers. Eve was still feeling shaky, but she and Viv went out to deal with them.

By the time Viv had told them off for being impatient, and Eve had sketched out what had happened, they were all sympathy and very happy to come back the following evening instead. At last, they decamped – mostly to the Cross Keys from what Eve gathered. The Falconers would be in for a busy night.

At some stage, Viv must have contacted Robin. He called her just after she'd finished telling her story for the fifth time.

'*I'm coming home right now.*'

'What about the raid?'

'*It's over. The guy who beat me up has been arrested.*'

'Thank goodness.'

Viv was fussing around Eve like a mother hen, trying to get her to eat three sorts of cake and drink tea, all at the same time. They were sitting in Sylvia and Daphne's cottage, where Greg had taken Eve to interview her. Gus had his head pressed firmly against Eve's ankles. Poor thing. She bent to stroke him.

Sylvia arrived with a shawl and tucked it round Eve's shoulders as Daphne leaned down to give her a hug.

'I'm so glad you managed to talk him down.'

Eve laughed, but she knew she sounded shaky. 'Me too.' She'd never met someone who could turn that quickly before.

Eve told them everything, her teeth chattering, then later that night, she told Robin too, over a large mug of hot chocolate. After she'd finished, he hugged her tight. 'Nice work, bringing him back from the brink.'

But Eve was haunted by thoughts of just before that. Seeing his expression switch, and knowing he was no longer in control. It had been a close call.

The day after the arrest, she, Robin, Viv, Sylvia and Daphne welcomed the villagers to Elizabeth's Cottage. Eve's head was in a spin. She was still coming down from the shock of her face-off with Theo, and everyone was demanding to hear the story. But her neighbours were sympathetic, and Robin and Viv were there as her lieutenants. Later, when Eve reviewed the evening, she mainly remembered Robin's warm, stoical presence – a protective arm around her shoulders – and Viv's fierce looks when the villagers' questions became too much. The event raised a lot of money, so it was all worth it. And there was something therapeutic about clearing up afterwards. Calmly collating the recycling, washing plates and stowing leftovers. Something simple she could control, when everything had been so turbulent.

At last, Eve and Robin's calm, treasured cottage was back to its reassuring self, dressed for the festive season. Eve had set a collection of golden glass baubles on her coffee table, nestled in a sea-green bowl Daphne had made. She and Robin put up the Christmas tree in the corner of the sitting room. She hadn't dared add those finishing touches until after the party. The danger of breakages had been too great.

In the days that followed, news came in dribs and drabs from Greg, and from Tabitha Osborne. Dora was horrified, of course. It was a terrible reality to come home to, though her closeness to Tabitha had helped. Tabitha had taken her in and held her tight, and she told Eve she had plans to help Dora recoup her losses, too. They were going to work together on some projects. Tabitha had withdrawn her offer on the house in Blyworth, but Giles had agreed to get help, and Hal was looking for his own place to live, now his earnings had gone up, and he could do it with his dad's blessing. He'd carry on at Arthur's Yard with the talented casual worker he'd mentioned as his second in command. Even in the short time since Theo's arrest, Eve had seen him grow in confidence. It was as though the enormity of what had happened had made him realise he could be strong. He was there for his dad, and for Dora too. His crew at the yard were treating him with respect, and Eve gathered he'd plucked up courage to contact his ex, Gabby. She hoped they might get back together. Giles had accepted he needed to take a step back, and that should make a difference.

Jackson Smith, the PI, had been in touch to say his job had been cancelled, but that he knew she hadn't given him away. He'd claimed he wanted to thank her, but then asked if she knew anyone who might want his services. She'd promised to ask around.

And Theo had confessed to everything. It meant Eve knew how Ada had ensured Hal wouldn't show Tabitha the fake love letter.

She'd included the words: *If anyone finds out about us, I'll have to tell Giles. It'll be too big a secret to keep.*

So Hal – if he'd found it – would never have challenged his stepmum, to avoid her revealing the supposed affair to his dad. Ada had guessed he'd protect him, and Eve was sure she was right.

Aside from the case, Viv had provided some much-needed happy news. Jonah and Stevie had been in touch to tell her officially that Stevie was expecting a baby. Viv had been so relieved and emotional that she hadn't taken them to task for holding back.

A week after Theo's arrest, Eve was fine-tuning her introduction to Anthony's and Ada's obituary. She wanted to get it out of the way before her twins and their partners turned up that afternoon. They were all spending Christmas together, and that ought to equal unadulterated joy, so she must get the sad piece finished first.

She'd debated about whether Ada deserved to share her brother's space. What she'd done was monstrous and Eve grieved for Anthony, but her work was all about telling the truth, and there were no complicating legal issues to stop her doing that.

Anthony Henry Mottram, owner and manager of Arthur's boatyard, and Ada Lisa Mottram, interiors worker-turned boatyard owner

Anthony Mottram, the well-loved and respected owner and chief engineer at the 100-year-old boatyard, Arthur's Yard, and his sister, Ada Lisa Mottram, who inherited the yard from him, have died. A man has been arrested for their murders.

Anthony and Ada were brought up in the boat repair business, learning their skills from a young age. As children, they were close, though even at that stage, Ada's character was demonstrably different from her brother's. Anthony was there for those in need, helping his lifelong friend Hal Osborne through bereavement and a difficult childhood and diligently learning his trade until he was one of the most skilled craftspeople in the county.

Whereas Ada hated authority and found it impossible to empathise with others. Anthony was kind and pragmatic, but Ada fought dirty. More than one person has alleged she was responsible for the terrible fire that caused such damage to Arthur's Yard fourteen years ago, the result of a spat with her father.

Their contrasting qualities explain why Peter Mottram left the yard to Anthony alone, and why Anthony bypassed Ada when recruiting his second in command, opting for Hal instead.

Horrifically, those decisions set Ada on a path to retribution. The cruelty she displayed and the damage she caused is hard to overstate. Meanwhile, the Suffolk community is mourning the loss of her much-loved and highly regarded brother.

Eve broke off. That worked, and she'd already reviewed the rest. It was done. As she emailed the file to *Suffolk Monthly*, there was an excitable rat-a-tat-tat at the door, met with equally excitable barking from Gus. She'd told him the twins were coming home. She dashed through to the sitting room to open up, Robin just behind her, Gus in front. Very much in the way, but in a manner that touched her heart.

She eased him aside to open up, and then the sitting room was a flurry of hugs and kisses, coats and scarves, exclamations and laughter, and pats and tickles for Gus. The dachshund was beside himself, rolling over onto his back, then leaping up again, rushing between her son Nick and daughter Ellen, Nick's wife Fiona and Ellen's partner Hugh.

It took at least fifteen minutes before anyone sat down – there was so much joy at just being together, and masses to say. At last, though, everyone squeezed onto the couches and chairs and Robin went to fetch drinks as the chat continued.

'By the way,' Ellen said, 'I saw Viv outside, just after we'd parked by the village green. She came up to give me a hug, but then blushed and went all weird. She was with a guy I'd never seen before...'

'Ah.' Eve found herself grinning. 'He didn't have a goatee and a piratical air, did he? Maybe even a top hat with a feather in it?' He might wear it all the time. Especially in this weather.

Ellen was laughing too. 'I see you've met him already.'

'Not yet. But I'm hoping I will soon.'

Her daughter grinned back. 'Got you.'

Robin appeared with a trayful of mulled wines.

'Sorry to be a pain,' Fiona said, 'but have you got something soft? I'm just so tired.'

'Of course. There's spiced apple juice on the go too.' Robin fetched her some.

Eve felt a wave of pure contentment rush over her. She was exactly where she wanted to be, with people she adored, and in the coming days she'd see Viv and find out all about her first date with Mr Top Hat. She hoped it was going swimmingly.

Later, as they all got ready for bed, Eve bustled about, checking if anyone wanted a hot water bottle or a glass of water.

'I think we've got everything we could possibly need,' Ellen said. 'Thanks, Mama!'

So Eve left them to it and walked hand in hand with Robin towards the steep cottage stairs. She happened to turn at the last minute, and noticed Fiona run a protective hand over her stomach.

Upstairs, after she and Robin had cleared the bathroom, and snuggled into bed, he held her close.

'Robin?'

'Hmm?' He kissed her on the nose.

'I don't want to tempt fate or anything, but Fiona didn't drink any wine at supper, did she?'

He frowned. 'No. I think you're right.'

A tiny thrill ran through her. It felt wrong to speculate. Despite regarding herself as rational, through and through, counting chickens before they were hatched would fill her with anxiety. But all the same, the idea of sharing the first-time-grandmother experience with Viv made the thought especially precious.

Robin pulled her in close. 'I'll buy some no-alcohol fizz for Christmas Day. Just in case.'

A LETTER FROM CLARE

Thank you so much for reading *Mystery at Mistletoe Place*. I do hope you had fun trying to sort the clues from the red herrings! If you'd like to keep up to date with all my latest releases, you can sign up at the following link. Your email address will never be shared, and you can unsubscribe at any time. You'll also receive an exclusive short story, 'Mystery at Monty's Teashop'. I hope you enjoy it!

www.bookouture.com/clare-chase

The idea for this book came to me after watching someone deliberately stir up trouble. I started to play around with scenarios, imagining how their actions might have unforeseen consequences, meaning they got more than they bargained for!

If you have time, I'd love it if you were able to write a review of *Mystery at Mistletoe Place*. Feedback is really valuable, and it also makes a huge difference in helping new readers discover my books. Alternatively, if you'd like to contact me personally, you can reach me via my website, Facebook page, Instagram or on Bluesky. It's always great to hear from readers.

Again, thank you so much for deciding to spend some time reading *Mystery at Mistletoe Place*. I'm looking forward to sharing my next book with you very soon.

With all best wishes, Clare x

KEEP IN TOUCH WITH CLARE

www.clarechase.com

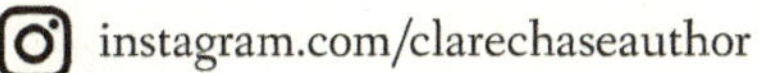 instagram.com/clarechaseauthor
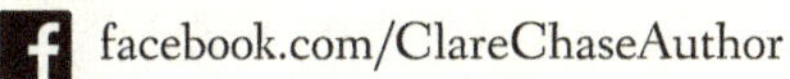 facebook.com/ClareChaseAuthor
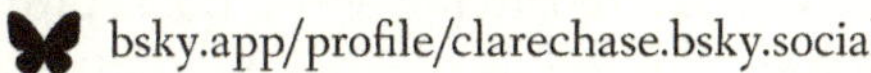 bsky.app/profile/clarechase.bsky.social

ACKNOWLEDGEMENTS

Very much love and thanks as always to Charlie, George and Ros!

And an enormous thank you to my brilliant editor Ruth Tross for her sharp-witted and creative thoughts that make such a difference. Big thanks too, to the entire Bookouture team who work on my novels. You can see what a fantastic group effort it is by looking at the following page, where everyone involved is mentioned by name. They are the most fabulous, skilled and friendly group of professionals and it's an honour to work with both them and Ruth.

Love and thanks also to Mum and Dad, Phil and Jenny, David and Pat, Warty, Andrea, Jen, the Westfield gang, Margaret, Shelly, Mark, my Andrewes relations and a whole bunch of family and friends.

I'd also like to thank the lovely Bookouture authors and other writers for their friendship and support. And a hugely appreciative thank you to the generous book bloggers and reviewers who pass on their thoughts about my work, including some who have been with me right from the start. Their support is truly incredible.

And finally, but crucially, thanks to you, the reader, for buying or borrowing this book!

PUBLISHING TEAM

Turning a manuscript into a book requires the efforts of many people. The publishing team at Bookouture would like to acknowledge everyone who contributed to this publication.

Audio
Alba Proko
Sinead O'Connor
Melissa Tran

Commercial
Lauren Morrissette
Hannah Richmond
Imogen Allport

Cover design
Tash Webber

Data and analysis
Mark Alder
Mohamed Bussuri

Editorial
Ruth Tross
Sinead O'Connor

Copyeditor
Fraser Crichton

Proofreader
Liz Hatherell

Marketing
Alex Crow
Melanie Price
Occy Carr
Cíara Rosney
Martyna Młynarska

Operations and distribution
Marina Valles
Stephanie Straub
Joe Morris

Production
Hannah Snetsinger
Mandy Kullar
Nadia Michael
Charlotte Hegley

Publicity
Kim Nash
Noelle Holten
Jess Readett
Sarah Hardy

Rights and contracts
Peta Nightingale
Richard King
Saidah Graham

Dear Reader,

We'd love your attention for one more page to tell you about the crisis in children's reading, and what we can all do.

Studies have shown that reading for fun is the **single biggest predictor of a child's future life chances** – more than family circumstance, parents' educational background or income. It improves academic results, mental health, wealth, communication skills, ambition and happiness.

The number of children reading for fun is in rapid decline. Young people have a lot of competition for their time, and a worryingly high number do not have a single book at home.

Hachette works extensively with schools, libraries and literacy charities, but here are some ways we can all raise more readers:

- Reading to children for just 10 minutes a day makes a difference
- Don't give up if children aren't regular readers – there will be books for them!

- Visit bookshops and libraries to get recommendations
- Encourage them to listen to audiobooks
- Support school libraries
- Give books as gifts

There's a lot more information about how to encourage children to read on our websites: **www.RaisingReaders.co.uk** and **www.JoinRaisingReaders.com**.

Thank you for reading.

www.ingramcontent.com/pod-product-compliance
Lightning Source LLC
Chambersburg PA
CBHW061520210726
48287CB00006B/1762